KU-248-920

A WIDOW'S VOW

1851. After her merchant husband saved her from a life of prostitution, Louisa Hill was briefly happy as a housewife in Bristol. But then, her husband has been found hanged in a Bath hotel room, a note and a key to a property in Bath the only things she has left of him. And now the debt collectors will come calling.

Left with no means of income, Louisa knows she has nothing to turn to but her old way of life. But this time, she'll do it on her own terms — by turning her home into a brothel for upper class gentlemen.

Enlisting the help of Jacob Jackson, a quiet but feared boxer, to watch over the house, Louisa is about to embark on a life she never envisaged. Can she find the courage to forge this new path?

30119 027 310 517

CHE

SPECIAL MESSAGE TO READERS

THE ULVERSCROFT FOUNDATION
(registered UK charity number 264873)
was established in 1972 to provide funds for
research, diagnosis and treatment of eye diseases.
Examples of major projects funded by the
Ulverscroft Foundation are:-

- The Children's Eye Unit at Moorfelds Eye Hospital, London
- The Ulverscroft Children's Eye Unit at Great Ormond Street Hospital for Sick Children
- Funding research into eye diseases and treatment at the Department of Ophthalmology, University of Leicester
- The Ulverscroft Vision Research Group, Institute of Child Health
- Twin operating theatres at the Western Ophthalmic Hospital, London
- The Chair of Ophthalmology at the Royal Australian College of Ophthalmologists

You can help further the work of the Foundation
by making a donation or leaving a legacy. Every
contribution is gratefully received. If you would
like to help support the Foundation or require
further information, please contact:

THE ULVERSCROFT FOUNDATION
The Green, Bradgate Road, Anstey
Leicester LE7 7FU, England
Tel: (0116) 236 4325

website: www.ulverscroft-foundation.org.uk

RACHEL BRIMBLE

◆

A WIDOW'S VOW

Complete and Unabridged

MAGNA
Leicester

0273105 1

SUTTON LIBRARIES
AND HERITAGE SERVICES
20 APR 2021
F
02731051

First published in Great Britain in 2020 by
Aria
an imprint of Head of Zeus Ltd
London

First Ulverscroft Edition
published 2021
by arrangement with
Head of Zeus Ltd
London

Copyright © 2020 by Rachel Brimble
All rights reserved

This is a work of fiction. All characters,
organisations, and events portrayed in this novel
are either products of the author's imagination or
are used fictitiously.

*A catalogue record for this book is available
from the British Library.*

ISBN 978–0–7505–4877–9

Published by
Ulverscroft Limited
Anstey, Leicestershire

Printed and bound in Great Britain by
TJ Books Ltd., Padstow, Cornwall

This book is printed on acid-free paper

This one is for my friend and most enthusiastic reader, Jackie Todd — you are the best fan a girl could have!

Love you,

xx

1

City of Bristol — February 1st 1851

Louisa Hill collapsed onto the chintz sofa in the dockside house she shared with her husband and her loyal friend, Nancy. 'Well, the windows are clean and the silver polished. We have, indeed, managed a good day's work. What do you say to a trip to the tea shop?'

'I'd say it's a miracle you're allowing yourself a treat.' Nancy raised her eyebrows as she puffed up a cushion, her auburn curls falling around her temples. 'You seem to be trying a little too hard to prove yourself to that husband of yours these days, Lou. You do believe he loves you, don't you?'

'Of course.' Louisa stood and smoothed her hands over her apron, uncomfortable with how Nancy's question poked so unerringly at her insecurities. 'I just owe him so much. The least I can do in return is keep a nice house for him.'

'Hmm, and an exciting bed whenever he deems to come home.'

Irritated, Louisa walked to the parlour door and tightly clenched the handle. 'I'll never forget what Anthony did when he rescued me and neither should you considering he agreed to take you in, too.'

'I agree, but how long do you intend paying him back? He gets more than enough for what he gives you.'

1

Louisa swallowed as guilt that she'd secretly been feeling the same way over the last few weeks pressed down on her. 'How can you say that?'

Nancy planted her hands on her hips, her grey eyes blazing with annoyance. 'Because he's constantly taking advantage of you, that's why.

It's one thing to gift you money and give you a roof over your head, but respect should come with that, too.'

'He does respect me.' She fought against the doubt that hovered around her heart. 'He treats me just as any man would treat his wife.'

'That's because you *are* his wife.' Nancy glared. 'Why can't you remember that? You're not his whore anymore.'

Locking gazes with her friend, Louisa had no doubt the fiery, streetwise rebelliousness in Nancy's eyes was mirrored in her own. No matter how much they battled to maintain the carefully tended, middle-class veneer they each adopted whenever out and about on the pretty squares and streets of Bristol, who she and Nancy had once been never shifted far from their minds.

Louisa marched into the hallway, her gaze darting over the high-polished side tables, the sparkling mirror and porcelain trinkets lining a high shelf.

Every painting was dusted, every square of the runner beaten and brushed until the pile was plush, every tile mopped and buffed until it shone.

But it didn't matter how much she scrubbed and cleaned, or how often she argued with Nancy, Louisa never felt she could completely wash away her previous life as a whore. Yet, if Anthony had dismissed Louisa's previous occupation, shouldn't she, too? She and Nancy both deserved to shed the skin that had enveloped them through misfortune and circumstances beyond their control.

Nancy's footsteps came behind her and Louisa turned, braced for another confrontation.

Her friend grimaced, her soft grey gaze filled with remorse. 'I'm sorry.

You know I'm only doing my best to look after you, right? I love the bones of you and always will. Fancy housewife, down-in-the-dirt beggar or wh — '

'Queen of Sheba.'

Nancy grinned. 'Absolutely.'

Louisa pulled the only friend, the only person she truly trusted in the whole world, into her arms and squeezed Nancy tight. 'Let us never fall out completely. I'd be lost without you.'

'Never. Friends for life.'

A loud and determined knocking at the front door drew them apart and Louisa frowned. 'That doesn't sound good.'

As she approached the door, Louisa brushed her hands over her skirts before smoothing some of her fallen blonde curls into place. She pulled open the door and smiled. 'Good afternoon, can I help . . .'

Further words stuck in Louisa's throat.

The constable was in his mid-thirties, his moustache as bushy as the two furry caterpillar-brows above his bulbous eyes. His expression was far from happy. 'Mrs Anthony Hill?'

Dread tiptoed up Louisa's spine at the stern tone of his voice even as Nancy, stalwart as always, slipped her hand into Louisa's. 'Yes?'

'Might I come in? I'd prefer that we not speak on the doorstep.' The constable cleared his throat. 'Under the circumstances.'

Louisa's foreboding gathered strength as she and Nancy stood back to let the constable step inside. She studied his face as she spoke. 'Nancy? Would you kindly bring some tea into the parlour?' She lifted her hand and gestured along the hallway. 'If you'd like to follow me, Constable.'

'Sergeant, madam. Sergeant Robert Williams, at your service.'

Louisa dipped her head and led the way into the parlour. 'Please, take a seat.'

The sergeant sat on the settee as Louisa lowered into Anthony's favourite wing-backed chair and pulled her trembling hands into her lap. The beige and cream walls seemed to slowly close in, the collective abundance of knick-knacks and framed sepia photographs dotted about the room adding to the suddenly stifling atmosphere. Despite the cheery chirping of the birds outside the open window and the fresh February air whispering through the room, Louisa sensed only bad news had brought the constabulary to her door.

She swallowed against the dryness in her throat. 'Can I ask what this unexpected visit is regarding, Sergeant?'

'Let us wait for the tea, shall we? I think it best you have your maid with you.'

Louisa's mind reeled with possible explanations of why he was here, each one more alarming than the one before. The seconds ticked by like hours until the clattering of china announced Nancy's return. She came into the living room, her intel-

4

ligent gaze momentarily meeting Louisa's before she placed the tea tray on the low table in front of them.

'Milk and sugar, Sergeant?' Nancy smiled, but her gaze was watchful and assessing. 'Although, I'm sure I'm right in saying that you are already sweet —'

'Just pour us each a cup, if you would, Nancy,' Louisa interrupted, knowing her friend's nervousness could easily lead to her natural flirtation which, considering the sergeant's unimpressed expression, would not be in any way reciprocated. 'I suspect the sergeant has come to impart bad news, rather than good, so a cup of sustenance will be most welcome.' She faced the sergeant, thinking she and Nancy would shortly be reaching for the wine decanter rather than the teapot. 'Please, I'd prefer you not keep us in suspense any longer.'

He took the cup Nancy offered him and cautiously sipped before slowly pushing it onto the table. Looking from Nancy to Louisa, the sergeant inhaled a long breath before extracting a cream-coloured envelope from his pocket. 'I'm sorry to tell you that your husband, Mr Anthony Hill, was found hanged in a Bath hotel room this morning.'

Louisa flinched and then an icy coldness shuddered through her, her fingers trembling harder. 'I'm sorry?'

The sergeant cleared his throat, his gaze dipping to the envelope. 'I'm afraid all I can offer you is this, along with my sincere condolences.'

A bitter taste coated her mouth as Louisa glanced at Nancy, her eyes wide and her mouth

5

dropping open. 'I don't understand. My husband is in London on business. He has no need to be in Bath.'

'Mrs Hill — '

'What is this?' She snatched the envelope from his hand, hating the way it shook in her fingers.

Two spots of colour rose in the sergeant's cheeks. 'A suicide note, madam, and the deeds and key to a property in Bath.'

'Suicide?' Louisa closed her eyes, confusion and shock making her breaths sharpen. A sudden and deep sadness threatened to close her throat.

Why in the world would Anthony choose to end his life? He would have spoken to her of his desperation. Wouldn't he? She shook her head.

'Anthony would never . . . what do you mean, a property? I don't understand.

This is our home. We have no home in Bath. I think you are mistaken, Sergeant. You must have the wrong address.'

Yet, possibility pressed down on her making her tremble harder. There had been times she was certain he'd lied to her, times he could not quite meet her eyes when he said he would ensure she was always taken care of . . . Surely, Anthony would not take his life and leave her alone any more than she would him. He had given her a good life, a better life, and would never abandon her. She had known nothing but Anthony for four years. His care and attention had ensured she did not have to think, plan or scheme for another day in her life.

Could he really be gone?

A sharp stab of grief pierced deep into Loui-

6

sa's chest; tears burning behind her eyes as her ignorance to Anthony's state of mind and distress threatened to overcome her.

'Mrs Hill, I assure you I have the right address. I would not be here if we weren't certain the man found was your husband.'

Second by painful second, the resilient armour Louisa had relied on for so many years before Anthony had taken her and Nancy in slid into place as though it had never disappeared.

She ripped open the envelope and a brass key dropped onto her lap. She picked it up, staring at it as though it was an alien creature before snapping her attention to the piece of paper, Anthony's handwriting unmistakable.

The house is entirely yours. I'm sorry.

Tears blurred her vision as she unfolded the other sheets of paper: official deeds to a Bath house she knew nothing about. The words jumped and leapt in front of her eyes, her tongue frozen as Nancy rose from her seat.

'I think it best you leave Mrs Hill to process her shock, Sergeant.' Nancy spoke as if from behind a thick cloud. 'Let me show you out.'

'Mrs Hill?'

Louisa slowly raised her eyes to the sergeant's.

His expression was filled with sympathy. 'I really am sorry.'

'Yes, thank you.' She dropped her gaze to Anthony's letter and crumpled it in her fist. 'My husband has written the exact same thing. Good day, Sergeant.'

7

He nodded and followed Nancy from the room as Louisa stared towards the parlour windows, numb and lost. Anthony was dead. She and Nancy were alone. Just as they'd each been before. How could she have not suspected more was going on in Anthony's life than he had told her?

Culpability whispered through her. Because she'd not bothered to ask. She had never allowed herself to fully trust him. Always retained just a little self-reliance, albeit internal. It had always only really been her and Nancy against the world. Her and Nancy side by side, come what may.

Her marriage had been one of convenience, both for her and most likely for Anthony. She closed her eyes. But there had been affection. There had been care. And there had been something that each had gained from the other.

Until now.

2

City of Bath — February 1851

The bandaged knuckles of Jacob Jackson's boxing opponent slammed into his jaw with such force Jacob stumbled backwards, a burst of stars momentarily fuzzing his vision. Unacceptable. It was time to finish this thing — he needed a pint. Adrenaline swept through him on a violent rush and he drew himself to his full six-feet-three-inch height. Tensing his muscles, Jacob revelled in the pop and strain of the tendons across his biceps. With a roar, he landed the other boxer a swift, sharp jab right in the very centre of his face.

Blood flew and sweat sprayed as the smoky, backstreet pub erupted into a barrage of cheers, jeering and stamping feet.

Jacob smiled as his opponent swayed to the left, then the right . . . before slowly falling backwards, his great bulk landing so heavily on the canvas that vibrations passed beneath Jacob's stockinged feet.

His manager leapt into the ring and pulled Jacob's head into the crook of his elbow, his knuckles rubbing over his crown. 'Yes, Jakey boy! Out with a single punch. Let's hear your appreciation, people.' His manager raised Jacob's hand. 'Your victor, Jacob 'The Man' Jackson.'

Jacob accepted the congratulations with a nod, his smile dissolving.

9

Fighting was a means to an end. Each punch a reminder of what his life was and always would be. He would never veer from the path determined for him at an age when a boy should not know the difference between a punch and a beating.

But Jacob did. Always had.

Violence bred violence. The lesson taught to him in no uncertain terms by his father.

He shrugged out of his manager's embrace and ducked between the ropes towards the bar, ignoring the congratulatory slaps to his tense shoulders and the flirtatious smiles of whores and the drinkers' wives.

'Do you have a pint for me, Maura?'

'Coming right up, my darling.'

With badly dyed red hair and teeth so few it was a wonder how the woman ate anything more than soup, Maura was the only person Jacob liked, or even tolerated, in the White Hart. Maybe it was something to do with her friendly blue eyes, always filled with humour, and the ready smile she wore for anyone and everyone, that kept him coming to sit at the bar where he'd talk to her night after night until closing. Set far back in a side street of Bath's busy metropolis, the White Hart was Jacob's second home.

The first was a small townhouse by the river, owned by the same man who liked to think he owned Jacob. His manager, Henry Bertrum — a crook, a scoundrel and swindler of the lowliest rank, yet Jacob kept Henry's company anyway. As long as he stayed with him, Jacob got to fight some of the best boxers on Bath's circuit, had bed

10

and board and the backing of Doreen, an eccentric housekeeper who he was fonder of than was good for him.

'So . . .'

Rolling his eyes, Jacob picked up his pint. 'What?' He faced Henry and tried not to squint under the glare of his manager's garish purple and green suit, his top hat shining like a black beacon. 'I finished the fight, didn't I?

Now I'd prefer to have the rest of the evening to myself, if you don't mind.'

Henry slipped onto a vacant stool. 'It makes no difference if you won this fight or twenty, you've got to up your game if we're ever going to make our fortune in London.' He gripped Jacob's shoulder. 'London is where the big money is. Don't you want to be richer than your wildest dreams? Have a woman on each arm, a carriage at your beck and call, the best clothes money can buy?'

'You're describing *your* perfect life, not mine.' Jacob supped his beer and wiped the back of his hand across his mouth. 'I'm happy enough here. I don't need a woman or fancy clothes, and certainly not a carriage when I've got a pair of working legs. You've got your cut, now leave a man to his beer, will you?'

Henry's fingers clenched tighter on Jacob's bare shoulder, his sharp nails digging into the skin. 'Now, you listen to me,' he growled in Jacob's ear. 'I don't see Bath as the be-all and end-all of the world. I plan to be rich, Jake, really rich — and you're looking more and more like the man to make that happen.'

Jacob slowly swivelled his head to the side and

looked straight into his manager's angry, dark gaze. 'I've told you before and I'll tell you again.

Not you, nor anyone else, will ever dictate how I live my life.'

'Is that so?' Henry sneered. 'You think you'd have anything without me?

I saved your arse from washing pots and clearing up puddles of beer for the rest of your life. I took your measly punches and taught you how to use them properly. You owe me, Jake. Big time.'

Jacob flicked his gaze to Henry's fingers, their implied possession making his pulse thump with suppressed fury. 'Take your hand off me.'

'Or what?'

'Or I'll have you sucking the beer out of the floorboards in two seconds flat.'

Their gazes locked and Jacob's heart picked up speed. He was tired.

Tired and feeling more than a little annoyed that Henry hadn't left him to have a quiet beer or three.

Henry's fingers lifted. 'I'm not your enemy, you know.'

'No? Then who is?' Jacob straightened and turned his back to the bar, stared through the thick, grey smoke at the drinkers and drunkards, pimps and labourers. 'You're the only one looking to control me, Henry. The only one whose roof I live under and the only person who takes a cut of what I earn. The way I see it, you leave me to do what I do best, and I'll leave you to do the same.' He faced him. 'I won tonight's fight quickly and cleanly, and you've done well out of it. If I ever want to be in London, it will be on my terms, not yours.'

Henry's gaze bored into Jacob's before he pushed away from the bar, a snide smile curving his lips. 'You're a born fighter, Jake. You live for it, revel in the heat of the violence. This life chose you. For Christ's sake, damn well use the rush. Bloody well thrive on it. Violence is at the heart of you. You know it, and so do I.'

Jacob lifted his tankard to his lips and sipped, carefully watching Henry as he strolled through the tavern, accepting the shoulder slaps and handshakes that Jacob had ignored. The man was a villain. A plunderer riding on the back of other people's misery. Yet, Jacob could not deny the man's words about Jacob's future.

Violence was the life he'd inherited from his father.

The life he was taught from the moment he could walk.

But it was his life and he would lead it on his own terms. Whether Henry accepted that or not.

He drained his drink and put the tankard on the bar. 'Another, Maura, please.'

The landlady poured him a refill and Jacob closed his eyes against the childhood memories that rose in his mind's eye, the remembered noises filtering through louder than they had for years. Twelve years had passed since then, too many brawls and professional fights to count and too much blood deeply embedded in the creases of his hands to ever erase.

His solitary life was a necessity. To be riddled with the sort of anger that beat through Jacob's veins meant he would never be close to anyone.

Not even the manager who had adopted his scrawny fifteen-year-old, near-emaciated body and made him the prize-winning, fairly wealthy boxer he was today. A man who used his fists, who'd failed to protect his mother from the murdering fists of his father, would never be accepted or normal . . . never be trustworthy or a man who would ever trust another.

3
City of Bristol — February 1851

Louisa and Nancy boarded the train at Bristol Temple Meads and entered their designated compartment, the rare silence between them illustrating the uncertainty and trepidation of what awaited them in Bath. Louisa sat on the red velvet seat as the close proximity of the walnut-panelled walls exacerbated her claustrophobia. She stared through the window at the bustling platform, steam hindering her view but not lessening the volume of shouts, whistles and general hubbub of the busy station.

It had been two weeks since she'd learned of Anthony's death and the numbness that had driven her to her bed for five days had finally begun to abate. In its path emerged a determination she had not known since her days soliciting punters. A dangerous humming had started in her ears two days before and she was all too aware of what its return meant.

Fate had called her to dig deep once again.

To accept that Anthony's love, which she had so often doubted, had only been skin-deep. He had not confided in her about his problems. Instead, he'd lied and kept secrets from her.

But, despite it all, she could not deny he'd given her a life a whore would never dare to dream of. No violence. A warm bed. A roof over her head.

Hot food on the table . . . He'd even asked for her hand in marriage.

Eventually.

But now she had learned of his debts, the depth of his secrecy and a life she knew nothing about.

A life he'd lived in Bath.

'Whatever we find in Bath, we'll manage it well enough,' Louisa murmured, her hands so tightly clenched, her leather gloves stretched uncomfortably against her knuckles. 'We're stronger than we think.'

'Is that a statement or a pondering?' Nancy finished fussing with her belongings and pushed her trunk onto the overhead shelf. She sat down, her grey eyes burning with resolve. 'Because I think whatever lies ahead might stink from here to Bath and back again.'

Louisa turned from the window. 'Maybe, but we'll manage it regardless.'

'Will we? We've had more gentlemen coming to our door this week asking for money than we ever had when that husband of yours was living.

'Not to mention the fact he's been sitting on a property you didn't know existed. Lord only knows what we'll find when we get there.' Nancy shook her head, her gaze furious. 'Why in God's name was I always trying to reassure you he loved you? You were right to doubt him. What sort of life has he been living without you, Lou? The notion he was gallivanting around another city makes me want to vomit.'

'Well, we'll find out soon enough tomorrow. I'm glad we're getting this later train and taking a night in a hotel.' Louisa stared through the window again. 'A good night's sleep will help us to deal with whatever we have to face in the morning.'

A shrill whistle blew outside the window and the train began a slow chug from the station into the bright February afternoon. Louisa sat back, her mind reeling. The state of Anthony's finances had become clear before she'd even buried him — which was why she was travelling to Bath the day after his funeral.

Barely a handful of people had attended the church ceremony, the lack of family and friends only enhancing her blind foolishness. Having always believed her husband to be a fine, upstanding businessman, she'd never felt she had the audacity, or even the right, to ask Anthony anything about his dealings, or even his day-to-day life. Now, her gratitude for services rendered was shaming.

Humiliation rose hot in her cheeks and she closed her eyes.

Despite her love for their home in Bristol, she quickly learned that Anthony had sold the property without her knowledge shortly before he died with the proviso that Louisa had one week from the date of his premeditated death to leave the premises. She could only presume his guilt in taking her home had been somewhat tempered, at least in his heart, by giving her the Bath house. The proceeds from the Bristol house had, of course, already been spent . . . both before he died and since, given to creditors and whomever else Anthony had owed money.

So, what little money Louisa had of her own

17

she had put into a locked box in her luggage and hoped it would buy her and Nancy a little time until they decided what to do next. The guilt that she had fallen short of her promise to always keep her friend safe and well was becoming more and more difficult to bear as the days passed.

'What will you do?'

Nancy's question was so softly asked, Louisa's shame deepened. Her usually forthright and candid friend was clearly making an effort to be gentle.

'I'm not sure.' Louisa sighed. 'I'll know more once we've seen the house.' She faced Nancy and sat a little straighter. 'At least we know this one is paid for.'

'I'm so sorry we've had to leave the house you loved, Lou.' Nancy squeezed Louisa's fingers. 'You took such pride in every room, every piece of furniture, every — '

'Everything that isn't mine. None of it is or ever was.'

'But — '

'But nothing.' Louisa turned to the window as they passed buildings and chimneys, the train picking up speed as they headed farther away from the city. 'Everything was Anthony's. Everything I had, that I thought was mine, was really his. I see that now.'

'To think I believed the man truly loved you . . . I feel such an idiot.'

Louisa's heart jolted painfully. 'As do I, but there is little point in dwelling on that now. Anthony's duplicity is just another lesson we must learn from. Maybe neither of us will ever be capable of

18

truly loving a man and there's no shame in that. After all, we've seen men as they really are.

It's hard to erase that experience from our minds or hearts.'

'Did you love him?'

'No, but I had come to rely on him.' Resentment rose bitter in Louisa's throat. 'I won't make that mistake again. He should have told me about the debt. About the trouble he was in. He knew where I came from. He knew how tough I am.'

'True, but he'd come to see you as a lady. A woman he wanted to keep and care for. You can hardly hate him for wanting to raise you higher. Wanting the world to see your beauty and grace.'

Louisa huffed a laugh. 'Beauty and grace? I don't think so.'

'No?' Nancy smiled, her eyes lit with teasing. 'Then why is it you can walk down any street and men turn? I've seen it a thousand times.'

Louisa shook her head. Anthony's betrayal had made her feel ugly, more tainted than ever before. 'If I am beautiful, then that will be my saving grace.'

'What do you mean?'

'I know now that without my looks I have nothing.' She inhaled a shaky breath, slowly released it. 'I've put my body and soul through so much for money, but now, after this, I don't believe the things I've done to be so wrong anymore.'

'Of course they weren't wrong. Each of us had to do what we had to do.'

Nancy's cheeks reddened as her jaw grew tight, pride glowing in her eyes.

'I feel nothing about sex. I feel nothing about

19

my selling it for a meal.

We're good, strong women, Lou. Don't you ever forget that.'

Louisa sat back in her seat, words catching like broken glass in her throat. How could she not have known that Anthony was so close to taking his life? How could she not have known his money had gone on bad investments, bad investors and a desperation for rescue at the card table? It didn't matter how much she wanted to feel angry, how could she when she'd asked for nothing, but Anthony had given her everything?

Tears burned behind her eyes. She might not have loved Anthony, but she had been so very fond of him. Had seen him as a kindly keeper rather than a lover and he had softened a small part of her hardened heart. He'd saved her from a life of prostitution. Saved her from having to ever again service one man after another. Although she'd been spared life as a streetwalker when a madam had taken Louisa into her brothel, when Anthony had begun to beg for her exclusivity, Louisa had quickly wanted what he had to offer and shunned the brothels and the madam who'd helped her, stupidly believing her life with Anthony would be safe and long-lasting.

How could she not when he'd so readily agreed to take Nancy in from the brothel too? Albeit as Louisa's maid and companion.

The truth was, Anthony hadn't trusted Louisa any more than she'd trusted him. Both of them keeping the worst of their secrets hidden, their shame branded on their lonely hearts.

And now she would live in Bath, in his secret

home, and start again.

She reached into her reticule and pulled out the envelope containing the deeds and key to what would become her new home. It was a large property with four bedrooms, an attic, lounge, parlour, kitchen and basement. A bigger house than Anthony had owned in Bristol. His solicitor had explained that property was a lot more costly by Bristol's harbour than on Carson Street, Bath.

The Bath house had become a silver lining around what had been an incredibly dark couple of weeks. With the Bristol house sold, a good portion of Anthony's debts had been paid, a few pieces of good jewellery and furniture taking care of the rest . . . unless someone else came knocking once she and Nancy were in Bath, which wasn't beyond the realms of possibility.

After all, once Louisa had searched Anthony's study and uncovered a plethora of hidden papers, the secrets had come pouring out like dung from a burst pipe.

Nancy had fallen asleep beside her, her soft snoring touching Louisa's heart. They were kindred spirits. Two young women who had fallen on hard times and found themselves working side by side in a seedy brothel, making money using the only constant they had available to them: their bodies.

Their looks and their youth. Louisa gently laid her hand over her friend's, sickness clenching tight in her stomach.

Anthony's agreement to also house Nancy had given Louisa indescribable relief considering she'd been prepared to reject his offer if he had refused to pay the madam for Nancy's release, too. She and Nancy had been friends through the best and worst of times for the last seven years and nothing would ever separate them. Louisa breathed deep. At least she could be certain of that, if nothing else.

Tears leaked from her eyes and Louisa quickly swiped them away.

She had a home and her best friend — the only friend she had ever found in her life. And, as God was her witness, she and Nancy would rise again.

4

City of Bath — February 1851

It had gone midnight by the time Jacob let himself into his lodgings.

Stepping inside, he closed the door and entered the dark hallway, the bare stairs and faded brown wallpaper doing little to elevate his bad mood. He strained his hearing towards the kitchen and a couple of seconds passed before the familiar sound of a match being struck filtered towards him.

Doreen, the housekeeper, would already be preparing a pot of tea, no doubt eager for their regular late-night chat.

Smiling, he shrugged off his coat and hung it with his hat on the hallway stand before walking into the kitchen.

Doreen greeted him with a smile and a wink. 'Tea or something stronger?'

'Tea will be appreciated.'

His housekeeper was part mother, part good-time girl, but if Doreen was home, Jacob, Henry and Colin, who shared the house, always received a maternal greeting.

With a nod, she left the kettle on the lit stove and moved to some hooks below a wooden shelf, lifting off two mugs. 'Did you win?'

'I did.' Jacob blew out a breath and moved his head from side to side to release the kinks in his neck. 'He went down in one.'

'Good lad.'

Jacob stared at her turned back as she made the coffee. *Good lad.* Doreen wasn't to know how every time she called him that it brought to mind his mother. A woman who had raised him as best and kindly as she could amid a home that also housed a drunk.

His father.

'Now, what's put that look of murder on your face?' Doreen slid a steaming mug towards him and sat down across the table. 'If it's Mr Bertrum bothering you, don't pay him no mind. He only likes to get the best out of you boys.'

'Why don't you call him Henry like the rest of us?' Jacob scowled as he picked up his tea. 'He doesn't deserve the respect of *Mr Bertrum* when he has no appreciation of all you do for him.'

She raised her eyebrows. 'All I do for him? Haven't I got a roof over my head? A bed upstairs and the company of you and Colin, two strapping boxers with muscles the size of boulders?' Her green eyes twinkled with mischief. 'I've landed on my luck and if it stays that way by calling Mr Bertrum, Mr Bertrum, it's no skin off my nose.'

Jacob sipped his tea.

'So, what has the so-and-so done now? I assume it's him you're all ruffled up about.'

Words and confessions battled on Jacob's tongue just as they did whenever he was alone with Doreen. She was the closest person he had to a confidante and the longer he knew her, the harder it became not to tell her a little about himself past his boxing, eating or sleeping habits.

But it wouldn't happen. At least, not tonight.

Jacob stretched out his legs and lounged back in his chair as though he hadn't a care in the world. 'It's not Henry. It's nothing. I'm just glad to be home.'

'Well, I would hate to see the expression on your face if you couldn't stand the place.' She blew across the top of her mug. 'You should count your blessings, you know. You haven't done badly under Mr Bertrum's guidance.'

Staring at her in disbelief, Jacob shook his head. 'Granted, the man taught me how to punch with intention, but he didn't teach me a damn thing about violence. I knew all about that way before I met *Mr Bertrum*.'

'Is that so?'

Jacob turned away from her wily gaze and looked towards the drapeless window and the darkness beyond.

'Do you know something?'

He waited, praying Doreen continued. He didn't trust himself not to blurt some home truths if he opened his mouth again.

'You are a good man, Jacob, but you've got one hell of a chip on your shoulder.'

Defensiveness rose and he faced her. 'What?'

'A chip the size of the Abbey, I'd say.' She sipped her drink, her gaze steady on his. 'You're twenty-seven years old, as handsome as they come and have a brain to match. Yet, you choose to spend your time punching ten bales of shit out of other blokes as stubborn as you. I don't understand it.'

He shrugged, hating the shame that tightened in his gut. 'Violence breeds violence. I don't know

25

anything else. Anyway, the pay is good and, like you, I've got somewhere nice enough to live. There are plenty of others who haven't.'

'So this is it?' She set down her mug, annoyance in her voice. 'You're not going to find yourself a nice, warm woman to come home to at night?'

She dipped her head towards his hands. 'Not going to let the broken skin around your knuckles and in your soul heal over?'

He swallowed. 'There's nothing wrong with my soul.'

'No? Then why do you keep fighting?' She softened her voice. 'Why can't you find another way?'

Jacob's heart picked up speed and his hands turned clammy around his mug. She was so good to him. Cared and shared. Laughed and loved. Yet, what did he give Doreen — give anyone — in return?

Self-loathing whispered through him and he looked into the depths of his tea. 'I need to prove something to myself, all right?'

'And boxing is the way to do that?'

'Yes.' He clenched his jaw. 'It's the only way.'

Her hand was gentle as it slid onto his forearm. 'Look at me, lad.'

Silently cursing, Jacob inhaled a long breath and met her soft gaze.

'Tell me who you are really trying to prove yourself to.'

The father who killed my mother. The mother who never doubted me. Not once.

He slid his arm from under Doreen's hand and stood. 'Myself, that's who.'

'But —'

26

Raising his hand, he cut off her words, guilt pressing down on him as he left the kitchen. The truth was, his mother would not be proud of how he earned his money. Not one bit. As for his father? Jacob could hear his damn laughter.

Hadn't he become what his father had always told Jacob he'd be? A nobody. A waif and stray. A bloke with no wife, home or kids.

'Well, to hell with you, Pa,' he muttered. 'I hope you're happy with my lot.'

Just as Jacob reached the bottom of the stairs, the front door swung open and a blast of cold February air accompanied his housemate and friend of sorts, Colin Beadon, as he swept into the hallway. Tall with dark blond hair, Colin was known on the boxing circuit for being a 'gentleman boxer'. A man of supreme skill and solid integrity. Any person or opponent who came in contact with him knew pretty quickly what they got . . . which was much the reason why Jacob liked him.

'Good God, it's bloody freezing out there.' Colin pushed the door shut and unwound his scarf from around his neck. 'All right, Jacob?'

'Good, what about you?'

'Yeah, all good. I've just come from The Star.' Colin frowned, his brown eyes filling with wariness. 'You heard of a boxer going by the name of the Killer?'

'The Killer?' Jacob huffed a laugh and crossed his arms. 'Is that a joke?'

'You'd think so, but after the stories I've heard, I'm not so sure there's much to laugh about if this bloke intends to make his presence known around here. He's come down from up North, apparently.

27

Here, look at this.'

Jacob took the newspaper Colin handed him and scanned the copy accompanying a picture of a giant of a man, teeth practically glinting from the page, his arm held aloft by a man Jacob presumed to be his manager. He continued to read; each word was more disturbing than the last.

He looked at Colin. 'He's done time in prison? Hard labour?'

'Yep. Apparently, he's been nicked several times for concealing and using home-made weapons in the ring. They can't get him for attempted murder because none of the wounds he's inflicted could be deemed near fatal, but the word on the street is, it's only a matter of time before the nutter successfully slays someone.'

Jacob looked at the paper again. 'And he's fighting here? In Bath?'

'And undefeated. I'm not looking forward to Henry getting wind of this.

You know what his first thoughts will be.'

'That it will be up to one of us to beat this bloke.' Jacob raised his head, unease knotting his gut. 'This is the sort of fighter we should stay well clear of.'

'Hmm, but I can't see Henry agreeing with that, can you?'

A scratch of a match being lit sounded through the open kitchen door.

Colin smiled and glanced along the hallway. 'That's my cue for a cuppa and a grilling from our lovely lady, I think. See you in the morning.'

'Yeah, night.' Jacob put his hand on the banister, his gaze lingering on Colin's retreating

28

back. The Killer. Maybe what was written in the paper had been blown all out of proportion, but it wouldn't hurt to be forearmed and forewarned. The least Jacob could do was watch the Killer's next fight . . .

5

Louisa looked at her map before squinting from her spot on Pulteney Bridge towards a terrace of beautiful Georgian houses just a short distance away. 'We must be in the wrong place,' she said, glancing at Nancy who stared in awe at the row of grand houses. 'With Anthony's finances the way they were, he couldn't have possibly lived anywhere near here.'

'We're not talking about Royal Crescent, you know. It's Carson Street.

Let's keep walking.'

Closing her eyes, Louisa clenched the map tighter. 'The anticipation of seeing this house is just too much. I feel sick.'

'Too much for us? I don't think so.' Nancy pushed her hand through the crook of Louisa's arm. 'If our new home is one of those houses we're off to a great start. Come on.'

The day had broken damp and cold and Louisa's harried breath puffed in plumes, yet the dank temperature failed to cool the heat in her cheeks. She had been humiliated, used and mistreated countless times during her time working in the brothel, yet tracing Anthony's second property — and the nuances of his second life — heightened her degradation to a new extent.

She saw now that she had just been something else he had bought — something else he had wanted to own and no doubt bragged of possessing when he'd been among his peers at the card table.

It shamed and sickened her, and in her heart of hearts, she longed to draw Nancy to a stop and beg that they return on the next train to Bristol. But what was there for them now?

Nothing. And the harsh reality was that, sooner or later, she and Nancy would need to find work.

They walked along the sweeping curved wall surrounding the gushing waters of the River Avon and a beautifully landscaped area known as, according to Louisa's map, the Parade Gardens. The barren trees were interspersed with evergreens, the soil beds empty of flowers in winter but imaginings of how the gardens might look in the summer months gave Louisa a flicker of optimism.

Continuing to walk along the cobbled street, she and Nancy neared the row of terrace houses they'd seen from the bridge.

'Carson Street.' Nancy pointed to a sign bolted to one of the corner houses adjacent to a busy thoroughfare filled with carriages, horses and pedestrians. 'This is it.'

Locating the right house wasn't difficult as Louisa had memorised the deeds so often and so intensely, the pencilled sketch of Anthony's property was clearly drawn in her mind. 'Anthony's house is — '

'Ahem, *your* house.' Nancy grinned.

' *My* house is about halfway along the street.' Louisa inhaled a shaky breath. 'Come on. I want this over with.'

She marched ahead of Nancy, pulling a brass front door key from her purse. Purposefully,

Louisa drew forth her anger at Anthony's lies, betrayal and cowardice. Lord knew, she would have to take strength from somewhere if she was ever to believe such a property was now hers to do with as she would. Lifting her chin, she shrouded herself in an invisible layer of protection against whatever further hurts were to come in her uncertain future.

But once she was standing outside the residence, her bravado floundered.

The house was beautiful. Built in a butter-coloured stone, its sash windows were flanked with velvet drapery, the front door painted a dark grass-green, complete with brass knocker and a stone ornament decorating its step. The longer Louisa stared, the more strongly inevitability enveloped her. She had survived this long and she would continue to survive, come what may.

After all, she and Nancy had the most pleasing of houses as their foundation.

She softly smiled as a whisper of positivity, of belonging . . . maybe even destiny, seeped deep into her heart. Could it be she was meant to be here?

That Anthony had known this house would one day be hers. Maybe her conceptions of his subterfuge were actually initiated in wonderful surprise rather than treachery.

'Could this really be it?' Nancy asked, gazing up at the house. 'For all my carrying on, this is so much grander than the Bristol house, Lou.'

'Indeed it is,' Louisa murmured. 'Let's go inside, shall we?'

She walked to the front door and slid the key

into the lock, her heart beating hard as trepidation swept through her. She and Nancy stepped into a large hallway, painted in the softest hue of lemon and white, the floorboards a beautiful dark wood.

As Nancy closed the door, Louisa's momentary notion that the house might have been meant for her wavered. There was something distinctly female about it whereas she had been expecting the décor to be entirely male. A bad feeling whispered through her even as she admired the colours, the spray of flowers in a porcelain vase, the framed embroidery on the walls and the floral, ruffle-edged umbrella in a stone stand.

A door farther along the hallway clicked open and a high-pitched gasp reverberated around the space. 'Who the devil are you and what are you doing in my house?'

Louisa flinched. A pretty, young woman strode closer, her cheeks mottled and her eyes wide with alarm.

'Oh, Christ,' Nancy muttered.

'I said, who are you? How did you get in?' The woman demanded before shouting over her shoulder. 'Mrs Armitage! Mrs Fairweather! Call the constable!'

Hurried footsteps emerged from below stairs and into the hallway and still Louisa couldn't find her voice or drag her stare from the semi-hysterical woman. She was attractive with dark brown hair, clearly defined cheekbones and big, green eyes framed with long, dark lashes. And she appeared two, maybe three years younger than Louisa's twenty-five years.

She had to be Anthony's mistress.

Sickness rolled through Louisa. Why in God's name had she ever believed he might have respected her? Clearly the monogamy he demanded of her when she left the brothel had been entirely one-sided.

Swallowing the bitterness that rose in her throat, Louisa forced her gaze to the two older women who now stood either side of their mistress. One was dressed in a smart, high-buttoned grey dress, a bunch of keys hanging at her waist and a cameo brooch at her throat. Presumably the housekeeper.

The other wore a white cap and apron, flour dappling the brown curls falling about her face. No prizes for assuming this woman to be the cook.

Slowly, Louisa faced the mistress of the house, her body slightly trembling as anger infused her, overtook her. 'Are you the mistress of Mr Anthony Hill?'

The woman opened her mouth to respond and then snapped it shut. Her eyes narrowed as she stared intently at Louisa, her gaze travelling over her from head to toe, only to return to her face. The abrupt change in her expression, her widening eyes and the vivid spots of red that leapt into her cheeks were all Louisa needed to see to know that whoever this woman was, she was fully aware of Louisa . . . fully aware that Anthony had a wife.

Whereas, once again, Louisa stood in ignorance of this newly revealed aspect of her husband's life.

She straightened her spine and held the woman's startled gaze. 'Well? Are you?'

'Of course, she is.' Nancy sniffed. 'Look at her.'

Louisa took a step closer, slowly unbuttoning her coat as the simmering fury inside of her gathered ferocity. Every ounce of her humiliation poured through her, igniting the self-preservation, the roughness and spine of steel she'd had to enforce in order to survive life as a whore.

Would she have to be that woman again in order to assert her authority over this strumpet who chose to live so openly — so richly — with her lover despite knowing he was married? It was one thing if a wife chose to tolerate dalliances, to accept that her husband might take a discreet lover or visit brothels, but none Louisa knew of would have accepted such blatant disrespect to live in such a beautiful house with staff no less. Who did this woman think she was? Surely Anthony had not loved this woman when he had left Louisa this very house and presumably his mistress nothing?

Louisa curled her hands at her sides, angry that there was every possibility she would have to once again resort to catfights, slaps and hair-pulling as a way to maintain her property and possessions.

She lifted her chin, her heart hardening, her muscles tensed and ready.

'Do you know who I am?'

The skin at the woman's neck shifted and she took a single step back.

'You're Anthony's wife.'

'That's correct. I'm *Mrs* Anthony Hill. And you are?'

'Caroline. Caroline Warwick.'

'And you are kept here by Anthony?'

The other woman nodded, her cheeks blazing red as her gaze darted from Louisa to Nancy, who undoubtedly wore an expression as threatening and hard-faced as Louisa's.

'I see.' Louisa released the final button on her coat. 'And these are your staff?'

Another nod.

'Is there anyone else here I should know about?'

'My maid.'

'Your maid?' Louisa laughed and shook her head. 'Well, Anthony really did keep you in the highest of households, didn't he? Considering I only ever asked for my friend here to stay with me as a companion.' She pushed her purse under her arm and plucked the fingers of her gloves. 'Of course, I was always happy to cook, clean and care for my husband myself.' Pulling off the first glove, she glared. 'He must have thought you worth every penny he bestowed on you. I can't help pondering why that might be . . . or what you did to keep him so wholly satisfied.'

Miss Warwick drew back her shoulders as her gaze filled with contempt.

'Anthony loves me. If he doesn't think you deserve staff then, quite clearly, you don't.'

Louisa's smile ever so slightly trembled. *Miss* Warwick had referred to Anthony in the present tense. *She doesn't know of his passing.* Yet, Louisa couldn't summon sympathy for her. How could she when the woman had been living so openly as Anthony's mistress? Clearly, *Miss* Warwick wasn't so well bred as she might pretend to be either. The determination and possession in her eyes spoke of someone who also knew how to protect what was hers.

A sudden calmness wound through Louisa.

36

She didn't want to behave as she had before; she didn't want to scream and shout, brawl and fight. She had come so far. Anthony had brought her so far. And, by God, his actions would not bring her down again.

She cleared her throat. 'I said *I* was happy to care for him without staff.

He offered to employ people to help me numerous times, only I refused on the grounds I cared for him deeply and wanted to run our house alone. It seems you felt differently.'

'Anthony isn't here, and you need to go.' Miss Warwick lifted her chin with a defiance that belied the uncertainty in her gaze. 'This is my house and I want you to lea —'

'Oh, no. You see, *Miss* Warwick, that is where you are wrong. This house is entirely mine.'

'What?'

'I think we'd better see about some tea, don't you?' Louisa placed her purse and gloves on the small side table beside her and took off her coat, taking her time hanging it on the hallway stand. 'I have some bad news to impart and I think it best you sit down.'

6

Through rain and drizzle, Jacob walked along one of the many paths that wound through the greenery of Victoria Park, his overcoat buttoned and his knitted scarf pulled up to his chin. From beneath the brim of his hat, he studied both the fancy and the fallen folk as they passed him. It never ceased to amaze him how Bath held such an amalgamation of status, wealth and poverty. As the years passed and Jacob became ever more embittered by the hand life had dealt him, it was hard not to scoff at the irony of how the rich were forced to cross the paths of the poor, unable to completely turn away from the sights, sounds and smells of depravity that strolled straight into their privileged paths every day.

A top-hatted gentleman and his beau edged away as Jacob came closer, their noses high and eyes averted. Jacob purposely lifted his hat and slid a wink at the young woman clinging to the toff's arm like her life depended on his salvation. Jacob somehow just about managed to swallow his laughter.

Taking a paper-wrapped pie from his coat pocket, he peeled it open and took a bite, savouring the rich gravy and meat, the heat welcome on his gloveless fingers.

He came into a clearing and watched five young lads playing a bit too roughly, a bit too freely on the frost-nipped grass. Something about the raised

38

colour in their cheeks, their furrowed brows and contorted mouths aroused Jacob's suspicion.

He glanced to what they kicked on the ground. Dark ruffled hair, a flash of cheek . . .

The pie slipped from his fingers and Jacob broke into a sprint. Adrenaline pumped through his body as he ran towards the melee, his teeth clenched and his anger at the injustice of what was being meted out in public sending his fury sky-high.

How many people had walked past these lads and turned the other cheek?

How many of the swells who talked endlessly about justice and the British way thought five boys kicking ten bales out of one was fair game?

'Oi! You lot,' Jacob shouted. 'What do you think you're doing?' He grabbed the collar of the closest lad and yanked him back, succinctly landing him on his arse on the grass. 'Get out of here, right now.'

The rest of his gang scarpered before the leader scrambled to his feet and fled after his friends.

Jacob glared after them before turning his attention to the beaten and bloodied mess of the youth at his feet. 'Here, my friend.' He offered the lad his hand. 'Let's get you to your feet, shall we?'

The boy couldn't have been any older than eleven or twelve and, despite the bulk of his too-large coat and boots, the scrawny inches of bare legs that flashed white beneath his too-short trousers showed the boy also weighed no more than a few stone.

Anger simmered inside Jacob as he fought to break a smile. 'Well, that was a fine mess you got yourself into.'

The boy picked up his flat cap before sliding his fingers into Jacob's.

When he'd straightened, the lad swiped the back of his hand across his bleeding bottom lip. 'Thanks, mister. Those boys think they got a right to my ma's shopping money.' He glared towards where his assailants had run, his blue eyes dark with revenge. 'But they would've had to kill me first.'

Admiring the lad's spunk, Jacob warmed to him. He crossed his arms as he studied the boy a little closer. 'That wasn't the first time you've had a run-in with them, was it?'

'No, sir. They go to my school.'

'So, they bully you there *and* when you're not at school? How did they know you'd be here?'

'They wait for me outside my house some-times.' His eyes flashed with unwavering spirit again. 'But if they think I'm going to hide from them, they can think again.'

Indecision warred inside Jacob even as he reached into his pocket for a coin to reward the boy for his bravery. The intelligent thing would be to walk away but . . . He stared in the direction the boys had run again, the image of what he'd come across when this young lad had been on the ground flashing in his mind's eye.

'Seems to me you need someone to show you how to put those lads in their places once and for all,' he muttered before facing the boy. 'What's your name, son?'

The boy narrowed his eyes, his gaze drifting back and forth from Jacob's face to the coin he

40

held. 'Thomas, sir.'

'Here. For your courage.' Jacob put the coin on the boy's outstretched palm. 'No one can take on five opponents at once. Do you understand? You're a strong, brave lad.'

'Yes, sir.'

'But this isn't a kind world.' Jacob hesitated as he debated whether or not what he had in mind to do was right or wrong. Did he really want this young lad to grow up as jaded, angry and alone as he was? He pushed away his doubts. The boy might as well learn the way of the world from him as anyone else. 'You've got to meet people where they are, Thomas. Defend yourself and look after what is yours.'

'Yes, sir. I try to look after my ma. Honestly, I do.'

The shame that the boy seemed to be succeeding where Jacob had so tragically failed cracked a splinter across his heart and he put his hand on the boy's shoulder. 'I don't doubt that, Thomas, not at all. In this city, there are ruffians, bullies and bad people ten to the dozen. So, if you are going to survive, you have to beat these people at their own game. Fight back. Stand your ground. Show them you won't take any nonsense.'

The confusion evaporated from the boy's eyes as they slowly lit with interest. 'What do you mean?'

'I mean . . . ' Jacob raised his fists in front of him and winked. 'You've got to learn to fight, son. It's the only way.'

The boy's eyes widened as he stared at Jacob's hands before lifting his incredulous gaze. 'And you'll teach me?'

41

'Well, a couple of punches, at least. What do you say?'

The boy brushed down the lapels on his coat, spread his feet and lifted his hands to mirror Jacob's. He grinned. 'I say yes, sir!'

Culpability pressed down on Jacob that he might be introducing the young lad to a different way of life, a different way of facing and dealing with his problems. But Jacob didn't know any other way than to treat violence with violence, anger with anger. What was he supposed to do?

Leave the lad to accept a second beating? A third?

To fight, to hurt, to maim, was the only way a man kept the wolf from his door, from his friends and lovers . . . from his mother.

Ignoring the stab of guilt that jabbed at his gut, Jacob stepped back and studied the boy from head to toe. 'Well now, let's see what you've got, shall we?'

7

Louisa sat in the Carson Street parlour, her patience stretched to breaking.

To say the atmosphere was tense would be an understatement. It was suffocating. Nauseating and frustrating.

She imagined a string attached to the top of her head and pulled her spine straight, her bosom high and refined ... but her insides shook while her foot, thankfully hidden beneath her skirts, bounced up and down on the oriental carpet. She and Nancy sat opposite Miss Warwick where she proceeded to lord over the space, her maid standing to attention behind her, jumping to her mistress's every instruction.

Tea had been poured and three plates waited beside a freshly baked, freshly cut sponge.

It was proving incredibly difficult for Louisa to resist swiping the entirety of the afternoon tea onto the fancy rug.

She held Miss Warwick's gaze. 'So, this is all very civil but a farce, I think. Don't you?'

'You should think yourself lucky I —'

'So, it would be best if I say what I need to say,' Louisa continued. 'And we'll see what is to be done thereafter.'

Muttering something incoherent — and suspiciously unrepeatable — Nancy shifted beside Louisa and reached for her cup of tea.

Louisa kept her gaze on Anthony's rat-faced

mistress. The woman had yet to pass even a slightly genial look Nancy's way and that irked Louisa immeasurably, considering Anthony's philandering had nothing to do with her friend and everything to do with the man himself. The least Miss Warwick could do was stand by her life decisions and show some friendliness to innocent bystanders.

Louisa cleared her throat. 'My husband is dead, Miss Warwick. Found hanged in a hotel room, right here in Bath. I take it as some measure of his character that he chose to take his life elsewhere rather than here where you might have found him.'

Maybe the brutal delivery of such news could be deemed cruel, but Louisa's directness had nothing to do with inflicting pain or distress upon Miss Warwick. The complete opposite, in fact. She wanted her to know the truth, without lies and omissions. After all, it was clear Anthony had been no more truthful about the state of his finances with his mistress than he had his wife.

Even though she should detest her, Louisa preferred that Anthony's deceit and shameful acts didn't affect Miss Warwick as irrevocably as they had her, considering the woman was no less guilty than Louisa of wanting a better life for herself. Of course, she knew nothing of Miss Warwick's history, but Louisa had yet to learn anything that might determine whether her beginnings had been in any way different.

Miss Warwick had paled, her lips so tightly pressed together they showed white, tears quivering on dark lashes that only served to enhance the woman's beauty.

She raised a trembling hand to her throat. 'Why

44

would you say such a thing?'

Nancy tutted and reached for a slice of cake. 'Because it's true. Why else?'

Louisa fought against her rising sympathy as a tear slid over Miss Warwick's cheek. 'Because, even though you were Anthony's mistress, you deserve the truth. The whole truth.'

'Which is?' She dabbed her cheeks with the heel of her hand before her maid offered a handkerchief from her apron pocket. 'How can there be more? What am I to do now?'

Miss Warwick's selfishly exclaimed question scratched over Louisa's patience like a sharpened claw. Clearly she thought nothing of her staff and their futures, only herself. Whereas Louisa's mind was consumed with Nancy's welfare and the future Louisa had promised her dearest friend.

'Anthony's death isn't about what you do now,' Louisa snapped. 'It should be about accepting the sort of man Anthony was, the debts and secrets he had. But maybe you are incapable of seeing past yourself.

Clearly, you knew about me, whereas I knew nothing of you. I can see finding out he took his own life has shocked you and I'm confident the gravity of his debts would, too.' Unable to remained poised a moment longer, Louisa stood and took a few steps about the room. She stopped and faced Miss Warwick. 'If I have to sell all this finery, furniture and decoration in order for my friend and I to start again, I will. You may keep your clothes and any jewellery or gifts my husband bestowed upon you, but everything else, Miss Warwick, is now mine.'

Nancy clapped. 'Hear, hear.'

Louisa threw a warning glare at Nancy, but she merely shrugged and returned to her tea and cake. Her satisfied humming could have easily been resisted if she'd wanted.

'But you can't!' Miss Warwick leapt to her feet, the colour rising in her cheeks and her eyes darkening with spite. 'This house is mine. Mine and Anthony's. He would've wanted me to have it. Your house is in Bristol. He told me so.'

Louisa's anger rose again. 'Is there anything he hasn't told you about our life together? Do you know my shoe size? Where I like to shop? My favourite piece of music?'

The other woman's colour darkened. 'He told me he loves you and would never leave you. That, *Mrs* Hill, was all I ever needed to know.'

Instead of triumph or happiness spreading through her, Miss Warwick's words sparked Louisa's sympathy for her. Anthony had clearly treated his mistress as a possession rather than a person, just as he had Louisa. And now Miss Warwick had fewer options than Louisa going forward.

She turned away and walked towards the window, looking out onto the street. 'He left a note saying sorry and that this house was now mine. I have no intention of contesting that or further questioning his decision-making. It is what it is, Miss Warwick.'

Louisa stared at a young couple as they passed the window, arm in arm, and closed her eyes. Had Anthony's written apology been for his suicide as she'd assumed? Or had he really been apologising for what awaited her when she pushed the key into the lock of this house in Bath? There was every possibility he was apologising not just for the dire straits he was leaving her in, but for Caroline Warwick, too.

Opening her eyes, resentment formed an icy chill around her heart and Louisa abruptly turned. 'You are — were — his mistress, Miss Warwick.

Surely, you understand I, of all people, am not under any obligation to you?

I'm sorry that Anthony — '

'Of course I understand that, but Anthony is no longer here, is he?' Miss Warwick snapped. 'But you . . . you . . . '

Nancy snorted. 'Cat got your cheating tongue?'

Miss Warwick flicked her furious gaze to Nancy and then Louisa. 'I have nothing but what Anthony gave me. You don't understand how we . . . where we . . . ' Her shoulders shook. 'I met him — '

'In a brothel?' Louisa swallowed against the dryness in her throat. No wonder she recognised the steel in this woman, the spirit and now the desperation. *Damn you, Anthony. Damn you.* 'Am I right?'

Miss Warwick nodded, her shoulders slumping before she collapsed into an armchair, her maid now standing a distance away, her mouth open and eyes agog.

Louisa swallowed against the compassion that thickened in her throat.

How could she just toss this woman into the street when Anthony had done exactly the same for Miss Warwick as he had for Louisa? For Nancy?

'Well, then,' Louisa sighed and resumed her seat on the settee. 'It seems Anthony has more than an affair to answer for. He has also left three whores living and, with his death, taken the lives he gave them.' She picked up her tea and sipped, her fingers trembling. 'But as his wife and the new owner of this house, I think it is up to me what happens next.' She looked to Miss Warwick's maid. 'If you could leave us alone for the time being, it would be appreciated.'

'Of course, madam.' The maid practically ran from the room, closing the door behind her.

Louisa, her heart thundering, laid her cup on the table and drew on every ounce of her strength. 'Now, first of all, do you have any family, any friends, who might be willing to take you in?'

'Lou, what are you doing?' Nancy gripped Louisa's forearm. 'This woman wouldn't give a fig about you if the shoe were on the other foot. Kick her out and be done with it.'

'And you'd be happy with that, Nance?' Louisa looked into her friend's eyes, willing her to trust her. 'I don't think you would, not really.' Nancy stared back, her glare gradually softening until she nodded, her hand slipping from Louisa's arm. She turned from her friend to Miss Warwick who watched them, eyes narrowed and clearly trying to calculate the dynamic between Louisa and Nancy. 'Miss Warwick? I asked you a question.'

Anthony's mistress slid her gaze to Louisa's, her green eyes cold. 'I have no one.'

'No one?' Louisa raised her eyebrows. There had been a slight hesitation in Miss Warwick's response. 'Are you sure?'

Again, Miss Warwick flitted her gaze back and forth between Louisa and Nancy until her

48

shoulders slightly slumped and she faced Louisa. 'There's a possibility John Hardman might help me.'

'John Hardman?' Nancy shifted closer. 'And who is he?'

'A friend.' Miss Warwick pinned Nancy with a glare. 'You'll find him any night in one of the taverns by the river.'

Nancy smiled wryly. 'A nice sort then.'

'Good, then I will track down this John Hardman later tonight,' Louisa said, placing her hand on Nancy's arm, silently warning her to keep her counsel. At least for now. 'While I am gone, Nancy will help you and your maids get your belongings packed and ready for your departure.'

'My departure?' Miss Warwick's eyes widened. 'You can't just throw me out! There is no guarantee that John will — '

'I'm sorry, Miss Warwick, my generosity does not stretch to ensuring your future. If you wish ill on anyone, wish it on Anthony.'

8

At the Bell Inn, Jacob snatched his shirt off the floor in the corner of the ring and pushed his way through a body of half-drunk men towards the bar, shoving his arms into his shirtsleeves as the adrenaline he'd needed to fight slowly seeped from his veins.

Around him, winning stakes were handed out to those who had bet on him to lose his latest fight. He squinted through a haze of smoke, the stench of ale and sweat clinging to the back of his throat. This fight had been considerably harder than the last. He should have had his opponent on the floor within the first two rounds. Instead the man, almost twice Jacob's size, had met his punch with every one of his own until Jacob had been forced to admit defeat.

His back and chest were slick with sweat, his lip split, and he had no doubt he'd have a shiner visible from the damn moon come tomorrow.

Well, he might have thrown in the towel, but any sense of shame he might have had didn't come. He wasn't prepared to die fighting, especially not on Henry's say-so.

Thankfully, his manager wasn't here to witness the loss as Henry was accompanying Colin at another fight across town. Jacob drew the back of his hand across his bloodied lip and gritted his teeth against the sting. He hoped to God Colin had fared better tonight. Henry's wrath, when they all returned home later, was a headache Jacob could do without.

An eruption of jeering and whistling turned him away from the bar to stare across the pub. A beautiful young woman with blonde hair and a frankly perfect figure was trying to fight her way through the pack of men surrounding her. Tall, slender and unmistakably female, her furrowed brow, flashing eyes and strategically placed elbows expertly nudged people out of the way.

Clearly a woman used to handling herself.

Yet, she wasn't dressed as though she frequented these sorts of pubs. Her hat was velvet and a bright sapphire-blue, decorated with flowers and a feather, her coat clean and smart.

One of the men made a grab for her and the response that came from her mouth sent the mob into fits of laughter.

Jacob approached her, fully aware his interceding might not be welcomed by the woman or the men, but his curiosity matched his concern, leaving him little choice.

'Hey, leave the woman alone,' he growled, gripping a man's elbow and pushing him to the side. 'I said, leave her alone.'

The woman's angry eyes met his. 'I am perfectly capable of looking after myself, sir.' She glared around the circle. 'These apes are as much of a threat to me as a leash of fox cubs.'

Another chorus of laughter and whistling filled the pub.

Jacob crossed his arms. 'Then maybe you'd like to join me for a drink?'

She narrowed her eyes. 'I did not come in here

for a drink.'

'Then can I ask — '

'Do not touch me!' She pushed her hands flat to another man's chest and sent his drunken arse stumbling backwards. 'Anyone else comes one step closer and I will not be accountable for my actions.'

Impressed, Jacob stepped back and raised his hands in surrender. 'I'm not sure about this lot, but I come in peace. Could you be looking for someone, by any chance?'

'Yes. Yes, I am.'

'Please, then let me buy you a drink and you can tell me his or her name.'

Drama over, the crowd around them slowly dispersed.

Jacob arched an eyebrow and waved towards the bar. 'Well?'

She studied him, her violet eyes hard on his. 'No, thank you.'

She pushed a stray curl under her hat and looked around, her jaw tight and her shoulders high. Her tension was palpable despite her bravado. 'I'm looking for a Mr John Hardman. Do you know him? I was told I'd find him in here or The Star.'

'I've not seen him, but I know of him. As far as I'm aware he prefers The Star over this place. I'm sure you'll find him in there at this time of night.'

Unease wound tight in Jacob's gut. From what he'd heard of John Hardman, he wasn't a man to cross and Jacob got the feeling this woman had no idea of the type of man she was looking for. He cleared his throat.

52

'Can I ask what you want with him?'

'No but thank you for your help.'

She moved to walk away, and Jacob stepped closer, not at all keen to let this beautiful, fiery woman walk alone about the streets at near ten o'clock, Hardman or no Hardman. 'Why don't I come with you? I was heading there after this pint anyway.' He quickly downed his ale. 'It's no bother.'

Planting her hands on her hips, she glared. 'I told you I am perfectly capable of looking after myself.'

'I realise that. But I could do with another drink. It's been one hell of a night.' He took a step towards the door. 'Are you coming?'

Jacob continued to walk through the crowds, praying she was behind him. He'd look a fool if he had to turn around and admit she had the upper hand. As he reached the door, he was just lifting his hat and coat from the stand when she pushed past him and stepped onto the street.

He smiled as he followed her out into the cold night air.

They hadn't been walking very long before she stopped and tipped her head back to look at him. 'How well do you know John Hardman?'

'Not very well at all.' Jacob rubbed his hands together, trying to think of something to say that might defer her hunt for Hardman. He suspected any reason this well-dressed woman wanted to find Hardman could not be good or moral. The man was a scoundrel. Worse, he was known for his heavy-handedness with women. 'Can I ask how you know him? I haven't seen you in The Star before and John isn't the type to be anywhere but in the pub.'

She studied him before her shoulders slumped and she sighed. 'The truth is, I don't know him at all. I need to find him for . . . a friend. We are relying on Mr Hardman to resolve a certain problem that has arisen.'

'What problem?'

'I have no wish to elaborate.'

They continued walking.

John Hardman was a drunk and a womaniser with very little money.

What he did have, he spent on alcohol, which only fuelled his inclination for violence — most likely to vent his frustration that he rarely had a pot to piss in.

Jacob glanced at this unmistakably shrewd and sharp-witted woman who had seemed inexplicably comfortable amid the drudgery of a backstreet pub. It was like putting a flower in a slag heap. Her demeanour and ease with The Bell's surroundings made no sense. Which meant he would have to see her safely home.

Clearing his throat, he looked to the star-spangled sky and stuffed his hands in his pockets, hoping to give the impression of indifference despite his disquiet. 'Did he do something to your friend?'

She stopped again. 'Why would you ask that?'

'Because John doesn't have the friendliest nature towards women and I'm not keen to introduce you to him, that's why.'

She raised her eyebrows, the steel coming back into her gaze. 'Is that so?

54

Then maybe it's best we say goodbye here and I'll make my own way to The Star.'

'That wouldn't be wise, Miss . . . '

'You have no need to know my name and I have no need to know yours.'

She walked away and Jacob cursed before hurrying to catch up with her.

What choice did he have but to go with her to The Star? All he wanted was a nightcap and then his bed, but God only knew what Hardman's reaction would be to her request for his help. There was something about this woman that told him every inch of her was steeped in right over wrong, protection over abandonment. And for that, he liked her and would see to it that no harm befell her.

The notion of her being alone with John Hardman when the man was so free and easy with his fists meant Jacob couldn't leave things be. The last thing he needed added to his deep-seated failures was the knowledge he'd practically introduced the woman to a man easily capable of assaulting her.

As they neared the pub, Hardman's distinctive orange hair, poking in every direction from beneath a battered top hat, caught Jacob's eye.

Hardman stood, tankard in hand, within a circle of drinkers outside the pub doors, smiling and laughing.

'That's him.'

She stopped and stared at the men. 'Hardman?'

Jacob glanced at her. 'Yes. The one with the flaming locks.'

'Excellent.' She pulled back her shoulders. 'Then I thank you for your help.' She held out her hand. 'It was nice meeting you.'

Smiling, Jacob lifted his eyebrows and crossed his arms. 'You think I'm leaving?'

She dropped her hand and glared. 'I can manage things well enough from here.'

'I'll introduce you and step back while you talk, but I'm not leaving.'

Before she could respond, Jacob slowly approached the group and assessed Hardman's level of intoxication. Hardman wasn't swaying, which could be an advantage or disadvantage. Maybe there was a small chance the man might listen to this woman, but his sobriety could also mean that any outburst from Hardman could result in Jacob having no choice but to knock the man down.

With the woman's footsteps behind him, Jacob raised his voice to be heard over the laughing banter of the group. 'Hardman. Mind if I have a word?'

John Hardman slowly turned, his tankard hovering at his lips. Meeting Jacob's gaze, Hardman's eyes immediately narrowed. 'What do you want?'

Having never so much as passed the time of day with him, Jacob was not surprised at Hardman's hostile attitude towards a relative stranger. This was not a place that people chose to be congenial to others they weren't familiar with.

Jacob stopped and the woman came to stand beside him. 'This lady would like a word with you.'

Hardman moved away from the other men, the suspicion in his dark eyes deepening as he stared her. 'What do you want with me?'

'A word if you don't mind, Mr Hardman.' She faced Jacob, her gaze steady. 'If you would just wait over there?'

Jacob was caught in her violet eyes, his protectiveness rising before he slowly turned to Hardman. 'I won't be far away.'

9

Louisa watched the gentleman who had accompanied her to see John Hardman stroll a distance away and lean against a low wall. The light spilling from the pub's windows illuminated his set expression, his stare firmly on Mr Hardman. Dragging her gaze from him, she forced herself to focus on the man she prayed would be willing to shoulder the care of Caroline Warwick.

'So?' Hardman growled. 'What do you want?'

Glancing again at her escort, Louisa pulled back her shoulders and faced Mr Hardman. 'I have recently taken ownership of a property where a friend of yours has been living.'

'A friend?' He smiled, his eyes lighting with amusement. 'I don't have friends.'

'Well, Miss Warwick claims to know you and has stated quite clearly that you would be willing to help her.'

'Miss Warwick . . . ' His gaze glazed in thought and then he huffed a laugh.

'Caroline? You've got to be joking.' He shook his head and took a hefty glug from his tankard. 'I don't think so. You've had a wasted trip if you think I'd help that woman.'

Disappointment dropped like lead into Louisa's stomach. 'But you have to.'

'I don't *have* to do anything, Miss . . . ?'

'There is no need for you to know my name, Mr Hardman, but there is a need for you to come to Carson Street in the morning and collect Miss Warwick and her belongings. Otherwise, she will be evicted with nowhere else to go.'

'Not my problem.'

Her patience thinning, Louisa planted her hands on her hips. 'Well, she certainly isn't mine.'

Footsteps sounded to the side of her and the man who had assumed himself her guardian came closer. 'Everything all right?'

'Everything's fine,' Louisa said, without looking at him, her gaze firmly on Mr Hardman's. 'We are just talking things through, isn't that right?'

Hardman took another sup of his ale. 'I'm done talking. Caroline Warwick is nothing more than a whore out for what she can get. My advice to you is to chuck her out on her ear and wash your hands of her. She's like a bloody cat. She'll always land on her feet. Trust me, you're better off without her.'

'Oh, I won't argue with that.' Louisa crossed her arms. What in God's name was she supposed to do now? 'But I am not the sort of person to throw anyone out of a place without knowing where they are going to sleep.

Now I suggest you — '

'Sorry, Miss, I'm done talking to you.' Hardman's glare burned into hers before he glanced at Jacob. 'Just get out of here and take your muscle with you. Caroline Warwick knows where to find me if she's that desperate.'

Louisa opened her mouth to say more but the man strolled back to his friends, leaving her standing there.

'Do you want me to drag him back here?'

She turned and stared into her new companion's frankly phenomenal blue eyes. 'No, leave him be.' She sighed, dragging her gaze towards Hardman and his cronies. 'The unwanted woman currently residing in my home will be gone in the morning, regardless.' She faced him again and offered her hand. 'It was a pleasure meeting you. Thank you for your help.'

He stared at her before a slight smile curved his lips. 'I think it best I walk you home.'

'Oh, there's really no need. I am perfectly — '

'Capable, I know but if it's all the same to you, I'd like to make sure you are safe for the night.' He held out his arm. 'And it's really not worth arguing.'

Knowing when she was beat, Louisa dropped her shoulders and slid her hand into the crook of his elbow, her fingers resting on his wide forearm.

The man was most certainly strong. Strong and imposing. A man, she hated to admit, who made her feel safer when he was beside her.

'Fine.' She exhaled a shaky breath. 'Then let us head back to Carson Street.'

They walked in silence through the streets, the darkness enveloping them as they walked farther from the light of the pubs and coffee houses and through the outskirts of the town centre. As they neared Pulteney Bridge and the Parade Gardens, Louisa was unable to bear the quiet between them any longer.

'I don't even know your name,' she said, tipping her head to look at him.

'Seeing as you have been so kind in your assistance tonight, it feels only right that we might exchange names.'

'Jacob. Jacob Jackson.' He looked down at her and winked. 'At your service, Miss . . . ?'

Her stomach treacherously flip-flopped, her cheeks slightly warming.

Although the quiet, brooding type, Jacob Jackson was also extraordinarily handsome and somewhat charming. The combination of brawn, clear intelligence and charisma suddenly felt incredibly dangerous.

She swallowed and looked along the street towards her house on Carson Street. 'My name is Louisa. Louisa Hill. Mrs, but . . . ' *Why am I telling him this?* 'I am widowed. My husband died recently, leaving me a house here.'

His gaze bored into her temple and her cheeks grew even hotter. It had been the silliest of things to tell him. It had sounded so purposeful. As though she wanted to make it clear she was unmarried.

'I see.' He coughed. 'Then I am glad you have somewhere nice to live, even if you no longer have the husband who loved you.'

Her stomach tightened and she pulled her lips together, trapping in the insane urge to tell him that Anthony in no way loved her. That his actions, debts and lies had proven that all too clearly.

'This is my house.' She drew him to a stop at the bottom of the steps.

'Thank you for walking me home.'

He stared up at the house's façade and protruded his bottom lip. 'Very nice.'

His expression gave nothing away, but Louisa had no doubt he was struggling to marry the grandeur of the house with her being out at night, scouring The Star tavern alone and exposed to goodness knew what.

She cleared her throat. 'Well, goodnight, Mr Jackson.'

'Yes, goodnight. Sleep well.'

Their eyes locked and Louisa's heart picked up speed, empty words dancing on her tongue. Yet, what else was there to say to him?

She climbed the steps, pulling her key from her purse with ever so slightly trembling fingers. Without looking back, she entered the house and closed the door, dropping her back against it and closing her eyes.

What in God's name was wrong with her? The last thing she needed was to be in any way attracted to the man. No matter Mr Jackson's size, appeal or charm. But he was so unlike Anthony or any man she'd ever met. His worldliness was obvious, a simmering tension emanating from him as though he was almost braced for a fight at all times.

Pushing away from the door, she took off her coat and hat and hung them on the hallway stand before walking into the parlour.

'At last!' Nancy stood from the settee, her grey eyes wide. 'Where have you been? I've been worried sick.'

'Sorry.' Louisa walked to the drinks cabinet and poured herself and Nancy a glass of wine. 'It took me a while to find Mr Hardman.'

'And? Is he willing to collect madam tomorrow?'

'No.'

'No?'

'No.' Louisa handed her one of the glasses and then dropped into an armchair. 'He wants nothing to do with her.'

'Well, that's just perfect.' Nancy sipped her wine, her cheeks mottling.

'What are we going to do with her now?'

Determination burned behind Louisa's ribcage. 'We tell her she is leaving tomorrow. We cannot allow Miss Warwick or her staff to become our problem, Nance. We have problems enough of our own.' She took a hefty gulp of wine. 'She has to go.'

'Thank God for that.' Nancy grinned. 'For a moment there, I thought I was going to have a fight on my hands convincing you to toss her out on her ear.'

Louisa shook her head and stared towards the window and the darkness beyond. 'No, no argument. Everything is about me and you from now on.

Everyone else can sort themselves out as far as I'm concerned.'

10

Louisa ignored the sickness in her stomach and stared hard at a painting that hung in the hallway. She refused to look at Miss Warwick, refused to falter and announce she had changed her mind about the woman's eviction.

Nancy had her hand firmly gripped to Miss Warwick's elbow and practically frogmarched her through the front doorway, her face a mask of indifference, even though Louisa knew Nancy must be feeling at least a little of the situation's injustice. Guilt continued to fill Louisa, and she swallowed hard, worrying that seeing Miss Warwick and her staff out on the street — with absolutely no idea where they were going — would haunt her for months to come.

But what choice did she have if she was to move forward? She had to rid the house of anything that had once been Anthony's. Including Miss Warwick. Once they were gone, only then would Louisa try to process the letter she'd received from Anthony's solicitor that morning. Only then would she share the true direness of their situation with Nancy, and what Louisa had decided they had no alternative but to do if they wanted to keep living at Carson Street.

'Just leave, will you?'

Nancy's shout cut through the turmoil spinning in Louisa's brain and she blinked, glaring at Miss Warwick. She could not stand to look at her a moment longer when she did not have the means to help her or her staff.

Straightening her spine, Louisa lifted her chin and followed them outside.

Even with her new plans, Miss Warwick had to go. Fellow prostitute or not, Miss Warwick would never have a place in this house.

Finally wrangling herself free of Nancy's grip, Miss Warwick faced Louisa, her face red with exertion. 'You'll pay for this. Do you really think I won't come back? That I won't find a way to have this house?' she screeched, eyes bulging. 'Anthony will be turning in his grave knowing how you have treated me. How you are slinging me out as though I was of no importance to him. He might have loved you, *Mrs* Hill, but he wanted me . . . for two years!'

Louisa flinched. *Two years?* Humiliation burned hot at her cheeks. *Two years? Anthony, how could you?* Hurt burrowed into Louisa's heart, threatening her fragile façade. How could she have been so naïve as not to have known?

She fought to hold on to her remaining dignity and marched along the short pathway, her guilt extinguished by the other woman's spite and venom.

Leaning so close to Miss Warwick she was forced to step back, Louisa spoke through clenched teeth. 'Now, you listen to me. I was Anthony's wife. He told you in no uncertain terms that he loved me and would never leave me. I have no idea why he saw fit to keep you living the high life for two years — '

'Because I satisfied him, that's why.' The woman's eyes gleamed. 'In ways that clearly you could not.'

Anger simmered and Louisa welcomed the inner strength it provoked.

'Well, now he's gone, leaving us both with uncertain futures. I will have to deal with whatever hardships might lie ahead for me . . .' She gripped Miss Warwick's arm, her nails pinching into the sleeve of her coat. 'As you and your staff will have to deal with yours. Now, go. And if I see you on this street again, I swear to God, you'll be joining Anthony sooner than you think.'

From the corner of her eye, Louisa could see curious spectators gathered on the street. The gawping audience were dressed finely, their colourful coats and hats illustrating their status. She inwardly cringed as her new neighbours stared, their eyes agog and their mouths twisted in disapproval.

Although, they certainly did not seem to be in any rush to leave while such a drama unfolded.

Shame threatened, but Louisa held fast. She had no qualms about resurrecting the person — the fighter — she'd once been, if it meant keeping a roof over her and Nancy's heads and ridding them of Miss Warwick. After all, there would almost certainly be worse things ahead of them than a street spectacle. She had a horrible feeling today was just the tip of a slowly melting iceberg.

'You'll pay for this,' hissed Miss Warwick, her face contorted in an ugly sneer. 'Mark my words. You'll pay.'

Louisa kept her feet planted, her back ramrod straight. Nancy shifted beside her, no doubt poised and ready to join in the fray if necessary.

Miss Warwick leaned down and picked up her suitcase and carpet bag, her chin high. With a scathing smile, she shook her head and walked away.

Louisa shifted her glare to the women who, up until a few minutes ago, had held the posts of housekeeper and cook. Miss Warwick's young maid had vanished some time during the ruckus, but the other women seemed frozen and clearly unsure what to do or say.

The trees shifted as a breeze whispered over the gathered crowd, the weak February sun slipping behind a cloud, shrouding the assembly in dank greyness. Tension inched across Louisa's shoulders as her old self began its rebirth, her survival instinct rising on an undulating wave. She might be down, but she wasn't out. If Cook and Mrs Armitage wanted to take on her and Nancy, so be it.

Cook was the first to look away and she glanced at the growing crowd of spectators, visibly flinching under the weight of their judgemental stares.

She touched Mrs Armitage's arm before the housekeeper too surveyed the onlookers. Finally, they looked at Louisa for a long, suspended moment before hurrying away along the street.

Louisa exhaled, the tension releasing from her shoulders.

'Right, show's over, ladies and gentlemen,' Nancy announced, her arms spread wide. 'If you want any more entertainment, I believe the Theatre Royal opens around eight.'

There was a burst of murmured laughter before the crowds dispersed, chattering and whispering, their genteel lives disrupted, yet heightened with something they would undoubtedly discuss over their dinner tables that evening.

A modicum of satisfaction poked at Louisa's pride and she sighed. 'Well, that's that then.'

'Indeed it is.' Nancy hooked her arm into Louisa's, and they walked towards their open front door. 'Why don't we open a bottle of wine? I'm in the mood to celebrate.'

'We need to talk first, Nance.'

'About what?'

Louisa stared after the retreating figures of Cook and Mrs Armitage, unable to face her friend. She had promised Nancy her full protection, both financial and emotional, and now Louisa had no choice but to admit failure and ask Nancy to re-enter a world they had both assumed gone forever.

Taking a deep breath, Louisa stepped inside the house. 'Shall we sit in the parlour?'

'What is it, Lou?' Nancy gently gripped Louisa's elbow, halting her. 'I know throwing Warwick and her cronies out like that won't be sitting well in your conscience, but to hell with them. Miss Warwick is vicious and deserves whatever she has coming to her.'

'Maybe, but — '

'There's no maybe about it. You care about people too much. You always have. And, although I love you for it, worry for that woman has to stop. Now.'

Louisa closed her eyes. 'It's not Miss Warwick bothering me, Nance.' As the adrenaline from the altercation with Caroline Warwick dissolved,

68

Louisa wandered to the stairs and sat on the bottom step. 'I received a letter from Anthony's solicitor this morning.'

Nancy frowned, concern seeping into her gaze. 'And?'

'And despite him saying he would do what he could for us, there is not a penny left. Of course, that alone is not a shock but it does mean . . .' Louisa swallowed, forcing her gaze to remain steady on Nancy's. 'We have to find a way to earn regular money and quickly.'

Nancy studied her. 'And from the look of you, I'm assuming you have a plan in mind. One you think I'm not going to like.'

'Yes.'

Nancy sat beside her and took Louisa's hand. 'I'll do whatever you ask of me, Lou. We're in this together, I promise.'

Louisa stared at her dearest friend, her heart heavy with what she was about to propose but knowing, deep in her heart, her plan could mean independence and freedom for both of them. 'Anthony's lies have proven I was just something else that he felt he could buy. That he saw me as his whore for the entirety of our marriage and I've come to terms with that. Accepted it, even.' Pride and anger rose, fuelling the determination Louisa would use whatever means she had to keep her and Nancy from having to answer to anyone ever again. 'We have one choice going forward, Nance.

We either sell this house and buy something smaller or . . .' Louisa swallowed as the rest of her suggestion stuck like rocks in her throat.

'Or what?'

A painful guilt bored into Louisa's heart and conscience. 'Or we make this house work for us.'

'What do you mean? Take in a lodger?'

'No, not a lodger. I don't want to open this house to anyone expecting a normal home.'

'I don't understand.'

'We have to make it *work* for us, Nance.'

'I have absolutely no idea . . . ' Her friend frowned, her grey eyes confused until, second by second, her expression changed as comprehension struck.

'You mean . . . we make it *work* for us.'

'Yes.'

'Is that what you really want to do? I mean, after all this time?'

Sickness rolled through Louisa's stomach, but she kept her gaze steady.

'What choice do we have? We're neither skilled nor experienced in any other work. We use what we have at our disposal or risk losing this house on top of everything else. Our attributes are not eternal. We both know that.'

'Meaning what exactly?' Nancy huffed a laugh. 'Our private parts aren't going to close up when we turn thirty!"

Louisa closed her eyes, unable to even conjure a smile at her friend's crassness. 'How much longer do you think our looks will last, Nance? How much longer will our corsets tighten as they do now? We must fight back the only way we can.' She opened her eyes as her voice treacherously cracked, a dark and bitter cloak of resentment shrouding her. 'I won't allow Anthony to take away in death what he gave us in life. Maybe neither of us was meant to live that life and if I hadn't known such joy, such freedom, I wouldn't miss it. But I *will* miss it, Nance. I don't want to go back to struggling through each day, not knowing if we'll have a decent meal or be warm in the winter. We have to create a new life on our own terms.'

She looked deep into her friend's eyes. 'We have to sell ourselves again.

It's the only way I can see to protect what we have. The only way to make this house pay for itself.' A lone tear slid over Louisa's cheek and she swiped it away. 'But, if you want to leave, I can spare enough money to give you a start. I'm not asking you to do this against your will. You're my friend and I love you, but I can't work for someone else again. I won't.'

'And neither will I.' Nancy brushed away her own tears and squeezed Louisa's hand, determination burning in her eyes. 'I wouldn't want to be anywhere else than right beside you. We can do this, Lou. I know we can.'

Louisa pulled Nancy into her arms and held her tight, pressing a firm kiss to her hair. 'We will find protection. Someone to stand at the door and ensure we come to no harm. The last thing I want to do is risk another man taking advantage of us, but I won't have either of us exposed to possible violence. Paid protection is the only way forward.'

'But that will cost, you do know that?'

'Yes, but . . . ' Memories of the violence they had endured at the brothel coated Louisa's throat in bitterness. 'Needs must. I'll find the right man for the job, trust me.'

'Always.'

Louisa pulled Nancy close and stared blindly ahead as Jacob Jackson's face appeared in her mind's eye.

11

Jacob threw another stone in the churning waters of the River Avon, his thoughts alternating between tonight's impending fight and the horrible, niggling loneliness that crept up on him more and more of late. His life had become an endless circle of waking, eating, fighting and sleeping, his only company, the drinkers at the pub, Doreen, Colin or Henry.

None of whom genuinely knew him.

Which was exactly the way he'd consciously set up those relationships.

Even now, he didn't really want to strengthen the tentative bonds he had with his fellow boarders or associates. It was one thing to superficially know a person, another to become too involved or invested in their lives, only to let them down in the future.

And he would let them down because he had yet to find a way of lessening the hardness that surrounded his heart and emotions. An enforced self-preservation to avoid ever feeling for someone the way he had for his mother. A woman who had died so young and had wanted so much for him.

Yet, living a distanced life was beginning to take its toll. His heart constantly failed his head by nagging him, reminding him that this was not the existence his mother would have wanted for him.

Jacob pulled up his coat collar and abruptly

turned from the river to walk along the pavement towards Pulteney Bridge. Horses and carriages trotted past him, sending rainwater and mud spraying from the gutters.

Two finely dressed ladies squealed and almost leapt into his path as the wheel of a passing carriage splashed through a puddle, showering muddy water. He gently gripped the arm of the woman closest to the deluge and eased her out of harm's way.

He tipped his hat, releasing her. 'Miss.'

She dipped her head, a flirtatious smile on her lips before she and her companion hurried on their way, giggling and nudging each other.

Jacob fought the moroseness pressing down on him as he continued to walk.

His moodiness was his own damn fault. The root cause that had re-awoken feelings he preferred remained buried was the house on Carson Street. The house and the woman he'd met living there.

Seemingly alone.

She had confessed to being widowed, but maybe she employed male staff — a butler or possibly a driver. Or maybe she had a female companion — a maid and housekeeper.

A woman living alone was far from usual and two and two seemed to make five as far as Louisa Hill was concerned. Tall, blonde and exceedingly attractive, yet there was a street-savvy wisdom in her eyes and in the way she'd squared her shoulders when she'd first spoken to him, as though constantly alert and on her guard. She held none of the grandiose or uppity attitude Jacob would

74

have expected from a lady living in one of the wealthier parts of town.

'Hey, mister!'

Jacob turned just as a young lad barrelled towards him, his dark hair lifting in the wind, his grin wide.

'Remember me?' he asked as he stopped in front of Jacob and swiped his hand over his rain-sodden face. 'We met at the park, remember? This is my pa.'

Jacob shifted his gaze to a man eight or nine years his senior, his green eyes shadowed with tiredness as he held out his hand. 'Pleased to meet you.

I apologise for my son shouting out to you in the street. He wanted to thank you for taking the time to teach him how to fight.'

Guilt slithered into Jacob's gut. There was nothing honourable about teaching a young lad violence, yet that was exactly what he'd done. 'Maybe I shouldn't have done that.'

The father placed his hand on his son's shoulder, pride obvious in his eyes. 'Maybe, maybe not, but the lad is all the happier for it.'

Jacob glanced at the boy who stared back at him, his eyes filled with misplaced adulation. 'The boys from school don't try to take my stuff anymore.' He beamed. 'Not since I socked Jack Bennet square on the nose like you taught me. Can you maybe teach me something else?' He looked to his father. 'Can he, Pa? You don't hit people, but this man does. He hits everyone, I reckon.'

Self-loathing twisted through Jacob and he coughed. 'That's not something to brag about, you know. I do what I do out of necessity, not choice. You'd be better advised to follow your father's path, rather than mine.' He touched his hat. 'I'll bid you both good day.'

As he walked towards his lodgings, the young lad's words circled Jacob's mind. It had been instinctual for Jacob to step into the fracas between the boys that day in the park; to teach the lad how to look after himself and put a stop to him being bullied. But what did that urgent need to intervene say about him? It said he had no skill, knowledge or care other than fighting.

A life of violence and isolation had always been enough, but with each month that passed, Jacob wanted more. His solitude grew more and more uncomfortable. As though his life no longer quite fit as it had before.

He continued to stalk through Bath's maze of streets, past shops and pubs, the theatre and the police station. Everywhere he looked, pasted billboards and flyer headlines drew his attention. Missing young women.

Wanted men. A boxing match. Warnings of the demon drink. On and on.

Violence, mistreatment and murder.

It didn't matter that the persona he'd worn his whole life was beginning to weigh a little too heavy, sit a little less easily in his conscience, Jacob saw little evidence to prove there was another way. If he didn't continue on this path, who knew if someone might be hurt or killed while under his watch?

He had no real friends, no lover or wife, no children and no good to honest job where he worked a day's graft and came home to a night of domesticity. All things his mother had wanted; all things Jacob had craved his entire childhood from a father whose lack of employment had led him to become frustrated, cruel and vicious. Sickness rose bitter in Jacob's throat as memories battered his mind.

His mother standing in front of him, protecting her son from his father's fury and taking the beating meant for Jacob herself. The muffled cries and pleas from behind a closed bedroom door as his father forced himself on his wife. Sounds that had confused and frightened Jacob then, but now haunted him until protectiveness towards all women became his mantra.

But his memories would forever be embedded in death.

His mother murdered and her killer, Jacob's father, hanging from a rope.

Jacob marched blindly onwards, rage burning in his chest. His father had given his son nothing but the destiny of a life alone, which had resulted in Jacob maturing into an angry, resentful adult who was paid handsomely to inflict pain.

Reaching his lodgings, Jacob let himself into the silent house and shrugged off his coat, thankful that no one else seemed to be home. Moving his head from side to side, he tried to release the knots of tension from his neck and shoulders as he walked into the kitchen.

After setting the kettle on the stove to boil, he sat at the table and stared at its wooden surface. Louisa Hill once again rose in his mind. Behind her bravado, he'd recognised a wariness, a carefully tended façade that he had concluded covered fear.

What was she scared of? Whatever it was, he could hardly blame her for her play-acting.

After all, wasn't he the consummate actor? A man capable of metamorphosising himself into whatever a situation warranted? Maybe it was because of this commonality that Louisa Hill's face continued to badger him — continued to reappear in his mind's eye, poke and prod at his consciousness.

He returned to the stove and took the kettle off the heat. It was no good; he had to go back to Carson Street. Had to make sure she was safe and well.

The fact she had sought out Hardman could only mean she was in some sort of trouble. No one in their right mind would want to be associated with that man unless they had no other choice.

Although Jacob was pretty certain his return to Carson Street and his interest in Louisa Hill wouldn't be welcomed, he feared his apprehensions wouldn't rest until he was convinced she had no further need of his help. He might discover there was a man in the house and she was well protected.

Maybe he would be sent away from her door with a flea in his ear. If that happened he would at least know he'd tried and he'd be happier — sleep easier — than he had these past few nights.

One way or another, he had to find an excuse to return to Carson Street.

12

Stopping by one of the dozens of stalls in Bath's market square, Louisa surveyed an array of apples and oranges, turnips and potatoes. The elderly woman standing behind the rudimentary table eyed her with undisguised suspicion. Louisa tried not to fidget under the unwanted scrutiny. The next time she ventured to this part of town, she would ensure she dressed a little less grandly. Appraisal and mistrust had followed her like a shadow for the last hour.

Louisa removed her purse from inside her basket and counted her coins.

Her and Nancy's money continued to dwindle at an alarming rate, which was why Louisa was at the market by the river. Shopping here, rather than the stores in the town centre, was a more frugal option as she searched for something for her and Nancy's dinner.

People jostled, cursed and meandered all around her. The stench from the river rose on the wind and mixed with the unwashed bodies of the poor.

Despite the bite of the February temperatures, women and children shuffled among the crowd, their hands outstretched for money or food, their haggard faces white with cold.

Guilt that she had not the means to help these people or the foresight to alter her dress pressed down on Louisa as she was forced to acknowledge just how proficient an actress she had become the higher Anthony had raised her. It was no surprise eyes swivelled in her direction and dislike darkened so many glares. What else did she expect? She knew all too well the depravity and desperation that so often gathered at a city's riverside.

Forcing a smile, Louisa met the woman's suspicious gaze. 'I'll have a cabbage, three parsnips and a half a dozen potatoes, please.'

The woman narrowed her eyes and sucked her teeth before reaching for the requested items. Louisa handed over her basket and the produce was haphazardly thrown inside. Clearly, the stallholder had no care for Louisa's return custom.

'Thank you.' Louisa handed over some coins. 'Good day to you.'

Yesterday's rain had passed overnight and now the sun shone brightly in a clear blue sky. It was one of those rare winter days when Louisa wasn't averse to spending some time outdoors. She walked through the market, glancing at the wares and offerings on the stalls either side.

Soon, the smell from the nearby river grew considerably less bearable, the putrid water rising in the air and crawling into Louisa's nostrils. Yet, she continued to walk. The people around her reminded her so much of a life she'd once known and she was curious to see whether women in the same trade as she'd once been solicited for business at Bath's riverside as so many had by Bristol's harbour.

Taverns offering cheap ale and gin stood alongside dilapidated coffee houses, rattily dressed men spilling from their doors onto the pavement, their grimy faces fringed by filthy beards and whiskers. No doubt each was intent on spending their last pennies on temporary escape, rather than handing their few coins over to their wives and children.

Bath was known for its butter-coloured houses, the lure of its theatres, grand promenades and healing waters, but she and Nancy had soon learned, when a person was emboldened enough to venture deeper into its seedier areas, this historical city was no different than any other.

Soot-blackened buildings rose out of the squalor, the stench of alcohol and excrement making Louisa's eyes water. Over and over again, she itched to pull her handkerchief from her pocket so that she might cover her nose and mouth, but she resisted, not wanting to raise any more attention or hostility from the people lying or standing about her. Men leered at her, their glazed studies passing over her body from head to toe, their mouths curved into suggestive smiles.

Louisa straightened her spine and stared ahead, surreptitiously gauging the women. It was clear many of them were selling sex, their dirty frocks a muted kaleidoscope of faded satin that might once have been emerald, ruby or sapphire-blue. The bodices were cut low, the hems higher than was strictly decent, showcasing an inch or two of stocking above mud-spattered boots.

The women eyed Louisa viciously, their possession over a squalid patch of cobbled street gleaming in their rheumy eyes. Nodding curtly at each prostitute, Louisa hoped the gesture relayed she wished them no ill harm or judgement and convinced them she was merely passing through.

It wasn't until she spotted a young woman, possibly twenty or twenty-one, sitting at the foot of an alleyway that Louisa slowed her pace. The woman sat with her knees tucked beneath her chin, her cascade of dirty, dark brown hair partially covering her face.

Louisa stepped closer, memories of herself in a similar sorry state reinforced by her rising tears. All that had happened in the past rushed through Louisa's mind and her steps faltered. Hitching her basket onto her arm, she reached for the stone post beside her as weakness threatened. The woman's emaciated state clawed at Louisa's heart, the vivid bruises on her face a painful reminder of the beatings Louisa had endured at the brothel.

When the house's madam had approached her, Louisa had been fifteen, selling trinkets on street corners as a way of keeping her hunger at bay after her parents had abandoned her. She'd slept nights on a neighbour's cold kitchen floor, kicked out every morning before the neighbour's husband woke and his wife felt the worst of his temper for taking Louisa in without his knowledge or permission.

Louisa glanced furtively around. Curious gazes came from some of the crowd surrounding her, others sneered in amusement. Pulling forth every ounce of her wavering strength, Louisa straightened and glared, lifting her chin as she walked defiantly towards the alleyway.

Cautiously, she approached the woman and put her basket on the cobbles.

Louisa lowered to her haunches. 'Hello there,'

she said gently. 'I'm Louisa.

What's your name?'

The woman continued to tremble, her knees hitched beneath her chin, tears leaking over her lower lashes to streak through the grime on her cheeks.

Louisa swallowed, her grief for this clearly distraught woman knotting her stomach as she touched her knee. 'I want to help you. Do you think you can stand?'

The young woman froze, her eyes darting to Louisa's, her sorrow turning to anger and her desperation to disdain. 'I don't need your kind of help.

Now, will you please go away.'

The almost middle-class tone of the woman's speech sent a jolt of shock through Louisa. A soft burr had surrounded her pronunciation as though she had known a good education and mixed with higher society. The scenario, considering her current location, state of being and distress, seemed ludicrous.

'Please,' Louisa said. 'I don't want to leave you like this.' She looked deep into the woman's eyes, protectiveness whispering through her. 'Is there anyone else who could help you? I will take a message somewhere if you like?'

'No, just go away.'

Louisa slowly stood and stared down at the woman, passionate determination stirring deep inside of her. One way or another, this woman was coming home with her. She might be one among a hundred others, but helping one had to be better than helping none.

'I just want to give you a meal and a bed for the night. After that, you will be free to leave my home.'

The woman rolled her eyes and tried to quickly push to her feet. She stumbled and gasped, pressing one hand to her ribs and the other to the wet wall beside her. 'Home? Do you think I was born yesterday?' Her gaze inched over Louisa's clothes, hair and hands. 'I know who you are, and I know exactly what you want from me.'

Louisa took a step back, warmth seeping into her cheeks. *She knows me?*

Did she know Anthony? Was she . . . had he? 'You know who I am?'

'Of course I do. Now, would you kindly leave me be.'

The woman edged along the wall, wincing with each step, the redness in her face that had risen in anger now fading to white in her pain.

Louisa stood in front of her and searched her ashen face. 'How do you know me?'

'You're a madam. You don't want to help me, you want to use me.'

'A madam?' Louisa blinked. Was her past displayed in her regardless of her fine clothes and pinned hair? 'Why would you think that?'

'Because people like you do not come to places like this without an ulterior motive, that's why.'

She brushed past Louisa and hobbled along the street, her head down and her shoulders raised. Momentarily stunned, Louisa stared after her before gathering her senses. She snatched up her basket and followed.

Louisa quickened her pace, the young woman's

dark, bedraggled hair moving farther and farther away. This woman needed her, and she needed Nancy. Although her perception about Louisa had not been entirely inaccurate, she and Nancy had once been whores and would soon be again.

Who else could sympathise and empathise more with this woman's plight?

Who else would understand more what this woman had endured and needed?

Finally, Louisa caught up with her and gently placed her hand on the woman's shoulder. 'It will take more than running away from me to make me disappear, you know.' She smiled, panting. 'Please, won't you take a chance and trust me? At least tell me your name?'

The woman whirled around, her dark eyes flashing with anger. 'It's Octavia, but are you mad? Just leave me alone.'

Louisa laughed a little hysterically. 'I quite possibly could be, Octavia, but I'm also determined that you accept my offer of a bed for the night.'

'Well, I don't know who you think you are, but I've got my own life to lead. Now, for goodness' sake, you don't need to mix your life up with mine.'

She shrugged Louisa's arm from her shoulder and walked away.

'I will come back!' Louisa shouted after her. 'I know you'll come to trust me in time.'

Dropping her shoulders, she met the inquisitive stares and wry smiles of the onlookers surrounding her. Oh, what did they know? There was something about the young woman that pulled at her and urged Louisa on in her determination to help her. She seemed so much like her. So much like Nancy.

There had been a spark of fierceness in Octavia's eyes, a guarantee that her life had not always been this way displayed in her articulation and manner. Louisa started to walk towards home, her mind reeling.

The house on Carson Street would be used for the purpose of sex. It would be used to sustain the life Louisa and her dearest friend had become accustomed to. However, this time around, what they earned would be used and managed as they dictated, no one else.

Surely this woman would understand the power in that?

Octavia needed Louisa's house, her establishment and she was determined that she saw sense.

13

Jacob crossed his arms and leaned back against a wooden post in the underbelly of a disused builder's yard on the outskirts of the city.

Henry had sent him to watch the Killer's latest match. His manager's summary of the fighter had been that he was big and looked kind of mean.

However, as Jacob watched the Killer bounce from one foot to the other on the sawdust, his eyes bloodshot and slightly manic, Jacob considered him suspiciously insane.

His black hair was shorn close to his scalp, his skin the colour of coffee and his eyes a startling pale brown. Judging by the way the men had assessed and the women admired the fighter when he had approached the makeshift ring twenty minutes before, the man was esteemed and feared in equal measure. Jacob narrowed his eyes and studied the Killer closer, his use of illegal weapons and time in prison resounding in Jacob's mind.

As he strutted around the ring, the Killer's smile never wavered as he periodically winked at the women in the crowd. Beneath the lamplight, sweat sheened over his chest and back, his teeth white against the darkness of his skin. Tendons strained in his upper arms and his legs, thick as tree trunks, rippled with muscle.

Rare unease passed through Jacob as he pushed away from the post, flexing and unflexing his fingers, gauging the girth and strength of the man.

There was every chance Henry would want Jacob to challenge the Killer and the prospect was far from attractive.

Not because Jacob thought himself incapable of matching the man punch for punch. Or that he didn't think there was a good chance he could even beat him. It was the mania in the Killer's gaze that unnerved Jacob, the way his eyes darted from his opponent to the audience as though his winning was a given and he didn't need to pay attention to the rules to which other fighters steadfastly adhered.

Skill. Methodical strategy and tactic. Lightness of feet and swiftness of fist.

No, this beast of man looked as though he wanted to maim, kill, and damn well eat his opponent like he was an exemplary cut of meat.

Ale-soaked sawdust shifted beneath Jacob's boots as he weaved among the crowd, his study never leaving the Killer. For a brief moment, the boxer's gaze met Jacob's and the Killer hitched his chin in recognition.

Jacob calmly nodded, somewhat pleased that he seemed to be aware of Jacob and how he fared on the circuit.

The Killer faced his opponent and slowly walked around him, the other fighter looking unsure whether to risk a jab or just curl into a ball until his inevitable beating was over.

The Killer's first punch came without warning before he dispensed his attack viciously and completely, the power and fierceness behind his onslaught bringing a sour bitterness to Jacob's throat. The boxer launched at his unprepared victim punch after punch, pummelling the man's face as blood sprayed and bones cracked, sending up a roar of appreciative cries from the audience. It had barely been two minutes before the fighters' prospective managers leapt into the ring and tried their best to pull the Killer from the bloodied heap on the floor.

But it was only when the Killer was spent, and the other man unmoving, did he stand back and raise his hands in mock surrender.

The Killer's gaze landed on Jacob a second time and he smiled.

Jacob nodded, even as sickness unfurled in his gut. It was clear the man was not entirely sane and there was a good chance Jacob's report to Henry would fall on deaf ears. Henry was determined that it would be one of *his* fighters who defeated the Killer. A man whose reputation of being unbeatable currently spreading like wildfire through the city. Jacob didn't doubt for a moment that his manager would become deranged in his pursuit of victory.

Walking from the yard and out into the night, Jacob's mind reeled with the ferocity of the Killer's tactics, the hysteria of the crowd and their unabashed revelry in witnessing his opponent's demise.

Light spilled onto the street from the White Hart's latticed windows as Jacob approached, his throat dry with need of a pint.

Just as he raised his hand to push the door, it opened and two laughing women stumbled out, their arms flung around each other and their heads tipped back in joviality. Recognition sent a jolt of shock through Jacob, the raucous jeers and shouts of the drinkers inside the pub quietening under his stupor.

Louisa Hill smiled, her gaze wandering over his face and chest as she slightly swayed. 'Well, look who it is. We're about to leave and the man we're looking for finally makes an appearance.'

Jacob clenched his jaw and slowly drew his gaze over her beautiful face.

Her violet eyes shone in the semi-darkness, her blonde curls moving about her face in the chilly breeze. His heart stuttered and he quickly glanced at her companion.

She grinned and stuck out her hand. 'Jacob Jackson, I presume?' She hiccupped. 'Nancy Bloom. You know, like a flower. Yep, that's me. All pretty petals with my feet in shit.'

She burst out laughing and toppled against Louisa Hill who deftly caught her. 'We are a little intoxicated as you can see.'

Jacob raised his eyebrows, words escaping him as he fought to not grab their arms and get them as far away from this cesspit of a pub as possible.

Did they have any clue how quickly trouble could break out in taverns like this one?

'What are you doing here?'

'Looking for you.' Louisa Hill stepped closer. 'And now we've found you.'

It had been over a week since he'd been at Carson Street and, in that time, something indiscernible had changed in her. Now she possessed a steeliness — a hardness — that hadn't been there when they'd last met. Even her accent was slightly changed: rougher, more demanding than when she'd been stood in front of her painted front door complete with highly polished brass knocker.

Uneasy, he crossed his arms. 'Have you had trouble with Hardman?'

'Of course not.' The redhead, Nancy, laughed. 'There isn't much trouble we can't handle ourselves, Mr Jackson.'

Slowly, Jacob's equilibrium inched back to normality and he lowered his shoulders in the hope he displayed nonchalance rather than gathering concern. 'Then why are you looking for me?'

Louisa's gaze lingered on his before dipping to his mouth and then she abruptly turned to Nancy. 'Why don't you go back to the house and leave me and Mr Jackson to talk?' She faced Jacob. 'I'm sure you'll walk me safely home, won't you?'

Walk her home? What in God's name is going on here? He nodded. 'I will, but don't you think I should also accompany your friend — ?'

'I'll be fine.' Nancy winked. 'I'm sure I'll be seeing you again soon, Jacob Jackson.'

Struck dumb a second time, protectiveness urged him to fall in step beside her, but he resisted as she sauntered away, whistling a tune from what sounded to be from some show or another.

Dragging his gaze from Nancy's retreating back, Jacob faced Louisa Hill.

'Is she going to be all right?'

She laughed. 'Nancy? Of course.'

Annoyed that she seemed to think very little of her friend's safety, much less her own, Jacob crossed his arms. 'So what do you want to talk to me about?'

'How about you give me your arm and we take

91

a slow walk back to Carson Street?'

The slight slur to her words and the way her bravado didn't quite ring true in her eyes raised Jacob's nerves. Slowly and against his better judgement, he offered her his elbow.

14

Louisa glanced at Jacob as they strolled along the street. Tall and broad, he carried a dominant aura of masculinity that both thrilled and scared her.

Whenever he looked at her, his dark blue gaze bored into hers with an intensity that was unnerving . . . yet strangely captivating.

She reflected once again that everything about him was so entirely different than Anthony . . . possibly different than any man she'd ever met.

His physical strength was, of course, undeniable and she had come across men of his shape and size before, but it was Jacob's quietness that appealed and intrigued. As though he had plenty to say but chose his words carefully and only spoke when he had something of importance to share.

And right now, she wished he'd speak again even if only to hear the deep, confident timbre of his voice.

Her fascination with him was worrying, but also necessary.

Louisa slowly exhaled, praying that the fresh air rid her of a little of the wine she had so enthusiastically consumed upon Nancy's urging. 'So, Mr Jackson, why don't I share the reason I'm so keen to talk to you?'

He turned, one eyebrow arched.

Immediate, senseless attraction washed through her, her breath ever so slightly catching. She quickly stared along the street, fearful that he would see the crack in her confident pretence. 'I'm not sure whether you surmised my situation at Carson Street during your brief visit the other day, but Nancy and I live alone. The house is mine. Paid for and in my name, but I still feel a certain . . .' She glanced at him and her heart stuttered to find him carefully watching her. 'A certain vulnerability by not having a male presence in the house.'

He nodded without comment.

Heat rose in her face under his powerful study. Nothing in his manner or gaze gave indication of what he thought or felt about her revelations and his emotionless expression unnerved her. How did someone become so self-contained? It was disconcerting but entirely what made her believe Jacob Jackson was the right man to stand at her door. She sensed he could be trusted with both muscle and discretion. That he would neither judge what happened in the house nor ask too many questions.

Although his clothes were a little tattered, the shadow at his chin indicating he was constantly due a shave, Jacob Jackson's eyes, Roman nose and broad physique made him a man impossible to ignore. He was an imposing presence. One she needed if she had the best chance of her and Nancy being protected.

She scrambled for her next words, for the feistiness and nerve of the woman she'd once been. Yet, the woman she'd once been had slowly softened under Anthony's care and the comfortable home life he'd provided. If she was honest, Nancy would be better equipped to tackle Jacob with their plans. Her stout demeanour and unwavering strength meant she was much at ease with stern words, unruffled by confrontation.

'Are you going to go on?'

His softly spoken question sent an shiver of trepidation through her and Louisa lifted her chin as she attempted to pull on her old persona like armour.

She stopped and steadfastly met his gaze. 'I hope, very soon, to have another young lady living with us and so the need for protection grows ever more urgent. I want to be able to rest easy that — '

'Protection?' His jaw tightened, his face set under the light of the streetlamp above them. 'Is someone harassing you?'

Louisa stepped back. 'No, and do not think for a moment that Nancy and I are not capable of dealing with whatever or whomever might choose to harass us.'

His gaze ran over her face and hair, her heartbeat counting the seconds before he turned to watch a carriage rumble past them on the cobbled road.

'If that's true, then I see no reason for you to seek me out. You speak in contradiction, Mrs Hill.' He faced her. 'Now, why would that be, I wonder?'

His knowing tone brought heat to Louisa's cheeks a second time, igniting her indignation. 'I will pay you handsomely, Mr Jackson. Would not a position as a doorman to a house in a nice part of town suit you better than fighting in filthy taverns and back-alley clubs?'

He stilled, his gaze boring into hers. 'How do

you know I fight?'

'I've ... been asking questions of the men in the bar. Questions about you.'

'Why?'

'Because when I first met you, I had the distinct feeling you are the person I need, Mr Jackson.' She looked away, battling to bring forth the confidence she'd once possessed in spades and would most certainly need again. She forced her gaze to his. 'When you were stood outside my house, it was as if you were meant to be there. I trust my instinct about that ... ' She took a long breath. 'Even if I have been given cause of late to doubt what I feel in every other aspect of my life.'

A nerve jumped in his jaw but then something she said brought a look of understanding to his eyes. Slowly, he nodded. 'I see.'

'Do you?'

'If you know I'm a boxer, why would you think I'd give that up to stand at your front door?' He shook his head. 'You and your friend are indeed unlike any other women I have ever met.'

Sensing a softening in his demeanour, Louisa pressed further. 'Surely, alternative employment away from the ring would appeal? Especially considering your time in life.'

'My time in my life?' He smiled, revealing perfectly white teeth, his eyes shining with sudden amusement. 'And what do you deem *this* time in my life?'

Louisa crossed her arms, determined not to be mocked or intimidated ...

or infuriatingly attracted. 'None of us are getting any younger, Mr Jackson.

I thought you might welcome an easier way of making a living than returning to wherever you live to nurse a split lip and blackened eyes.' She shrugged and dropped her arms, taking a purposeful step along the street.

'But if I was wrong, then . . . '

'I would need more information from you to make a decision.'

Louisa fought to hide her delight and turned. 'You will consider my proposition?'

'I didn't say that. I earn good money boxing, Mrs Hill. *Really* good money, and I like what I do. Tell me why I should give up that to be the hired protection of women I know nothing about. You say you are widowed, yet I sense no grief in you. You and Miss Bloom dress like you have money but then I find you practically falling out of the White Hart half-cut. Who are you?'

She hadn't expected questions about anything other than what she would pay him and on what terms. Embarrassment and indignation bloomed inside of her. The last thing she wanted was to be forced to reveal any more about herself or her plans until necessary. Who she was and the real purpose of the house, and what would happen within its walls, could be shared in time, once she knew her ambitions would succeed. Yet, the canniness that shone in Jacob Jackson's eyes and his obvious intelligence were appealing, and it suddenly felt like months since she lain with a man in abandon . . . had strong hands touch her and pleasure her without expectation or remuneration.

Blinking, she pushed away her incongruous

97

and unexpected thoughts and fought to embrace the boldness that had kept her moving forward when she'd been at the brothel. She could not defer from her right to once again, one day, be the same carefree, loved and happy woman she had become under Anthony's care.

Even if it was now clear that her life then had been founded on lie after lie.

She pulled back her shoulders. 'I will pay you handsomely, Mr Jackson.

More than you could earn in the ring. In fact, I vow, right here and now, to match the maximum you have ever earned in a single fight to be your weekly wage. The same money without the need to have your face battered.

In addition, you will receive full bed and board.'

He protruded his bottom lip as though considering her terms, amusement glinting in his eyes.

She put her hands on her hips. 'Something funny?'

'No, not funny.'

'Then — '

'Ridiculous. I'm a fighter, Mrs Hill, not a guardian. I break men's jaws and noses. I walk through their blood to grab a pint or two of ale at the end of the night. I have no idea why you think I might be the man to stand on your doorstep in case some random hooligan decides to knock on your door, but I wager I am entirely the wrong choice.'

His derision only swelled her resolve. 'Do my reasons matter as long as you are paid? Am I not free to pursue a life of my own making? I'm no shrinking violet and neither am I afraid of hard work or doing whatever it takes to ensure my prosperity. I am a businesswoman, Mr Jackson, and someone who cares deeply for those I love. I need you because I would not be able to physically disarm a man who may become violent.'

'Violent? Why do you think you or Miss Bloom could be subjected to violence?' His expression darkened. 'What aren't you telling me?'

Louisa swallowed. If she told him she intended to run the house as a brothel, would he bolt? It was too soon for such a revelation. She needed to persuade him that an alternative way of life was within his grasp in the hope the prospect would be too good to resist.

She lifted her chin. 'All you need to know is you will be there to dispel any potential violence. I hazard a guess that any trouble will be rare.

However, if you cannot see the benefit of earning a wage *in case* your skills are needed, then maybe we should say goodnight.'

'Maybe we should . . . ' He considered her before a little of the irritation left his eyes. 'But not before I see you safely to your door.'

She laughed, although entirely frustrated. 'Now you are the one full of contradiction.'

Turning away from him, Louisa headed along the street, the thud of his heavy footsteps behind her. She walked quickly in the hope Mr Jackson might return towards town and thus feel their conversation unfinished. In her experience, there was nothing more enticing to an individual than unfinished conversation. But he did not, and by the time she'd reached her front door, she was riled and angry that his questions continued to bother her.

'Well, here we are, Mr Jackson. I thank you for your company.'

'And I for yours.' He touched the brim of his hat. 'Good evening, Mrs Hill. I hope you find the man you're looking for.'

'But —'

'Goodnight, Mrs Hill.'

Louisa watched him saunter back along the street, her heart beating fast and her cheeks stinging from the icy wind. Somehow he had managed to turn the tables, her plan backfiring and leaving her frustrated and curious.

Damnation.

Well, it was of no matter. The one thing she was absolutely sure of was she had found the man she was looking for.

Jacob Jackson *would* be hers.

15

Jacob tightened his grip on the back of the kitchen chair as Henry continued to rant, pacing from one end of the small kitchen to the other.

'God damn it, Jacob. The club is offering a fortune for you to fight the Killer. This could be the fight that makes you a name in this city. You win, and *you* will be the one to fear. The one to esteem.' Henry abruptly stopped, glaring. 'Are you afraid of him? Is that it? Judging by your summary of him the other night, I can only assume —'

'I'm not afraid of him.' Jacob swiped his hand over his face and straightened, his irritation growing with every additional second he had to look at his manager. 'I'm telling you the man is not all there. Something isn't right in his head.'

'And it is in yours?' Henry laughed, saying nothing about Doreen's tut as she continued to prepare their dinner in front of the stove. 'Well, I never had you down as a coward.'

Jacob sat at the table and clenched the engineering periodical he'd been attempting to read. 'I'm not a coward and I'm not stupid. You've heard enough about this bloke over the last week or so to know his type. He had a bloody blade hidden in his glove in the last match. The man doesn't care about the rules, about honour. He's out for a reputation.' Jacob looked pointedly at his manager. 'As are you.'

Henry's jaw tightened. 'I look out for you,

don't I?'

'And you think sending me into the ring with a nutter is looking out for me? I don't think so.'

'But think of the money.' Henry sat down beside Jacob and gripped his forearm. 'Think of the prestige and choice of fights beating the Killer will bring you. It will be a certain step to London, Jake. I'm telling you, accepting this fight is what we need to do.'

'We?' Doreen gave an inelegant snort as she emptied water from a pan into the sink. 'There ain't no *we* about it, Mr Bertrum. It's Jacob and only Jacob who will face this maniac.'

'Since when did I ask for your opinion?' Henry snapped. 'You keep your mind to your work, and I'll do the same.'

Jacob restrained a smile as Doreen stuck out her tongue and wiggled her hips behind Henry's back.

'I don't know why we're arguing about this,' Henry continued. 'I'm your manager; I line up your fights and fighting the Killer is your next move. He wants to fight you three nights from now at the underground club and you're going to oblige. Jake, for the love of God. This is the chance to — '

'How much?'

Henry eagerly sat forward, his scowl vanishing. 'More than we've . . . *you've* ever earned in a single match. Enough to pay your rent upfront for the next six months, take a trip to London and stay in one of the top-notch hotels. Come on, what do you say?'

Jacob glanced at Doreen. The housekeeper's

brow was creased, her soft green eyes worried beneath her dyed blonde fringe. Her words to Jacob urging him to settle down and leave his current way of life behind resounded in his head. Then his contemplation drifted to Louisa Hill's proclamation that she would match anything he'd ever earned in a fight.

The trouble was, he still wasn't sure what she really wanted with him. He should forget he ever met her, but now that she'd inferred she wanted him to protect her, forgetting her was impossible.

Of course, on the other hand, it could be that whenever she looked at him, she saw nothing more than a man of violence. A man she could rely on to punch, hit and pummel on command. Jacob swallowed, uncomfortable that for the first time in a long time, he wanted someone — Louisa, of all people — to see him as something more than that. She was a beautiful woman. Classy and intelligent. But she hadn't seen anything more in *him* ... which only further proved violence ran through Jacob's blood and was plain to see as the nose on his face.

He drew in a long breath and gave Henry his full attention. 'All right. I'll do it if the price is right. I want everything you've promised me and a few pounds more, do you hear? I won't risk my career or life for anything less than a quarter fortune.'

Henry pushed to his feet, his eyes gleaming with triumph as he clamped his hand to Jacob's shoulder. 'I'll go and see the Killer's manager right now and hammer out a deal. Leave it to me to see you right.'

103

Jacob met Doreen's irritated gaze as Henry swept out of the kitchen, the slam of the front door behind him making her flinch. 'You are a fool, Jacob Jackson,' she said, turning to the stove and attacking a pot of soup with a wooden spoon. 'An absolute fool.'

'I'm a boxer, Doreen. It's what I do. What I was born to do. This fight will be a challenge, but I'll win. You know I will.'

She came towards him so quickly, Jacob barely had time to draw his next breath.

'Now, you listen to me.' She thrust the dripping spoon to within an inch of his nose. 'They say this bloke has no conscience or morals. No fear or foible. A man like that isn't a fighter, Jake, he's a killer. This won't be a match of honour among thieves or whatever the bloody code is for boxers, it will be a fight to the death. You are better than this. For Christ's sake, you know he's already done time for nearly killing someone. What if he goes the whole way this time?'

'He won't. And who says I am better than this?' Jacob abruptly stood, his chair legs scraping along the flagstone floor as he snatched his periodical from the table and stuffed it in the inside pocket of his jacket. He hated the concern in her eyes that no amount of anger in her voice could hide. 'You don't know me. Nobody does. Which is just the way I like it.'

'Don't you think all of us have had our crosses to bear? That we've seen and done things we're not proud of? That doesn't mean we go along day after day, year after year, not wanting more. Do you know where I come from? Do you?'

104

Not wanting to hear anything from Doreen that might make him care for her more than he already did, Jacob forced hardness around his heart and turned away from her unrelenting glare to stare towards the window.

'I came from the seed of a man who took children from mothers so desperate that they entrusted my father with their care. I was born from the womb of a woman who promised these same women that she would treat those poor mites as her own until the mothers came back to claim them.'

Jacob faced her. 'How in God's name does coming from charitable people like that make you a bad person? My father was . . . ' He snapped his mouth closed.

'Was what? A man who then sold those children into slavery, child labour and God only knows what else? I ran from my parents, Jacob. Ran for my damn life and made the life I've got myself. Now, here I am, a housekeeper to a man who pays a fair wage and under the protection and love of you and Colin. What else could I want? But you, you seem hellbent on going on along on the same path until you're dead. You were *not* born to fight. Do you hear me? You are kind and warm. Handsome as the devil and strong. Inside and out. Reach for more, Jacob, before it's too late.'

Tears glinted in her eyes before she returned to the stove. Dumbstruck, Jacob stared at her turned back. God damn it, the woman really cared for him. How could he have let that happen?

He had to get out of here.

Had to leave.

Stalking from the kitchen, he snatched his overcoat and hat from the stair newel post and left the house. Sucking in a breath against the freezing night air, Jacob walked and continued to walk.

When he found himself in Carson Street, he stood across from Louisa Hill's house. What the hell he was doing here? Yet, the longer he stared at the house, the more satisfaction he drew from imagining Henry's face if he told him he had taken a position as a doorman at a private residence. A residence owned by a woman.

Could Doreen be right? Was it time to quit the ring and try a different way?

Jacob smiled.

16

Louisa sat on Nancy's bed and fingered the floral coverlet. 'We need him. That's the bottom line.'

'But why Jacob Jackson, in particular? There must be a hundred fighters as good as him in this city. Not to mention a hundred other scoundrels who will be willing to protect and look after us once the house is up and running.

Especially if they think there's a chance they might get a free turn or two. If Jacob turned your offer down, I don't understand why you want to go looking for him again tonight.'

'Because it's been three days since I last spoke to him. Maybe I've lingered in his mind as much as he has in mine.'

Nancy turned from her dressing table mirror, her eyebrows almost brushing her hairline. 'Lingered in your mind? That's an unusual way to describe your thinking about a potential employee. Do you have something to tell me?'

'Of course not.' Louisa stood and walked to the window, purposely turning her back to her friend. 'There's just something about him . . . ' *His face, his height, his shoulders . . .* 'Something I trust.'

'Trust? God above, Lou, how can you easily trust a man so soon? You barely know him.'

'I know . . . ' Louisa closed her eyes, completely agreeing with her friend but unable to quiet her certainty about Jacob Jackson. The sincerity in his eyes, the way he held her gaze so openly told her he had nothing to hide.

She suspected what you saw in Jacob was what you got and, after Anthony, there was nothing more she sought in a man. 'But we don't have a lot of choice if we're going to do this. We haven't got the time to dither, Nance.'

'So we need some muscle on the door, but that doesn't mean Jacob Jackson is the only man to provide it. I don't want to be in gratitude to a man again. Do you? Let's find someone eager to take the job. Better still, who *needs* the job. Someone who doesn't question anything, earns his money and clears off at the end of his shift.'

'No, I want Jacob.'

'But why?'

'Because he's already shown his concern for women's safety by insisting on walking me home and worrying about you. Plus, he has a candidness that I respect.' She crossed her arms, steadfastly ignoring her friend's protestations and her own suspicions that she had very little on which to hang her instinct about Jacob. 'I also suspect he'll like that I'm trying to forge a future for us once he learns of the circumstances in which we've found ourselves.'

Nancy's eyes slightly widened. 'You intend telling him about Anthony's suicide? His debts?'

'Maybe. In time. Jacob has intelligence, a look about him that speaks of consideration and care, regardless of his current vocation. I think he's a man of integrity and without prejudice.'

Nancy turned back to the mirror and readjusted her hat, setting the feather just so. 'Well, if you want

108

me to help you look for him tonight, I will, but I advise you to keep an open mind with regards to other men we might come across.' She stood and put her hands on her slender hips, her brow furrowed. 'There's nothing to say that Jacob Jackson won't take complete advantage of your pursual of him. In my experience, a man is a man. They have excessive egos, and if he understands it's only him you want at our front door, he'll be the one in control. Not you.'

As Nancy gathered her purse and umbrella, Louisa had to admit her friend was right. It would pay to apply caution as far as Jacob was concerned. At least for the time being. She trusted her instincts about him, but it would be foolish to give away even the tiniest amount of her power.

This business would be hers and she planned for everything to be carried out on her terms.

The only thing worrying her was that even though she and Nancy were returning to whoring, she had never possessed her friend's steeliness and someone like Jacob, a man clearly used to living his life his own way, could easily take umbrage with Louisa's instruction. Worse, he could take a fancy to one of the girls he was there to protect. After all, as Nancy testified, a man was a man. Yet, his immediate refusal to her proposal to work for her told Louisa that female wiles provoked no weakness in him; clearly his head ruled his heart and he only made decisions on what he considered right for him and him alone.

And that was exactly the type of man they needed as protection.

Someone focused and unconcerned by the

physical activities that would go on behind the house's closed door.

Decision made, Louisa nodded towards to the door. 'Come on. It's time to go.'

She and Nancy hailed a hired cab into town. As the horse pulled the carriage along the edge of the River Avon, past the Abbey and closer to the poorer areas, Louisa contemplated the new city she now called home, her thoughts bouncing back and forth to her meeting with the young woman by the river.

When she'd told Nancy about Octavia, she had asked a few questions and Louisa's answers had eventually satisfied her friend enough that Nancy had agreed they should try to offer Octavia their help one more time. Louisa intended for that to happen sooner rather than later.

But for tonight, everything was about Jacob.

Even though she had thought that living away from Bristol, a city she adored, and adjusting to life as a widow in a new home would prove difficult, Bath had somehow welcomed her. If she stopped fretting that more of Anthony's creditors might arrive at her door, Louisa could almost contemplate her future being as happy as it had when she'd believed herself content with Anthony.

Now, more than ever, she wanted to provide the same for Nancy and Octavia. Maybe, one day, she would be in a position to give help to even more whores on the street.

Nancy unceremoniously banged on the cab's roof with her umbrella.

They had arrived at the White Hart tavern.

Alighting from the carriage, Louisa stepped

onto the rain-sodden street and met the curious stares of the drinkers outside, their eyes wide at the sight of a carriage in this part of town.

Louisa inwardly grimaced. This was the second time she'd not considered how such extravagance might be interpreted by certain people.

Her insensitivity was shaming and there would not be recurrence of such lack of thought again. But, for now, she must brazen out any reaction.

'Order the driver to wait a moment, Nancy,' she said quietly. 'It might be that Jacob isn't here. In which case, we can be on our way all the quicker.'

Her friend nodded and turned back to the carriage.

Louisa approached a group of men who appraised her with varying degrees of lust, dislike and suspicion. 'Good evening. Would any of you gentlemen happen to know if Jacob Jackson is here tonight?'

One of them stepped forward, spitting a lump of tobacco onto the paving.

Louisa fought not to recoil and kept her face impassive.

The man stared at her bosom before slowly raising his gaze to hers.

'Jackson will most likely to be found beaten to a pulp in the next half an hour or so. But if it's company you're looking for, I am more than willing to do what I can for a woman who looks like you, sweetheart.'

Louisa smiled, knowing exactly what was expected of her. 'Well, I'll bear that in mind, but for now I really need to speak with Mr Jackson.' Her stomach tightened with tension as the man

111

grinned, showing more gum than teeth. The few he had were almost black. 'Why do you say he will soon be beaten to a pulp?'

'Clearly you've been living with your head in the mud for the last three days if you haven't heard. Jackson's taking on the Killer at the underground club the other side of the river. He's a dead man walking.' He leaned closer, his eyes dark with menace. 'They say the Killer can break an opponent's neck with just a twist of his elbow.'

Louisa mouth dried, fear for Jacob whispering through her. 'And this club is the other side of the river?'

'Yeah, but it's easy enough to find if you know where to look.'

'Which is where?'

'A few hundred yards past the King's Head Hotel. It's a black door between a grocer's and a barber's but, if you take my advice, you'll steer clear.'

'Well, thank you. I'll be careful, don't you worry.' Louisa returned to the carriage and gripped Nancy's elbow. 'Let's go.'

She tumbled her friend inside with a shout to the driver to take them across the river.

'Bloody hell, Lou, go careful, will you?' Nancy snapped as she attempted to pull her crumpled skirt from beneath her. 'There is little chance of me replacing this frock any time soon.'

'It seems Jacob is embroiled in a fight with a maniac. We have to find him and quickly.'

'Good God, this bloke has well and truly caught your eye, hasn't he?'

After a short journey over the bridge and across

the river, Louisa and Nancy managed to charm their way past the doorman of the club. Louisa led the way along a dark corridor, her eyes slowly adjusting to the dimness as her ears filled with muffled grunts and whacks from behind a second door.

She put her hand to the door and faced Nancy. 'Ready?'

Nancy gave a curt nod, not a trace of fear or apprehension in her grey eyes. 'Any idea what we are likely to see in there?'

Pulling back her shoulders, Louisa shoved open the door. 'None at all.'

She was immediately enveloped in a thick blanket of smoke, so potent her eyes watered. She put her hand over her mouth in an attempt to stem her coughing.

'Good God . . . ' Nancy shouted behind her. 'This place is like hell.'

Louisa shouldered her way through the mass of bodies shouting and jeering around a ring erected in the centre of the room, as the bloodstained straw covering the floor shifted and slipped beneath her feet. The stench of sweat, pipe smoke and blood was rife, assaulting her nostrils and coating her throat. Louisa closed her mouth on the urge to gag.

She stopped close to the ring, the men around her and Nancy so engrossed in the bloodbath ahead of them that they didn't seem to notice, or care, that two women dressed in silks stood among them.

Where in the world was Jacob? She scanned the dirty faces around her, but she couldn't see him anywhere. Was he in the ring? One half of the fight currently in full flow? She edged closer. The boxers were on the floor, their knuckles bare and blood covering their faces to the extent that recognition was almost impossible.

Almost.

'Jacob . . . ' She whispered his name just as the man currently astride Jacob's lifeless body slammed his fist into Jacob's face, spurting so much blood it sprayed like a fountain upon the delighted faces on the onlookers.

'My God.'

The entire place erupted.

Blood was everywhere as Jacob lay unmoving on the floor. His opponent grinned and barrelled out of the ring, hotfooting it away with no one having the courage or gumption to hinder his escape. Louisa bolted forward, Nancy right behind her, as they shoved the men surrounding Jacob out of the way.

'This man needs help,' Louisa shouted as she tore a strip from her petticoat and pressed it hard to the slash across Jacob's abdomen. 'Find a physician. Call the constable. He's been cut. Somebody find help. Now!'

It was as though she had shouted that the devil himself had just walked into the room. Men scattered, fleeing for the door, blood staining their clothes, their ale and gin jugs flung to the floor forgotten.

Louisa stared around her in disbelief. 'Where are you going?'

'For the love of God, Lou,' Nancy said, crouching down beside her and stroking Jacob's dark hair from his brow. 'You don't mention calling a constable in a place like this.'

Three men remained and they came forward, one of them looking over Jacob, his brow wrinkled in worry. 'Let's get him into the back room. I can stitch him well enough to get him out of here, but then he's your responsibility. I don't want nothing else to do with it.'

Louisa nodded, her heart thundering. 'Thank you.'

The men somehow managed to get Jacob onto their shoulders and carry him through the door. Louisa followed, fear clutching at her heart.

She angrily swiped at her treacherous tears. How dare she get so upset over the state of a relative stranger? A stranger who had refused to help her.

Louisa lifted her chin against the dangerous emotions stirring awake in her heart. She couldn't care again. She was not allowed to show weakness.

'God, help him,' she murmured. 'And if you can't help him, help me.'

17

Jacob tried and failed to open his eyes, his lids swollen and heavy.

An unfamiliar aroma drifted around him, something heady and sweet.

Like flowers mixed with a smell he was much more familiar with considering the frequency of his injuries — medicinal ointment.

Again, he fought to open his eyes and managed to crack them open to slits. He lay in a bed in semi-darkness, a sliver of light spilling across his face from a gap in the drapes sending a sear of pain through his brain. He slowly turned his head to one side, tightening his lips against the burning in his ribs. A vase of pink and white blooms sat in a water jug on the chest of drawers beside him explaining one half of the smell.

The other half . . . He turned his head in the other direction.

And his heart damn near stopped, his aching eyes popping wide open.

Louisa Hill stood at a bureau in front of the window, the low winter sun casting her face in half-shadow as she poured water into a bowl. She plunged a cloth into the liquid, her pretty features strained with what he thought either fatigue or concern. As she worked, her teeth worried her bottom lip, her shoulders stiff and her back rigid.

Jacob closed his eyes, his heart pounding. Jesus Christ, was he in her house?

His eyes shot open a second time and he slipped his hand beneath the covers, a pain shooting through his side. He gritted his teeth and stilled. His cock and balls were bare.

'Oh, you're awake.'

Jacob snatched his hand from beneath the covers with such force a jab of hot pain shot through his back. 'Fuc ...'

'Don't move.' Louisa came closer, the corners of her mouth lifting as she clearly fought her smile. 'You're black and blue all over.'

All over... Jacob scowled. 'Where are my clothes?'

'Well, you were shirtless and barefoot when we picked you up off the straw. And your trousers were torn and bloodied beyond belief, so I threw them out. It's safe to say you weren't wearing many clothes at all, but I'm sure I can find something of my husband's for you to wear.'

He tried to move up the pillows propped behind him and slumped, the agony of his ribs too much. 'Two questions ...' He grimaced. 'Who is *we*? And where exactly is *here*?'

'Nancy and I, and you are at my house, of course.'

'Well, of course,' he said dryly. 'Would you mind helping me to sit up?'

She leaned over him, the scent of her hair and the soft warmth of her breath brushing over his face sending a quiver of awareness skittering over his skin in a way that was entirely unwelcome.

With her help, he managed to sit half upright and accept the cup of water she put to his lips. He took a few sips before collapsing back against the pillows, exhausted but determined not to fall back asleep. 'I need to go.'

She cast her study over his face, concern clouding her extraordinary violet eyes. 'Could you manage a little soup? I have some on the stove. Maybe a little bread and cheese?'

'I said —'

'You're going nowhere until you've at least eaten something.'

He held her gaze, the determination in her eyes impossible to contradict.

He slumped against the pillows. 'Soup sounds good. Thank you.'

As she moved to walk away a thought rushed his mind and he caught her wrist, the sudden movement sending another stab of pain through his body.

He stared at her, not liking the attraction that enveloped him. She really was astoundingly beautiful.

'How did you get me here?' he demanded as he released her. 'More importantly, why am I not in my own home?'

She lowered onto the side of the bed and clasped her hands in her lap. 'I took over your care. I didn't think that manager of yours would be much help to you or show much sympathy had you returned home.'

'You met Henry? I didn't see him before the fight and assumed he'd been waylaid somewhere.' Jacob closed his eyes, a headache rousing in his temple. 'But if he was there, then I can only guess at his reaction to the state of me. The Killer had the upper hand from the minute the fight started.'

118

'No, I didn't meet your manager.' She scowled. 'And thank God I didn't, considering the way that fight ended. The men at the club told me what kind of man Henry Bertrum is and I surmised you'd be better looked after here.'

Jacob moved and softly cursed as his ribs screamed with pain again.

'Damn, what in God's name is wrong with my ribs? Did he pummel me in one place or something?'

'It's not your ribs, it's your side. A gentleman at the club stitched and bandaged you. I have changed the dressings, but goodness knows — '

'Stitched me?' Jacob frowned. 'Why would he need to stitch me, for crying out loud?'

'That monster you were fighting had a knife.' Her eyes turned steely.

'The cut isn't too deep, and you are sufficiently stitched. The doctor is confident there won't be any infection, but I would like to see the other boxer dragged in front of a magistrate. Surely, there are rules against weapons?'

'He cut me?' Jacob slipped his hand beneath the cover and tentatively lowered his hand to his left side. The bandage was dry and thick against his fingers. 'Bastard.'

'Indeed.' She stood and walked to the bureau, picking up the bowl. 'But you were lucky he didn't cut you more severely.'

'A cut is nothing compared with what Henry will want to do to me. He'll be cursing that the Killer didn't finish me off. Well, at least until he calms down and then realises there will be more money to be had if I demand a rematch.'

'A rematch?' Her knuckles turned white around the bowl in her hands.

'Don't be ridiculous.'

'It's the way of the boxing world. I lose, I want a rematch. Simple.' Jacob glared towards the window. 'And this son of bitch cut me.' He faced her, adrenaline making his heart beat faster. 'I can't let that go without doing something to back up my reputation.'

'You care more for reputation than you do for your life?'

The disappointment in her eyes twisted at something in Jacob's chest.

Something that felt too much like shame. 'Something like that.'

'Then you really need to take a long look at yourself.' She stepped towards the door. 'I'll go and see about that soup.'

'There's something else.'

Her pretty eyes flitted over him as though considering whether or not to open the door and flee downstairs or remain. She slumped her shoulders and came closer to the bed, looking expectant.

'I want to leave. Before dark.' He coughed and winced. 'I'll also need a pair of trousers, a shirt, some socks and boots collected from my lodgings. I live at the house with the green door on Sydney Place.'

She crossed her arms. 'You won't be needing anything like that for at least a few days yet. I can get some nightclothes for you, though. I didn't dress you before because you were a stone weight asleep and we barely managed to get you undressed.'

He arched an eyebrow. 'So, you were more determined to undress me than dress me . . . duly noted.'

She smiled, a twinkle glinting her eyes. 'Needs must, Mr Jackson.'

He couldn't drag his gaze from hers and his treacherous groin twisted with need. He looked past her shoulder to the wall. 'I can't stay here.'

'You can and you will. At least for a few days.'

'A few days . . . ' He snapped his gaze to hers. 'What makes you think Henry will step aside and let you take care of me? The man is under the delusion that he owns me. He'll be knocking at your door in no time, expecting me fit and well and ready to fight again.'

'That may be so and if he comes here, he will be sent quickly away. I asked the man who stitched you to pass on a message to Mr Bertrum that I will be taking care of you for a week.'

'And you think he will agree to such a thing?'

'I told him I owe you a debt of gratitude and I couldn't possibly let you out of my sight until you were recovered.'

Jacob laughed, winced and laughed again. 'He'll never believe that.

Henry is the most cynical man I know. He wouldn't think anyone would owe me anything, let alone gratitude.'

She smiled, her eyes shining with delight. He couldn't tell what had pleased her so much, but, in that moment, he wanted to stop time just to look at her bright eyes and wide smile a while longer.

'Well, he sent a message back saying I was welcome to you.' She put her hand on his knee on top of the cover, sending another quiver through his groin. 'For a week, anyway. After that, I'm hoping neither of us will have to worry about your return to him.'

'What do you . . . ' Jacob shook his head. 'Oh no, I see where this is going, and you can halt whatever plans you've got going on in that pretty head of yours.'

'Pretty head?' She raised an eyebrow and grinned. 'Well, thank you.'

Inwardly punching his knife wound as punishment for unwittingly telling her he found her attractive, Jacob scowled. 'I said no to your offer and I meant it.'

'But — '

'No.'

'If you just let me expl — '

'You have proven by getting me under your roof, naked and lying in one of your bedrooms, that you are perfectly capable of making a man bend to your will. However, if it's a protector you want, you'll have to look elsewhere. My answer is a firm no.'

The light he'd enjoyed so much in her eyes faded and guilt knotted Jacob's gut, but he held firm . . . even if his study kept dropping to her exquisite mouth. There was no question of him becoming her doorman now that he had a score to settle with the Killer.

'Let me at least explain why I want you and what I intend to happen in this house.' She stood and walked to the foot of the bed, her fingers curling

122

round the iron bedstead. 'I told you before that I was widowed . . . '

'But you're not?' Irritation simmered inside him. He wasn't sure if he was more angry that she'd lied to him or that she was married. Christ, was her husband away on business somewhere? Was he staying in a man's house who could return at any moment? He moved to shove the blankets aside and stopped, remembering his current state of undress.

She pulled her lips together, her infuriating gaze dancing with amusement.

He glared. 'This isn't funny, Mrs Hill.'

'Louisa, please. And I agree, nothing about this is funny — that's why I need you. But to answer your question about whether I lied to you. I did not.'

'So you are widowed?'

'Yes, and my husband left me this house, but nothing else.'

'And?'

'And I need to earn a living. I am young, reasonably attractive and intend to make this house work for me, Mr Jackson.'

'I don't understand.' He fought against anything she might say to weaken his resolve not to work for her. 'What does that have to do with me?'

'Because you're perfect.'

'For?'

'Standing at the door of a brothel.'

Shock reverberated through him sending pangs through his wound and every other part of his body. He stared at her, looking for some indication she jested him. Yet, her eyes remained firmly on his, her chin jutted and staunch pride glowing in her eyes.

'Very soon I will open this house to the upper-class men of the city,' she continued. 'You will stand at my door and walk the house, protecting my girls and ensuring no undesirables find entry. The job will be well paid, will include bed and board and the position will give you the oppor-tunity to use your handsome looks, charm and strength in a better way than thumping other men around a boxing ring. Now . . . ' She walked to the door. 'I'll go to the kitchen and get your soup.'

She disappeared and Jacob stared dumbstruck through the open door, his mind reeling.

A brothel?

Louisa Hill was a prostitute?

She'd said *my girls*. Did she intend being the madam of this house? The overseer? Her expres-sion had been unwavering as she'd spoken, her tone confident and assured as though she knew exactly what would be involved in running such an establishment and the protection the house would need in the face of its clients and workers.

A prostitute . . . it seemed impossible.

She carried herself with an elegance he'd not seen in the girls he passed almost daily on the streets. Had she once worked in a house as grand as the one he now lay abed in?

Well, whatever she might or might not have done, she had thrust her future plans in his face without so much as a blink of her eye. The notion of deterring her was laughable, judging by her determination.

It was clear Louisa Hill had been left to fend for

124

herself to the best of her ability — to protect what was hers, and herself, the only way she knew how.

Unwanted admiration rose inside him.

He had thought them to be poles apart. Different people with different lives. Yet, maybe they weren't quite so unalike, after all.

18

Dusk closed in as Louisa made her way past the prostitutes touting for business along the dank, dingy street where she'd found Octavia a couple of weeks ago. Louisa's turbulent past shadowed her as she walked, provoking a fierce affinity with each and every woman out here on such a bitterly cold night. Many returned her nods, some with friendliness, others with blatant hostility.

Louisa knew only too well how the inherent hierarchy worked, how important it was to note and be wary of a new face. Each of these women would be getting their measure of her, considering whether or not she was a potential friend or foe who might take food from their mouths and money from their pockets.

She searched among them for Octavia, her face imprinted on Louisa's memory. Thoughts of how the young woman fared had badgered Louisa until she couldn't ignore the feeling fate had led them to meet that night.

With Nancy at home tending to Jacob, Louisa's need to find the girl had grown ever stronger until she'd slipped out of the house. The brief times Octavia had left Louisa's thoughts were when Jacob and his refusal to be the house's protection intruded.

Well, she hadn't given up on securing his acceptance yet. Just as she wouldn't on her insistence the young woman came to stay with her and Nancy.

Once Octavia had been fed and slept in warmth and comfort, if she wanted to return to the streets, Louisa wouldn't stop her. If the young prostitute had every intention of continuing to trade out here in the danger and the cold, then Louisa would respect that.

After all, how could she doubt the woman's shrewdness or intelligence?

She had assumed Louisa a prostitute — a madam — on their very first meeting.

Whoever Octavia was, she was clearly street-savvy and didn't suffer fools gladly. Her posh way of speaking had thrown Louisa, but now curiosity about Octavia's background was all-consuming.

But whatever her previous station in life, it was clear she needed help now.

Louisa pulled her coat tighter around her, dipping her face away from the cut of the icy wind. Only the brave or the desperate would be in one of these dark doorways or standing on a half-crumbling street corner on such an evening.

'Who are you looking for, missus?'

Louisa stopped and faced a woman who looked to be in her early thirties, although it was hard to be certain. Her ravaged skin was tightly drawn across jutting cheekbones, her eyes sunken and glazed.

Pulling back her shoulders, Louisa confidently met the woman's rheumy gaze. 'I'm looking for a young woman named Octavia. Dark brown hair, pretty. She spoke . . . well.'

'Ah, you mean Upper-Class Polly.'

'Is that what you call her?' Hope and amusement unfurled in Louisa's stomach, but she kept her face impassive. 'Do you know where I can find her?'

'She'll be at the theatre.'

The theatre? Surely, someone dressed so ragged, her hair unkempt and her face unclean wouldn't be allowed access to the Theatre Royal? 'Why would she be in the theatre?'

The woman laughed, showing a flash of yellow teeth before she hacked a cough into her gloved hand. Once she'd regained her composure, the woman shook her head, mirth glinting in her eyes. 'Why do you think?

She'll be hoping for a handout from the toffs at chucking-out time. You'll find her hunkered down in the alleyway by the side of the Royal. With her looks and voice, lots of those sorts take pity on her, even if they'd take her home on a night they weren't arm in arm with their wives.'

Louisa reached into her pocket and extracted some coins. 'Here. For your help.'

'Thank you, missus. Anytime.'

Louisa hurried away in the direction of the Theatre Royal.

When she arrived there, crowds swept out of the theatre's gilded doors in a stream of overcoats. Men resplendent in black top hats and pristine white scarves, the women beautiful in an array of feminine shawls and feathered hats. Light from the theatre's lamps spilled onto the street, gaily illuminating the frosty pavement and the faces of the audience.

Louisa quickly walked to the side of the theatre and along a cobbled street. Vagrants — children dressed in rags and women cradling babes beneath their coats — lined both sides of the narrow street. Their hands were outstretched to the privileged, their faces drawn with hunger and exhaustion.

Despite the need for frugality in her present circumstances, the desperate people around her needed money more than her, and Louisa dropped coins into palms as she walked.

Then she saw Octavia.

Slowing her pace, Louisa studied her as she spoke to a gentleman, a little way back from the crowd. He was finely dressed and appeared to be addressing Octavia with kindness, but Louisa suspected their exchange was neither fine nor gallant.

She edged closer just as Octavia shook her head and turned to walk away.

The man lunged and gripped her roughly by the arm, sneaking a surreptitious glance over his shoulder.

Louisa stalked forwards, prepared to intervene.

Octavia wrenched her arm from his grasp. 'I said, leave me be or I'll scream. Is that what you want?'

'You're a fool.'

'And you're perverted.'

Louisa stood behind the man and firmly prodded her finger twice into his shoulder, praying Octavia didn't flee. 'I think it's best you be on your way, sir.'

The man swivelled around, his face momentarily contorted as though vicious words danced on his tongue. Whatever he saw in Louisa's eyes stilled him. She raised her eyebrows. He looked from her to Octavia and back again.

'I believe you want to walk that way,' Louisa

said, pointing ahead of her.

'There's trade to be had all over the city, but not here, sir. Not tonight.'

He hesitated, looking back and forth between Louisa and Octavia again . . . before scurrying away like a rat into the night.

Louisa dropped her tense shoulders and faced the other woman. 'Hello.'

'You again. What do you want?' She drew her canny gaze over Louisa's face, her blue eyes intensely suspicious. 'I told you I don't need your help. Now, I'd kindly thank you to leave me alone.'

'Why won't you at least listen to me?'

'Why should I?' Octavia huffed a laugh. 'Out of all the people who need helping on Bath's streets, you chose me. Well, aren't I the lucky one?' Her smile dissolved and she leaned in close to Louisa. 'I do not work for anyone else, do you understand? I'm my own woman and always will be.'

Louisa fought to hide the euphoria that burst inside of her. This young woman was clearly made of the stuff Louisa wanted and needed at her house. Octavia had fire in her eyes and a spirit that told Louisa she would be right at home at Carson Street. She had no doubt that Nancy would like her very much, too.

Octavia exhaled heavily, pushed a dark curl behind her ear. 'Look, I do not have time to stand here exchanging niceties. I need to go.'

'Where?'

The woman glared. 'I'm sorry, but I fail to see how that is any of your business.'

Louisa stood firm, but she knew the way of the streets and if she misjudged Octavia, there was no saying whether or not she would thump Louisa clean on the nose.

She stood a little taller. 'I'd like to offer you a bed for the night, along with a warm meal this evening and breakfast in the morning. If you find my house isn't to your liking, or you have no wish to entertain the proposal I'd like to discuss with you, then you are free to leave and I'll never bother you again.'

Octavia narrowed her eyes. 'So it's as I thought — you wish me to work for you.'

'Not for me. *With* me.'

The rush of exiting theatre-goers had dwindled and with them the vagrants hoping for a modicum of charity. The lessening of the noise evoked an intimacy to their solitary conversation and Louisa prayed Octavia trusted her.

But the longer Octavia stared, the more her eyes darkened with open cynicism. Louisa couldn't help questioning again what had happened to such a clearly educated, articulate and pretty young woman that Octavia had come to be selling herself on Bath's streets.

Octavia exhaled a long breath. 'I must admit, there's something about you that interests me.'

Hope flickered inside Louisa. 'Good, because there's something about you that interests me, too.'

Octavia's set features marginally softened, and she nodded. 'Fine. I'll accept your invitation of a bed and food but once I've heard what you have to say, the decision of what happens next is mine alone.'

Louisa smiled. 'Agreed.'

131

19

Jacob watched Nancy as she sat across from him in Louisa Hill's parlour.

The room was over-feminine, flowers and embroidered decoration covering every surface, a fancy mirror of a questionably large size over the fireplace. Even the cushions behind his back were satin and the most godawful shade of pink.

He had overheard snippets of conversation between Nancy and Louisa that the rooms would soon be altered to Louisa's taste. The redecoration made no sense considering the time she must have lived here with her husband before he died. He couldn't imagine any man dictating his home to be decorated in this particular fashion. Then again, who was he to judge?

Yet Jacob's confusion further fuelled his curiosity with regards to the set-up inside the house and the companionship within it.

Of course, there was every possibility her husband had never lived here . . .

Many middle-class couples chose to live separate lives and the same could have been true of the Hills. Jacob took a sip of brandy. He had so many questions about so many things but was reluctant to ask too much for fear of what he might learn and how he would feel about any gained knowledge. He liked Louisa, was man enough to admit he was attracted to her and he was fond enough of Nancy.

There was no guarantee that if he learned too much, he could come to care too much.

Yet, despite the knife wound to his stomach healing well, his bruises and cuts fading, still he remained at Carson Street.

Nancy's fingers remained busy at her knitting needles, her brow free of line and worry. He scowled at her apparent tranquillity. How in God's name could what Louisa had planned for Nancy's future not bother her?

The fact these women were intent on becoming prostitutes sure as hell bothered him.

So much about Louisa's plans to turn the house into a brothel made no sense. What were her and Nancy's histories? Why did they think themselves capable of running such a place? And what on earth had led them to believe selling themselves was their only option?

He couldn't deny their individual charm and allure, plus both were good-looking women with figures to turn a man's eye. Yet, so much more than those things would be needed to run a damn brothel. Experience, street-savvy, guts and quick thinking. He had the distinct feeling Louisa Hill had known the good life for a long time, even if he didn't completely disregard the possibility that she might once have known a different life. Who could say if she had the skills to cope with such a potentially dangerous business?

She'd certainly handled Henry well enough and he was an arsehole at the best of times. The fact Jacob had been in her house three days, and Henry had seemingly abandoned him, meant there must have been more to Louisa's message to him than she had shared. Unless, of course, there had been very little dialogue between her and Henry and more an exchange of money.

Henry barely left Jacob alone for more than a day before haranguing him into his next fight. His manager lived and breathed money and success. He wouldn't give a shit about Jacob's bruises, cuts and wounds. He would normally be doing all he possibly could to have Jacob back in the ring by now.

So how had Louisa managed to keep Henry from her door?

'If there's something you want to ask me, Mr Jackson, spit it out,' Nancy said, her focus on her stitches. 'Your glare is boring into my cheek and it's not particularly pleasant.'

Jacob sipped again at his brandy, its effects lowering his guard. Fine, if the woman wanted him to stop glaring, she could answer his questions. Of which he had many. 'Do you know what Louisa has in mind for this house?'

'Of course.'

She still didn't look up from her knitting. Instead, she continued in her work as though nothing disturbed her peace.

Jacob fought his frustration. 'And what do you think about it?'

'I think Louisa will prove herself an astute businesswoman . . . even if she's yet to have that confidence in herself. She's kind and fair and will only ever have my best interests at heart.' She finally met his gaze, her grey eyes challenging him to contradict her summary of a woman who clearly meant a lot to her. 'Let me put it this way, Mr Jackson. We both have some experience of what's involved in running such a house and, have no fear, Louisa and I will give all we have to making a success of it.'

'You were prostitutes.'

'Indeed, Mr Jackson, we were.'

There was no shame in her tone, rather pride, and Jacob couldn't help but admire her. 'And Louisa feels no regret about what she might have done in the past?'

Nancy's face darkened as she lowered her knitting into her lap. 'Why should she?'

Jacob battled not to fidget under the weight of Nancy's tight-lipped irritation. He cleared his throat and lifted his glass. 'I just wondered.'

'Well, you can wonder all you want. Louisa did what she had to do to survive, as did I. As we will again.'

'That's something to be admired.'

'It is. Louisa might not be as accepting of her past as I am of mine, but she is not ashamed nor remorseful. Unfortunately, though, she continues to believe all she has in this world are her looks and figure. She couldn't be more wrong, of course.'

'Meaning?'

'Meaning she is so much more than that.' Nancy pinned him with an unwavering and defensive stare. 'However, I do question her assurance that you are the man to look after us. Even more so after your questions.'

Jacob turned towards the window, his mind filled with Louisa and her safety. 'Believe me, you're not alone in that doubt, Miss Bloom.'

'But, if Louisa wants you here, you'd be a fool

135

to turn down her proposition.'

Jacob looked back, his interest piqued. He needed to know more about Louisa and her reasons behind so avidly seeking him out. It was the fact she'd chosen *him* that concerned and confused Jacob. 'Why?'

'Because Louisa only helps or asks for help from people she knows need her just as much as she needs them. She isn't a taker by any means and if she's selected you to help us, Mr Jackson, there's every chance you will gain more by her association than she will by yours.'

It was like unravelling a damn riddle, but he wouldn't give Nancy the satisfaction of witnessing his confusion. He leaned back in his chair and swirled his brandy, his gaze on hers. 'Why should I embroil myself in a house of vice where men will be teased and coerced until their blood is hot with lust and their minds in their cocks? I might be a fighter, Miss Bloom, but the majority of my opponents are in the ring to win honourably. The violence of the men who Louisa intends to entertain will be fuelled by frustration or possession. That, is an entirely different animal to tame.'

She smiled, the challenge in her eyes softening to what looked to be reluctant respect. 'Good, I'm pleased you understand what we will be facing. Maybe Louisa was right in her judgement, after all. She must have seen something in you that I hadn't until now. If you understand the nature of our business before you've been properly exposed to it, then you are a fine choice to defuse any situation that has the potential to become out of control.'

She picked up her knitting and resumed her work, seemingly no more rattled by his questions than she'd been before. Jacob carefully watched her.

He had to understand more of who Louisa really was . . . even though he was determined to be out of this house tomorrow, come what may. Yet, until he was convinced she wasn't under threat, he felt duty-bound to help her after she had tended to him so diligently.

As for her proposal, he needed to be in his own home to consider the prospect more closely. Being around these women skewed his judgement.

The fact he was still sitting here was proof enough of that.

'More questions, Mr Jackson?'

The amusement in Nancy's voice irked him and Jacob put down his glass with a little more force than intended. 'As a matter of fact, yes.' He sat a little straighter, not really comfortable with what he wanted to ask, but sick to the back teeth of wrangling about the truth of these two women. 'This house is nicer than most. Mr Hill clearly had money.'

Slowly, Nancy raised her head and frowned. 'He did, yes.'

'Yet he left none of his money to his wife.'

'No.'

'But he left the house.'

'Yes.'

It was the least forthcoming Nancy been since he arrived and, judging by the irritation in her eyes, she was either annoyed with him asking about Louisa's husband, or else, hadn't been an admirer of the man.

'You didn't get along with Mr Hill?'

She held his gaze, her jaw tightening.

The clock on the fireplace mantel suddenly sounded loud in the room, horses' hooves on the street outside filtering through the window.

She exhaled a shaky breath. 'No, I didn't like him.'

'Why not?'

'He treated Louisa well enough and tolerated me, but I always suspected him of having secrets and I didn't like that. I've cared for Louisa too much to stand aside should the man who promised her the damn world have a mind to hurt her. And I like him even less now that he's left Louisa with no choice but to resurrect the life she had assumed behind her.' She lifted her chin, her expression turning steely. 'But be under no disillusion that Louisa won't triumph in her plans, Mr Jackson. With or without you, she will prevail.'

'I don't doubt that. She has guts and determination. The fact I'm here and still under her care illustrates her single-mindedness.'

'It also illustrates your indecision about her proposal.' She smiled teasingly. 'Do you find her intriguing? Is that why you are sitting in *her* parlour, rather than in your own?'

Rare heat warmed his cheeks and Jacob turned away from Nancy's wily gaze to stare into the fire. 'So, was it Mr Hill who saved Louisa from a life on the streets?'

'Who said Louisa was ever on the streets?'

'She wasn't? Then how . . . ' Comprehension dawned, and Jacob nodded.

'She worked in a brothel.'

'We both did. That's where we met and have remained firm friends ever since.'

Protectiveness for Louisa rose inside him. 'Was she Hill's whore? Then his mistress until he eventually married her?'

'You certainly have a lot of questions.' She sighed. 'But I am under no obligation to answer any more. If you can't accept mine and Louisa's word that the business she has in mind will provide you with a good income and a position that is highly unlikely to result in you being in the state you were when we brought you here, then you are free to turn down her offer and walk away.'

'Agreed, but in order to consider the offer properly, I want a little reassurance that two women who appear on the surface to be wealthy and living the high life have actually lived a real life, with real people and real problems.'

Two spots of colour darkened Nancy's cheeks and anger shone in her eyes. 'Well, rest assured, both Louisa and I know that and more.'

Although he took no pleasure in his persistence, Jacob pushed on.

'Because?'

'I was streetwalker before I came to the brothel where Louisa worked, Mr Jackson. The rest, as they say, is for you to trust.'

Jacob forced himself to take another casual sip of his drink. Just the thought of Louisa living such a hard life made his gut knot with anger.

'Look . . . ' Nancy leaned forward and picked up her wine. 'Louisa's husband gave her an escape from the brothel and she took it, taking me with her. But don't make the mistake of thinking her husband's generosity was in any way honourable. Anthony Hill wanted Louisa for himself and Louisa knew that but, still, she selflessly insisted that the only way that was going to happen was if I came as a part of the agreement. That's the sort of person she is, Mr Jackson. She does nothing without other people in mind. Trust me, the same will undoubtedly be true of her reasons for wanting you.'

'That's what I don't understand. My life is fine just the way it is.'

'Is it?' Her mouth lifted at the corners, her eyes glinting with knowing.

'Are you happy?'

The sound of the front door opening filtered into the room, followed by female voices. Jacob looked at Nancy.

She smiled. 'Seems Louisa is saving your backside at every turn.'

Before he could retort, Louisa entered the room followed by a young dark-haired woman of no more than twenty or twenty-one. Louisa looked happy, her eyes bright, and her cheeks red. Jacob's heart stumbled. God, she was beautiful.

She looked between him and Nancy. 'Jacob, Nancy, this is Octavia. She will be staying with us for the night.'

Jacob's heart sank. Now he understood Louisa's happiness. Judging by the visitor's bedraggled and dirty hair, the state of her low-cut dress beneath a woollen shawl, and scuffed boots, this was another woman Louisa wanted to give a chance to get off the streets. Another person she couldn't

140

resist giving an opportunity for more. Was Nancy right? Did Louisa look at him and see a man who needed saving?

'Jacob? Won't you say hello to Octavia?' Louisa's smile faltered, her eyes burning with irritation. 'She is my guest and I would like her to feel welcome.'

Jacob cleared his throat and dragged his study from Louisa. 'Miss Octavia.'

The young woman nodded before shooting her attention to Nancy as she rose from her armchair. 'Nice to meet you, Octavia,' Nancy said. 'Why don't you take a seat next to Mr Grumpy over there and I'll get you a plate of hot food?'

Jacob glared after Nancy as she swept from the room. When he looked at Louisa, she widened her eyes with expectation.

He forced a smile as he turned to Octavia. 'I apologise. Come and have a seat.'

She walked forward and Louisa nodded her approval.

20

Louisa tapped her foot upon the parlour floor as she silently willed Octavia to finish her meal. Considering her undernourished state, her slightly sunken cheeks and overly thin wrists, one might have been forgiven for thinking Octavia would demolish the hot buttered toast and tea Nancy had given her in no time at all.

Yet, the young woman's manners and decorum hadn't faltered in the last half an hour. She'd politely flitted her gaze between Louisa, Nancy and Jacob, giving the impression of interest in their somewhat stilted conversation about the day's weather, the comings and goings of their neighbours and whether Jacob's manager might or might not knock on their door tomorrow. Octavia's breeding was obvious, her manners incomprehensible considering where she had been living and the awful, inadequate state of her threadbare clothes.

And, those facts escalated Louisa's concern of what Octavia must have endured to come to be selling herself.

At last, Octavia slid her plate onto the low table in front of her and picked up a napkin. She dabbed her lips, her eyes closed and her expression supremely satisfied.

Louisa smiled. 'Better?'

Octavia's eyes snapped open and she blushed. 'Yes. Thank you.'

142

'You're welcome. Would you like more?'

'No, that was perfect.'

Louisa glanced at Nancy and Jacob, both of whom stared back at her expectantly. How else were they supposed to react to Octavia's arrival? It was hardly their fault that Louisa had disappeared almost two hours before, claiming to need some fresh air, only to return with a new boarder.

She felt guilty that she'd made the sudden decision to find Octavia that night without speaking to Nancy first, but Louisa's instinct that she had to act fast had become too insistent to ignore. Also, she wanted to strike while she had Nancy's agreement that having Octavia live with them was the right thing to do. Because, as much as Louisa loved Nancy, her dearest friend also had the occasional tendency to chop and change her mind. Something engrained in Nancy from past disappointments according to her friend's throwaway explanation about her indecision. The fact of the matter was, Louisa believed that they needed Octavia. The reason for that sentiment might continue to elude Louisa but she was confident that, in time, all would become clear.

Louisa picked up her tea. 'Whenever you're ready, I will show you where you will be sleeping. We usually breakfast around eight, but if you'd like to eat earlier, I will show you the kitchen and where everything is. I do not keep a maid or cook so I'm afraid it's each to their own.'

'Eight o'clock is fine.' Octavia shifted uneasily and glanced at Jacob as he continued to stare into the depths of his empty brandy glass. She picked up her tea from the table and faced Louisa. 'Why

143

don't you tell me why I'm here?'

Jacob and Nancy's stares bored into Louisa's temple, but she ignored them and instead concentrated her entire attention on Octavia. 'As I said before, I have a proposition for you.'

Octavia lowered her cup and saucer to the table, her shoulders stiff and her blue eyes turning cold. 'And, as *I* said before, I will listen but promise nothing.'

Admiring the woman's steeliness, Louisa nodded. 'I expect nothing more. Your life is your own and I have no desire to change that.'

A flicker of disbelief broke Octavia's steady gaze. 'That remains to be seen.'

'When we first met, you assumed me to be a madam. Well, you are very astute because becoming a madam is exactly my intention. I wish to establish this house as a brothel. The business will be mine. Should you come to work with me, I will ensure you are looked after, safe and never have to do anything you don't want to do. Neither will I ever ask you to service any client you'd prefer not to.'

Octavia continued to stare, her brow furrowed. 'You expect me to believe that I would have a choice in clients and whether or not I will acquiesce to their desires?' She smiled wryly. 'You will forgive me if I find that incredibly hard to believe.'

Louisa placed her hands in her lap and held the other woman's gaze even if nerves tumbled in her stomach. She had no real idea of what she could guarantee any of them, but she did know she would always do everything in her power to protect Nancy and Octavia.

'You can believe or disbelieve me, but I am fair and possess a good instinct for people. You will be given one night off a week and keep half of the money you earn, plus any extra gifts your clients might wish to give you. You will have a room of your own from which all your business will be conducted. Bed and board will also be included. All of these things I promise for the duration that you might wish to stay here. Of course, you are free to leave at any time. In return, I ask for your promise of absolute discretion about the gentlemen who come here during your employment and, should it occur, after your departure.'

Interest mixed with suspicion in Octavia's bright blue eyes before she glanced at Nancy and Jacob. 'That is very generous offer. Too generous, in fact. I am no fool. What is the catch?'

Knowing she had no choice but to share a little of her own life if she had any possibility of Octavia trusting her, Louisa cleared her throat. 'A few years ago I found myself in dire circumstances but was then taken in by a madam. That eventually led to a better life than I ever could have imagined.

I just wish to do for you what someone else did for me. I am offering you an opportunity. Nothing more, nothing less. If you do not wish to accept it, then we will simply say our goodbyes in the morning.'

Second by silent second, Louisa's heart picked up speed as she willed Octavia to trust her. Let her help her. Octavia could have no idea how much she reminded Louisa of the woman she'd once been. It seemed quite clear that Octavia

145

had been wronged, possibly abandoned by her parents, as Louisa had been. But the young woman's background was nothing but conjecture for now. Hopefully, Louisa would one day have the opportunity to go some way in helping heal the wounds that showed so clearly in Octavia's hostile gaze.

Octavia straightened her spine and looked directly at Jacob. 'And what is your role in this? Are you a cull?'

Louisa pulled her lips together, trapping in the bizarre urge to laugh.

Nancy was not quite as subtle.

She laughed aloud and grinned at Jacob. 'Are you a cull, Mr Jackson?'

Jacob's cheeks reddened, his gaze burning with agitation as he glared at Nancy and then Octavia. 'I am a boxer and here under duress. But don't you worry, I'll be gone first thing in the morning.'

Disappointment knotted Louisa's stomach as she fought to maintain nonchalance. 'Mr Jackson is currently considering my offer that he become our live-in protector. He is a fine fighter and a good man. I have offered him terms and a better way of life but, like you, he suspects my motives run deeper than a mutually beneficial business arrangement. But also, like you, he is free to leave at any time.'

Louisa faced Jacob, his handsome face set in irritation and his gaze steady on hers. His thoughts were indecipherable, but she sensed his hesitation. It had been a slight ploy on her part to do all she could to get Octavia to the house before Jacob's inevitable departure. She wanted

146

him to understand her intention for any woman who might come here was that her life be better, happier and more independent than it was before.

That she was not setting up a house to profit from their suffering or degradation but enabling self-sufficiency and hoping that they might take pride and hope in their endeavours. To prove to them that independence and financial freedom is possible for any woman willing to work hard and sacrifice what she must in order to succeed.

Passion and determination burned deep in Louisa's heart as tears frustratingly pricked her eyes. 'Sometimes all women have to rely on is their youth and looks, Octavia. Yet, I see no wrong in a woman applying whatever she has, in any way she sees fit, in order to propel herself out of a life she hates and into one she adores.'

'And you really think that is possible?' Octavia scoffed and shook her head. 'I'm grateful for your hospitality, Louisa, but you have no idea what you're talking about. Some things can be altered or changed, but others mark a woman like a brand. One that everyone can see the moment they look at her.'

'That's not true.'

'No? Then if I were to come to live and work here, would it not be that one day you will say I owe you something? Even if it is just my gratitude. There is always a price. Always.'

Louisa's mouth dried as she studied the certainty, the cynicism in Octavia, a woman so very young. 'If you never feel the need to thank me, I won't be hurt or upset. As much as I want to help you, I also need you to help me. It will take money

147

to make this house work and it will also take commitment from everyone who works here. I wish to live independently but know nothing more than the trade and intend to use that experience to ensure the life I want.'

'So you are using us for financial gain. To live the life *you* want.' Octavia sneered. 'As I thought.'

'I am asking for your help.'

'Yes, to line your pockets.'

Annoyance and guilt swirled inside Louisa as she held Octavia's canny gaze. 'Line my pockets, yes, but also line your own while working in a place that is safe, warm and protected. I promise I will not want anything more from you than what you are willing to do to contribute to the success of this house, including your trust and discretion. If you feel that you cannot do that, then — '

'You can trust her, Octavia.' Nancy stood and crossed her arms. 'Louisa is someone you want on your side, believe me.' Her gaze hardened.

'However, if you wish to leave, there will be plenty of others willing to take your opportunity.'

Grateful for her friend's loyalty, Louisa breathed a little easier, her frustration easing. 'I am asking that you join Nancy and me in a bid for each of us to create a life of our own making. One that no one can ever steal away from us. Please, Octavia, won't you at least give me a chance to prove I am not the villain you assume me to be?'

Louisa could hear her own rapid breathing. Her voice had treacherously cracked on her last words and she couldn't bear to look at Jacob, lest he see her fear and weakness. She had to be strong. Had to make him *and* Octavia believe her unafraid of anything . . . even if Nancy knew differently. Even if Louisa knew herself to be afraid of *everything* that lay ahead of them.

'I'd like to be shown where I am sleeping now.' Octavia stood and looked at each of them in turn, her gaze considering. She nodded at Louisa.

'I appreciate your honesty and what it is you'd like to do. I promise to give you my answer in the morning.'

Hope sparked in Louisa's heart, part of her already believing Octavia would soon join her and Nancy and become as good a friend to them as they were to each other. 'Wonderful. Let us go upstairs.'

21

Jacob left Carson Street at dawn, leaving the women asleep and ignorant of his cowardice. Cowardice served by indecision. A state of mind that didn't sit well with him at all. Considering the tactical, underhanded way Louisa had got him into her house in the first place — without his knowledge or compliance — his decision to leave should have been firm.

Even if she had nursed him, fed him, shown him kindness and care . . . she was still a shrewd woman whose persuasion — when she looked at him with those big violet eyes — he somehow could not resist.

Turning up the collar of his overcoat, Jacob stalked through the cold winter wind towards his lodgings. The bruises on his face had begun to yellow and his cuts to scab, the wound on his side aching a little less. Yet, his stitches tightened every day, and soon he would have to go back to the underground club and hope that whoever had stitched him could also *unstitch* him.

All night his mind had whirled with what he had witnessed and heard during his stay at Carson Street. From Louisa's honest declaration that the need for money and independence lay behind her motivation for opening a brothel, to her canny instinct about people, to her apparent need to help others in conjunction with helping herself. Then there was Nancy. Straight-talking with a glint in her eye, yet deep inside, Jacob sensed a lingering, barely subdued anger about something that haunted her. And finally, Octavia, a young woman whom Louisa had sought out with the hope she might provide a considerably safer environment in which Octavia could work.

Three women who were now constantly on his mind. They were unprotected, had certainly been exploited in the past and now seemed consumed with desire to create a house — a brothel — that Louisa was undeterred would be successful.

He didn't doubt her strength or tenacity. Neither could he deny that she had got under his skin.

How was he to turn away and leave them exposed to God only knew what?

Picking up his pace, Jacob's gut knotted with his past failures. The murder of his mother once more reared in his mind in all its gory detail. She had been murdered and his father hanged. Yet, justice had neither been served nor closure given. Nor would they ever be. He had to stay away from Louisa and Carson Street because a man filled with violence and hatred would only spread his poison and these women deserved so much more than that.

Why couldn't Louisa see what was inside him? Yet hadn't Nancy boasted of Louisa's ability to know who needed help? Jacob scowled. Well, he could not imagine anyone in more need of help than him.

He was better off returning to Henry, the man who had taught Jacob to channel the hatred he held towards himself and his father and earn money from it. A good income that had served both his manager and Jacob well up until now and to wind Henry up by walking away from the ring to stand at the door of a brothel was not sound reasoning.

He reached his lodgings and let himself in.

Laughter came from the kitchen as Henry's raised voice regaled Doreen and Colin with some story or another, Doreen's high-pitched cackle joining Colin's deep laugh in rare joviality.

Purposefully lowering his tense shoulders, Jacob tried to free his mind of Carson Street and walked into the kitchen.

'Jacob!'

'The wanderer returns.'

'My prodigal son.'

Jacob shook his head, raising his hand in acknowledgement of their mockery. 'Yes, I'm back.' He nodded towards the bowls of porridge on the table. 'Any of that left for an injured man?'

Doreen leapt to her feet, her eyes shining and her smile wide. 'Oh, you're a sight for sore eyes and looking well cared for, I see. Sit yourself down, I've made plenty.'

He pulled out a chair and met Henry's steady gaze. 'Well, let's hear it then.'

Henry's gaze ran over Jacob's face. 'You've recovered then? I assume you're fit and well if your nursemaid released you?'

'Well, this is a first. Aren't you going to yell at me?' Jacob leaned back in his chair and winced as his stitches gave a sharp tug. 'Never known you to be concerned about my wellbeing. Or Colin's for that matter.'

152

'Would you rather I gave you a clip around the ear?'

Jacob took the bowl of porridge and spoon Doreen offered him. 'What I'd prefer is you telling me what Louisa Hill wrote to you . . . or gave you . . . for you to allow me languish in her home for the last five nights.'

Henry narrowed his eyes, defensiveness seeping into his gaze as he glanced around the table. 'Who am I not to take a lady at her word that you would be well cared for?'

'How much?'

Picking up his mug, Henry sipped his tea, steadfastly avoiding Jacob's gaze. 'How much what?'

'Did she give you?'

Henry shrugged, put down his mug and stood. 'Not much. I was interested to see how long you lasted with her, that's all.' He winked.

'Clearly, she was as good in person as she was on the eye, eh, Jakey?'

Henry walked to the door. 'I'm out of here. I'll speak to you later about your next fight. It's all lined up for next week.'

Jacob let him go, having neither the energy nor inclination to start a row at this hour in the morning. No doubt heated words would be exchanged by evening, which was soon enough.

Colin pushed back his chair and carried his bowl and mug to the sink.

'It's good to have you back, Jake. I've got some things to sort out. We'll have a pint at the White Hart tonight.'

'Sounds good.'

The minute Colin's footsteps sounded on the

stairs, Doreen walked to the kitchen door and firmly shut it. 'Right then, it's time me and you had a chat, don't you think? I'll make a fresh pot of tea.'

Knowing when he was cornered, Jacob settled back in his chair.

Once the teapot and cups were on the table, Doreen folded her hands on the table. 'Right, this Mrs Hill . . .'

Jacob stirred his porridge. 'She's a good lady. At least, I think she is.'

'You *think* she is?'

'Let's just say, there seems to be more than my feeble brain can determine about Mrs Hill and the other two women who live there.'

'There's three of them?' Doreen's eyebrows rose and she leaned eagerly forward. 'And no husband to any of them?'

'She's widowed.'

'Mrs Hill?'

'Yes.'

'And the others?'

'No idea.'

Her face hardened. 'Jacob Jackson, are you going to make me drag what I want to know out of you?'

Jacob stared into his bowl, his stomach vibrating with the effort needed to retain his laughter. 'She looked after me well enough.' He met Doreen's glare and smiled. 'She's pretty. Kind. Tough as nails from what I can tell and . . . ' His smile dissolved. 'Half out of her mind.'

'What? Why?' Doreen's green eyes lit with avid interest. 'Did she have a turn? Try to seduce you?

154

Ooh, was she in need of some slap and tickle considering she's without a man?'

Jacob swallowed his mouthful of porridge so quickly, he winced against the burn. 'For crying out loud.'

'What?'

'She's half out of her mind because she has the idea to turn her fancy house on Carson Street into a brothel.'

Doreen's eyes widened to terrifying proportions. 'But I heard she dresses finely. A lady, no less. I know they like the good stuff as well as the rest of us, even though most of that uppity lot deny it. But a brothel? Are you sure?'

'Yes, and that's why she took me home the other night, not because she was fearful for my next breath.'

'What are you talking about?'

'She wants a protector. Someone to stand at the door.' Jacob glanced at the newspaper beside him on the table, an article about the so-called Crystal Palace being erected in London's Hyde Park catching his eye. 'Chuck out any undesirables. That sort of nonsense.'

When Doreen's expected opinion wasn't immediately forthcoming, Jacob raised his head. She stared at him, her eyes narrowed, and her arms crossed.

He put down the paper and picked up his tea. 'Go on. Spit it out.'

'What about your boxing?'

'She claims that she'll pay me more for my protection, including bed and board, than I've ever earned in the ring.'

'Do you believe her?'

'Yes.'

'Then why the hell have you come back here?' Doreen rolled her eyes.

'For the love of God, Jake, you should be grabbing an opportunity like this with both hands. She's got her own money, her own house and willing to pay and keep you.' She leaned over and gripped his collar. 'Why have you come back?'

'Unhand me, woman and loosen your corset. I haven't given her an answer yet.'

Her hand slipped from his collar and Doreen sat back in her seat. 'Do you really think Mr Bertrum is going to wait while you decide if you want to carry on fighting? Once he gets wind of this, he'll have you in shackles. You're his biggest earner, Jake. He won't let you go again now you're back.'

Jacob swallowed another spoonful of porridge. 'Do you really think he could stop me?'

She picked up her tea. 'Probably not, but I could do without a full-blown fight in my kitchen.'

'*Your* kitchen?'

She gave a dismissive wave. 'Don't split hairs. What's wrong with you? You have the chance to get out from under Mr Bertrum's control. Why didn't you say yes to this woman? You said she's kind and pretty. What's holding you back? It makes no sense.'

Jacob could never resist Doreen's care for him. She might be less than twenty years older than him, but for the six years they'd known each other, she had become the closest thing to a mother he had. She supported him and Colin with love and that

156

was something neither of them took for granted in a world they knew to be dark and mean.

'What's holding me back is my ability to do the job, what else?' He focused on his food, not wanting to see judgement in her eyes. Doreen knew him better than anyone and had the knack of looking into his eyes and immediately knowing his feelings. 'There are three women in that house.

There could end up being more. How can I protect all of them? Louisa Hill is hellbent on opening a brothel, but I'm not convinced she knows what she's exposing herself to. That's the bottom line.'

'So your answer is to let her find out alone?'

Her jab was quick and deep, slicing him deeper and harder than the Killer's knife. He slowly raised his eyes to hers, irritation simmering inside him. 'I said, I haven't made up my mind yet.'

'You're not getting any younger, Jake. It's time you found different work than something that could end up killing you. Didn't the knifing you took from that boxer teach you anything? Fighting is getting meaner, slyer, and you could be killed next time.' She shook her head, her eyes glinting with tears. 'I don't want to see that. I want to see you walking through that door with a wife on your arm and kiddies at your feet for a visit with their Auntie Doreen. Don't you want that, too?'

Sickness mixed with unwanted longing and Jacob abruptly stood and walked to the sink. He put his bowl and spoon on the countertop and turned on the tap, words sticking like rocks in his throat.

'Look.' Doreen sighed. 'I just want a better life for you. One where you are free to walk around town without violence hanging over you like a big, black cloud.'

He snatched up the washrag from the drainer. 'Working at that house will inevitably mean violence, too, you know. If any of those men get out of hand with — '

'But it is much less likely, isn't it? These men will be there for the women. For the sex and a good time. They don't go to these places looking for trouble, they go there for some titty and arse.' Her chair legs scraped along the stone floor and then her hand was on his arm, easing him around to face her. 'You're a good-looking man, Jake. Gentle, but as strong as an ox. You put yourself out there for love and the girls will come flocking. Please, think about this chance.'

Fear slid through his veins, shaming him. 'All I want is a quiet life.'

'A quiet life does not come with boxing. You know that.'

'It also doesn't come in a houseful of prostitutes.'

She stared into his eyes before lifting her hand from his shoulder and raising it in tired surrender. 'You do what you have to do but tell me this.

How will you feel if anything happened to one or all of those women now you've met them? Now that they've cared for you?'

Dropping her hand, she pressed a firm kiss to his cheek and walked from the kitchen.

Jacob gripped the sink and tipped his head back, closing his eyes.

Louisa's face appeared behind his closed lids. There was something about her. Something about

158

the way she looked at him. As though she already knew he belonged at Carson Street in a way he'd never belonged anywhere before.

Then Nancy and Octavia's faces appeared alongside Louisa's . . .

Jacob screwed his eyes tighter. 'For Christ's sake.'

22

Louisa strode into the lobby of the Theatre Royal ahead of Nancy and Octavia. Her blue satin dress was the finest she owned and the three of them had been meticulous in their ministrations to ensure Nancy and Octavia were also dressed elegantly and enticingly. They had arranged each other's hair and adorned their tresses with pearl-tipped pins and feathers, their jewellery appealing, but not overly flamboyant, their makeup light and the curve of their bosoms just visible.

Now that Octavia had agreed to work alongside her and Nancy, Louisa felt she had not just gained an associate but also a new friend. Together, they would be invincible.

The house on Carson Street would be open for business in one week and it was time to start making its existence known among the class of gentlemen Louisa was determined to attract.

Nerves tumbled through her stomach and a slight sickness coated her mouth. *Everything is going to be all right. You can do this.* Curious glances assessed her and her friends, and Louisa met the theatre-goers' stares from beneath lowered lashes, her smile gentle. It scared her just how easily she could re-employ the rules of the game. How quickly she remembered that men liked women to be sexually alluring, yet demure. There for their use, quiet and subservient.

Resentment threatened as it pulled at her every

fibre, urging her to grasp Nancy and Octavia's hands and speed them away from their mission. Was she wrong to revisit this path? To be pulling her friends into a situation with no idea of how it would play out? Her heart pounded but Louisa fought back as she inhaled a slow, strengthening breath. They could do this. It would turn out to be the best decision for all three of them. It had to be.

Turning to Nancy and Octavia, Louisa ensured her smile remained in place, her awareness continually vigilant to the people around them.

'Remember,' she whispered. 'We're here to provoke discussion about the house. There is to be no negotiating or direct invitation. We want to arouse the gentlemen's curiosity. Ignite their need to be first at the door on opening night.' She caught the eye of a hatted gentleman and nodded demurely. 'We need to present an enigma. Be appealing yet composed, so we become women they are eager to engage in conversation. It's imperative their appetites are left unsated.'

Nancy nodded, but her eyes flitted around the lobby, her face noticeably pale.

Louisa gently touched her friend's arm. 'What is it?'

'Nothing.' Nancy smiled, but it was strained. 'I'm perfectly capable of doing everything you've asked.'

Louisa lowered her voice. 'If anything is bothering you, you must tell me. I don't want to do this without you.' She turned and took Octavia's hand. 'Either of you.'

Nancy's hand trembled as she pushed a fallen tendril from her cheek.

'I've spent time in theatres in the past, that's all.' She briefly closed her eyes. 'Unfortunately, my memories are not in any way good or welcome. But I'm fine. Truly.'

Uncertainty whispered through Louisa. She hated seeing Nancy anything but confident, her smile flirtatious and her pretty eyes alight with adventure.

'Nancy, if you want to leave, we can. I won't make you do anything that makes you uncomfortable. You both have my word on that.'

'It's fine. *I'm* fine.' Nancy pulled back her shoulders and met the gazes of several men staring at her. 'Rousing the required interest won't be any problem at all as far as I can tell.' She faced Louisa, her grey eyes dark with determination. 'Are we to separate or walk together?'

'Together.' Louisa looked at Octavia who stared confidently back as though she had been a part of this theatre, this company, her entire life. The contrast between her and Nancy could not have been more different or surprising, but Louisa could not waste this opportunity finding out why.

There would be time for that later. 'We will present more of a spectacle, a fantasy, if we stand together. We are blonde, dark and red-headed. Together, we offer something for every appetite.'

Nancy and Octavia nodded their understanding. They each had a job to do if the proposed business venture was to succeed. The three of them had the chance to make something entirely their own and, as Louisa looked at her friends, she sensed that their determination to live their lives on their own terms matched her desire completely.

She scanned the finely dressed crowds as their laughter rang and their champagne glasses clinked. 'Let's get to work, ladies.'

Red-carpeted stairs led to the stalls and main theatre, with corridors to the upper circle and boxes. Money was spent by the upper classes in order to remain inconspicuous. Outwardly, at least. Therefore, Louisa's chosen clientele would undoubtedly wander the landings and seating upstairs.

As they emerged onto the Grand Circle landing, the noise and chatter was close to deafening. Clearly, the propriety downstairs was abandoned the moment the audience found their seats. The smell of alcohol mixed with cigar smoke and the tart scent of oranges as the sellers walked among the wealthy offering refreshment. The stalls below were rife with the lower classes, sitting or standing upon the wooden benches, their stained caps and bonnets and well-worn clothes a clear disparity and indication of the audience spectrum.

Yet, the raucous and bawdy behaviour among all the classes was not in any way dissimilar.

Feminine laughter screeched around her, men leering and women openly flirting from behind fans and beneath the brims of their hats. The silk and satin of the ladies' dresses gleamed beneath the gaslight, amber reflections dancing across rouged cheeks and revealed décolletages.

As Louisa and her friends walked, conversation waned either side of them, glasses halted and hovered halfway to gentlemen's and ladies' mouths as they dropped open, much to Louisa's satisfaction. Leading her friends to a darkened corner, the three of them feigned interest below, their gazes trained on the stage.

When they had left Carson Street, Louisa had been confident of the visual impact the three of them would make whenever they walked along the street or anywhere else together. Each of them could be deemed attractive, pretty even, but it was so much more than their looks that demanded attention. For a prostitute, beauty was only a hook. The first cast of her line to draw in her client. After that, she needed more. She needed a quiet confidence, a master of the strong and the innocent that inevitably fanned the flames of male intrigue.

She, Nancy and Octavia surpassed this parody when they stood together.

They were strong, united and confident in their undertaking. Together, their secret fears buried and hidden beneath lace and silk, they radiated poise and power.

Men were clustered in circles, their wives or beaux carefully watching their reaction to Louisa, Nancy and Octavia. The intensity of their audience's gazes burned through Louisa's back and bosom, disintegrating her nerves as her old persona encapsulated her, forcing her previous theatrical skills forward in all their practised sexual inducement.

Two actors walked on stage and the theatre lapsed into a modicum of civility, the noise levels dropping as audience attention focused on the stage. Pleased that glances continued in their direction, the men's eyes glinting with lust, the

164

women's with curiosity or envy, Louisa stood a little taller.

Facing front, she discreetly nudged Nancy and Octavia either side of her.

They both turned and Louisa winked, satisfaction burning deep inside.

Nancy grinned before turning back to the stage, seemingly happy once more. Octavia merely nodded, her eyes purposefully hooded and a slight smile playing at her mouth.

'Good evening, madam.'

Even though her heart stuttered, Louisa forced herself to turn slowly towards the gentleman who stood at her side. Beside him, a woman smiled.

Louisa presumed her to be his wife, even if her husband's gaze incessantly dropped to Louisa's breasts, his face clearly flushed in the semi-darkness.

Louisa dipped her head. 'Sir. Madam.'

The man stepped closer, his hand still tightly clutched to his wife's where it lay relaxed upon his forearm. 'I couldn't help noticing you and your lovely companions.' He nodded at Nancy and Octavia. 'I am quite certain I would remember if I had seen any of you before. Might you be new to the city?'

Louisa knew to take each step methodically and carefully. They needed the man's interest to be irrepressibly aroused if he was to find his way to Carson Street . . . along with his peers, of course. 'We are, sir.'

His smile faltered. Her reply was purposely succinct so that he would be forced to instigate further conversation. A prostitute's best tactic was

165

to be coy, quieter than her client in order that he might feel superior. An unfortunate requirement of their trade.

His eyes fell to her lips. 'And you are finding Bath to your liking?'

'Very much so.'

The noise gathered in volume as something amusing occurred onstage, yet the steadily increasing chatter and laughter did nothing to divert the gentleman's interest from Louisa or her friends. He glanced at his wife whose eyes remained kind and gentle. A woman who accepted her husband's flirtations? Or a woman who actively encouraged his sexual diversions? It was hard to tell.

Louisa cleared her throat. 'Well, it was nice meeting you, sir, madam. If you'll excuse us, we — '

'Would you like some refreshment? I would be happy to — '

'Oh, we are quite refreshed, sir.'

When he looked sufficiently desperate that he might lose her attention, Louisa reached for Nancy and Octavia, sliding her arms into the crooks of their elbows, their differences open for his judgement or selection.

'However, you and your lovely wife might be able to assist us in another way.'

'Well, of course, my dear.' He grinned, his eagerness clear. 'I am at your service.'

'Well, we would love to learn what is a popular night-time diversion in the city. What people . . . gentlemen such as yourself . . . like to do after dark.'

She smiled and nodded at his wife. 'And ladies,

166

of course, madam.'

The woman laughed, though she was distracted by the stage. 'Of course.'

The gentleman assessed Nancy and Octavia, his tongue poking out to wet his bottom lip. Louisa fought the lurch in her stomach and held fast to the character she'd possessed so many years before. She must not falter. No matter what. Only focus on the future. On the prosperity of herself, Nancy and Octavia.

'Sir?' She raised her eyebrows. 'Do you have somewhere in mind that might suit my friends and I to be after dark?'

His gaze bored into hers. Slowly, comprehension of what Louisa implied dawned and the gentleman's eyes brightened with hope and lust.

'My dear . . . ' He addressed his wife, but his eyes remained on Louisa. 'I believe I saw Mrs Oliver along the way. Might you like to speak with her?'

'Oh, I would.' His wife smiled at Louisa, Nancy and Octavia. 'Will you excuse me?'

The moment his wife had walked away, Louisa hardened her resolve. The gentleman seemed neither surprised nor discouraged by the change in her.

Instead, he stood taller now that he found himself free of his wife.

He stepped closer. 'You are working ladies?'

'We are, sir.' Louisa slipped her hands from Nancy and Octavia's arms.

'We have an establishment on Carson Street that will open its doors one week from tonight. We would welcome you and your friends for an evening's entertainment, if you are so inclined.'

His whiskers lifted with the breadth of his smile. 'I do believe I will be able to find some acquaintances who might find your company most inviting.'

'Very good. Then we will bid you a good evening and look forward to seeing you again very soon.'

Louisa walked along the theatre landing, Nancy and Octavia following silently behind. Their delight and stemmed laughter passed like vibrations through Louisa as she fought to disguise her sudden nerves, awareness she had been brought back down to where she began burning hot at her cheeks.

Somehow, some way, she must reinvent herself just as Nancy would. How her friend continued to love Louisa rather than despise her after such a change to their future was unfathomable.

But Louisa's gratitude to Nancy was eternal.

Maybe Nancy already knew what Anthony's death had forced Louisa to learn.

Women only survived in this world through their looks and appeal. There was no other reliance but what men saw and felt about them. An injustice, but the truth.

Breathing deeply, Louisa lifted her chin and spoke over her shoulder.

'Right then, the first cull is caught, ladies. Let's see who else we can talk to, shall we?'

23

The banging on Jacob's bedroom door had him sitting bolt upright and wincing as the stitches in his side stretched. He reached for the candlestick on his bedside table as a weapon, his sleep-riddled brain imagining the Killer had come back for round two. 'For Chr —'

'It's gone ten, Jakey,' Henry shouted from the other side of the door.

'Open up, will you?'

Another sleepless night of tossing and turning, his mind filled with morally tangled decisions and implications, had kept Jacob awake for hours. The last time he'd heard the hallway clock strike, it had been three in the morning. The last thing he needed was any of Henry's crap. Cursing, Jacob replaced the candlestick, grabbed his trousers from the bedstead and struggled into them.

Another bang hard enough to splinter wood. 'If you don't open up right now, I swear before all that's holy —'

Jacob yanked open the door. 'Do you want me to punch you out?'

Henry pushed past him into the room. 'Put a shirt on. We're going out.'

'I'm going nowhere until I've had some breakfast, and then I plan to head over to the club to get these bloody stitches removed.' Jacob walked to his chest of drawers and pulled out a white vest. 'Anyway, I've nothing to say to you that I haven't said before. I'm in no mood to hear about the next fight or anything else. Not yet.' He removed a folded shirt from the drawer below, shook it out and shoved his arms into the sleeves. 'The Killer did his best to finish me off. I deserve some time to myself for a while. Don't you think?'

'Not when there's money to be made you don't.' Henry swiped the newspaper Jacob had fallen asleep reading to the side and sat on the bed.

'You've been back two days and I've already cancelled one fight at your request. Not to mention your little holiday at Carson Street. It's time to get back in the game.'

His little holiday? Jacob scowled. His stay with Louisa and Nancy had been anything but a holiday. Those four nights had stuck like wax to his brain cells and somehow travelled through his blood stream and straight into his conscience. Worse, he couldn't rid his head of Doreen's words of wisdom about finding a better life for himself, or the fact he wanted, rightly or wrongly, to see Louisa again. The woman had burrowed deep inside his stupid head and taken up apparent permanent residence.

He opened his mouth to tell Henry just what he could do with the next fight, but his manager spoke first.

'It seems people don't care how the Killer won that fight, they like you and want you back in the ring.'

'The man's a criminal, Henry. Slicing me was not his first time fighting dirty. Seems to me the man is hellbent on covering up murder under the guise of boxing. The whole circuit is aware of his

170

tactics and he's giving the game a bad reputation. If the constabulary gets wind of him openly cutting people, they won't leave us alone as they have been. Mark my words.'

'What are you talking about? The constabulary couldn't give two figs about what goes on in the ring. They've got a lot more on their plate than blokes willingly smacking each other about.'

'Yeah? Well, the Killer isn't just smacking people about, is he?' Jacob glared. 'He can't be allowed to carry on without being called up on it.

Boxers box, Henry. They don't cut and maim.'

'So what do you intend to do about him, Jakey? You want justice, fight the bloke.'

Their gazes locked.

Jacob shook his head and marched towards the bed for his boots. 'Seems to me, all you care about is making yourself a bit of money for doing absolutely nothing.'

'Doing nothing?' Henry's cheeks mottled as he pointed his finger at Jacob. 'I do plenty. I give you a place to stay, food on the table, scout out your work and damn well — '

'Stand by the ropes while I get beaten from here to next week. Or else, I beat someone else half unconscious. How much longer do you think I can fight?' Jacob pulled on his boots. 'I'm getting too damn old for it, Henry.

Maybe it's time I retired.'

Silence fell like a shadow. As though the room had been lit with sunshine and the moon eclipsed it. The sudden tension heavy and thick, Jacob stood in the half-light of the room and held Henry's angry gaze.

'You think you can just walk away after everything I've done for you?'

His manager's voice was quiet and measured, his brown eyes boring into Jacob's. 'You owe me, Jakey. You'll owe me the rest of your bloody life.'

'I've found work elsewhere. I want out.' Jacob's heart picked up speed.

The decision burst into his head and out of his mouth before he could stop it. Was he really doing this? He was going to accept Louisa's offer and stand guard outside a brothel? Live in her house? Eat her food? He inhaled a long breath and surrendered to the inevitable. He had to do what he could to protect those women. 'I've had enough.'

Henry pushed to his feet and stalked to the window. He shook his head and planted his hands on his hips before whirling around, his face a mask of fury. 'This is about that woman, isn't it? The one whose house you didn't seem in any hurry to leave. Jesus, Jake, get your head out of your cock and think straight, will you? Women come and go. Go to her if you have to, take her to bed and get rid of your frustration, but for crying out loud, don't throw away everything we've built. Not for a bit of scrumpet.'

Clenching his fists at the jibe, Jacob trembled with anger. 'I'm doing this for me, not her.'

'Yeah? Then why the sudden change of heart? You've been fighting for years. Damn well relished it. Now you want out? I'm not buying it.'

Jacob tipped back his head and closed his eyes, fighting to keep hold of his temper. Maybe Henry was right and Louisa was the catalyst for Jacob's sudden desire to get out of boxing once and for

172

all, but his manager had no idea *why* she was the catalyst. The fact was, there was something behind her eyes that reminded Jacob of the sorrow he'd so often seen in his mother's kind blue eyes. As though she and Louisa passed through life waiting for disappointment — waiting to be shown they were not worth any more than the hand they had been dealt. Both were strong, yet vulnerable. Brave, yet so very afraid. He'd witnessed an underlying pain in Louisa and now he couldn't erase it from his stupid heart . . . couldn't forget his mother and how he'd failed her.

He opened his eyes and dropped his chin. 'Do I have your blessing to walk out of here with a wish for my prosperity? Or do we go our separate ways with bad blood between us?' Jacob shrugged. 'Either way, I'm leaving today.'

Assurance he was doing the right thing firmly settled in Jacob's gut.

There was no going back. He would return to Carson Street and whatever happened thereafter was in God's hands. The pull he felt towards Louisa, to the house, to doing what he could for those women, ran stronger than anything Henry could say or threaten.

If Jacob didn't do this now — today — the feeling that he could finally try to atone for failing his mother could disappear forever. He would not allow that to happen.

'Do you know what?' Henry walked past him to the door. 'Do what you want. You've got money and at least a scrap of sense left in your head, I hope. Get her out of your system. You know where I am once you're thinking straight again.'

His manager's boots stomped down the stairs and a few seconds later the front door slammed.

Jacob released a shaky breath and walked to his wardrobe.

Withdrawing a large hessian sack, he filled it with his belongings, emptied his cash box, filling his pockets with coins and notes. Finally, he shrugged on his overcoat and walked downstairs into the kitchen.

Doreen stood with her back to him at the stove, still as a statue.

Concerned by her apparent paralysis, Jacob started towards her.

'Doreen?'

She picked up a wrapped package from the side of the oven and slowly turned. Her eyes glistened with tears, sending a jolt through Jacob's chest.

'When I encouraged you to work for that woman, I didn't expect you to leave so soon.'

He swallowed against the sudden dryness in his throat. He cared about Doreen so much and now felt he was abandoning her. Another woman who needed him. 'It feels right.'

'Then you should go.' She walked closer and cupped her hand at his jaw, looking deep into his eyes. 'I love you like a son, a brother. You're special, Jake and I hope she sees that.'

'It's not for her care that I'm going.'

Scepticism shadowed her eyes. 'No?'

'No. I'm going because — '

'She's struck you like no woman has before or since. I understand. Just promise me you'll be careful.'

Words, explanations and excuses flailed on his

174

tongue, so Jacob closed his mouth and nodded.

'Good.' She flashed him a wobbly smile and a wink. 'Then take this and get out of here. It's toasted bread and a cut of cheese. All the breakfast any man ever needs, right?'

He forced a smile in return. 'Right.'

She turned away and Jacob stared at her back for as long as he could stand before heading into the hallway and out the front door.

24

Wrapped in a wool coat and scarf, Louisa rubbed her hands together, the fingers of her kid gloves doing little to protect her hands from the cold February wind. Bracing against the chill, she pushed a wooden flower box onto the parlour windowsill and stood back, trying to visualise how the box would look once the seeds she'd planted bloomed in the spring.

A touch of colour would be a welcome enrichment to the house's otherwise austere exterior. As lovely as the Georgian houses of Bath were, Louisa loved colour and the golden stone wasn't satisfying enough alone.

She was about to return indoors when she sensed a presence at the gate.

Her heart raced a little faster, her face growing warm even as she fought to act nonchalant.

She turned, already knowing the face she would see would be Jacob Jackson's.

He stood with his hand on one of the stone pillars flanking the black iron gate, the other holding the ends of the hessian sack over his shoulder. His brilliant blue eyes stared at her, his face absent of emotion, his broad shoulders rigid, his entire body unmoving.

Inside, she wanted to leap for joy. His being here could only mean he had come to accept her offer of a position at the house. And just in time. The brothel would open in two days.

Inhaling a shaky breath, Louisa crossed her arms and approached the gate. 'Good morning, Jacob.'

'Mrs Hill.'

'Louisa, please.'

He nodded and finally drew his gaze from hers towards the parlour window. 'Window boxes in February?'

She didn't turn to follow the direction of his gaze. She couldn't. Her body was immobile, but her heart was beating a tattoo. Instead, she utilised his distraction to study him more deeply. He really was so extraordinarily handsome. Big and broad. Imposing . . . yet absurdly, inexplicably approachable. Dark hair and olive skin. His stubble of beard accentuated strong cheekbones and a slightly crooked nose — one she assumed must have been broken numerous times.

His gaze swivelled to hers. 'I guess you know why I'm here.'

She nodded. 'The position.'

He smiled, sending a wave of awareness over every inch of her body, unnerving her and shaking her casual pretence. Somehow, she managed to move her legs and walk to the front door.

'Then you'd better come in.'

She preceded him inside and, once they removed their outer garments, led him into the parlour. 'Take a seat while I make some tea. Would you like anything to eat?'

'No, I'm fine. Thank you.'

His gaze slowly grazed her face, lower until she had to quickly exit the room lest she lose her carefully controlled façade. A woman unaltered by a

177

man; a woman in ownership of every aspect of her body and mind. That was who she wanted to be — *had* to be — now and forever. She knew enough of men to have learned how fickle and unfaithful they could be. As a whore, she'd slept with husbands; as a wife, she'd slept with a liar. She could not weaken once again. Self-loathing burned inside and Louisa marched into the kitchen, bumping straight into Nancy.

Nancy stumbled over the leg of a chair at the kitchen table in her haste to disguise that she'd been eavesdropping. Her friend snatched up a rag from the sink. 'Everything all right, Lou?'

Louisa rolled her eyes at her friend's turned back and walked to the stove. 'Perfectly, thank you. Well, if I don't think about Jacob Jackson sitting in our parlour.'

Turning, Nancy grinned, her eyes filled with triumph. 'He's here for the job, isn't he? He's going to be our doorman.' She tossed the rag into the sink. 'I knew he'd given in the moment I saw him through the window.

He's the right man for the job, no mistake.'

'I thought you weren't keen on him.'

'I wasn't until we had our little chat the night you went to fetch Octavia.'

Nancy glanced towards the door, her gaze considering. 'There's something about him. You're right. He's quiet, yet those eyes of his seem to catch everything. He'll see we're all right.'

Louisa put the kettle on the stove, pleased by her friend's summary. 'I couldn't agree more, but now I'll have to listen to his terms. A man like Jacob Jackson does not accept anything without

178

conditions. Would you mind bringing us some tea? I don't want to leave him alone too long in case he bolts.'

'Of course. Go on. I'll be as quick as I can.'

As she returned to the parlour, Louisa paused at the doorway and watched Jacob where he sat on the settee. He'd kept his hat on at the door, but now he'd removed it and drew the brim in circles with his fingers as he gazed towards the window, his thoughts seeming to be far from Carson Street. Yet, even as her concern grew that he might not yet be certain in his decision to stay, Louisa couldn't dismiss her body's response to him, no matter how much she wanted to.

He turned and immediately stood, his beautiful blue eyes intense on hers.

She stepped into the room and waved towards the sofa. 'Sit. Please.'

Lowering onto the sofa, he stretched his arm across the back of the seat and exhaled. 'So, are you open for business?'

His direct question seemed loaded with accusation. If he disapproved of her intentions, why was he here? She would not allow him to waste her time. Jacob was who she wanted beside her, but if he thought he could stand in judgement of her, she would find another protector soon enough.

Defiantly lifting her chin, Louisa sat beside him, pride pulsing through her. 'Not yet, but our efforts to spread the word over the last few days will prove fruitful, I'm sure. Word is most definitely spreading.'

'I see.'

'We haven't had any gentlemen come to the

house asking questions. At least, not yet, but a few girls have come by looking for work. That tells me people are discussing the house and know the nature of its services.'

Something akin to dread flashed in his eyes. 'You've employed more women? How many do you intend having here exactly?'

Louisa tried to gauge what his brusqueness meant but deciphering anything about Jacob Jackson continued to elude her. Everything but the certainty he was meant to be here. With her. 'In time, I'd like to think I'll be in a position to give more working women a safe haven but, for now, I need to concentrate on earning enough money to keep a roof over our heads.'

She raised her eyebrows. 'And, of course, yours. If you should choose to live here, as I'd prefer.'

'Hmm.'

His indecision was clear, and Louisa's nerves stretched at the idea that he might leave. 'The thought of more women here displeases you?'

'Not so much displeases as worries me. More women means less chance of me being able to ensure they are all unharmed.'

'Your presence will be enough to ensure they are unharmed.'

'Why would you assume that?'

She forced herself to hold his gaze with confidence. 'Look at you, Jacob. You are big, strong and sombre enough to make any gentleman think twice before he raised his hand to one of my girls.' She paused, wanting him to know it was more than his physical strength that had drawn her to trust in him. 'You

180

are a good man. A loyal man. One who, I sense, doesn't flee from difficulty but faces it. Deals with it.' She sighed. 'We need a man like you here. Side by side with us . . . ' She held his gaze. 'With me.'

He didn't look away from her but he showed no reaction to her speech either. 'And if I agree to bed and board, will I effectively be at your beck and call?'

She hesitated. His face was unmoving and unease knotted Louisa's stomach. Her unwavering self-assurance had to be in place at all times. Had to be present from the very beginning or else he would think her a fraud.

'Yes.'

Louisa struggled not to squirm under his intense study. This was a test.

His first jab at her authority.

'Tea is served.'

He ever so slightly jumped as Nancy came into the room carrying a tea tray. Louisa tightened her lips against the urge to smile. She'd seen Nancy from the corner of her eye and thus had had the upper hand. One she would have to thank her friend for later.

'Thank you, Nancy.' Louisa inched forward towards the table where Nancy had placed the tray. 'You can leave us.'

Nancy scowled and huffed as she left the room.

Louisa picked up a spoon and lifted the lid of the teapot. 'So, is being at my beck and call something you think you could tolerate, Jacob? You will be paid well for your service.' She laid down the spoon. 'I need you to keep Nancy and Octavia safe. Their wellbeing matters more to me than

181

anything.

Money, status, success . . . none of it will ever concern me more than the women who work here.'

He slipped his arm from the sofa and leaned forward, staring at the carpet for a long moment before facing her. 'And you? What about your wellbeing?'

Louisa stilled. No one had ever asked about her wellbeing. Not her parents when they'd left a note saying they weren't coming back. Not her madam at the brothel. And not Anthony, she realised now.

She busied herself with the tea, porcelain clinking porcelain as she lifted the trembling teapot against a cup. 'I'll be perfectly fine. I always am.'

His ensuing silence brought a humiliating heat to her cheeks. She stared at the cup, not daring to pick it up while her hands continued to shake. What was it about Jacob, about his penetrating gaze, that made her falter? Had she made a huge mistake insisting he was the right man to care for and protect her friends?

'Then I promise to look after Nancy and Octavia.' His voice was soft and low, barely audible above the pulsing in her ears. 'But I need to say something before we go any further.'

She swallowed, her throat dry. 'Which is?'

'How often will *you* be taking . . . clients?'

Rather than disapproval this time, his expression relayed concern, care.

Louisa cursed the heat that rose in her cheeks. His care was considerably harder to endure than his displeasure.

'As often as I need to. For now, my most important role is to ensure the house is a success. Look after the money coming in and out. Ensuring our clients are happy rather than assuming or abusive.' She put down the teapot and exhaled a shaky breath. 'I want this house to be exemplary, Jacob. What will occur here will be neither easy nor acceptable to most of society. No matter how wrong or unfair it might be, a woman's body has always been her end option for survival. I hope, no pray, that one day that won't be the case, but now, in 1851, it is the case entirely.'

His gaze lingered on hers, dropped for a brief moment to her lips, before he lifted the teapot, filling the second cup. He held it out to her, steady and unmoving. 'I'll accept your offer and willingly take bed and board, but . . . '

She took the cup, pleased that it did not tremble. Now he had agreed to her terms, relief rather than pitiful insecurity filled her. Yet, that only proved her weakness. That there was every possibility the house would not succeed without a man's presence. No matter how much she might want to prove herself worthy — Nancy and Octavia worthy — of living independent lives she wanted Jacob here for them. For her.

She lifted the cup to her lips. 'But?'

'In time, I will want to review the importance of *your* wellbeing.'

25

From Louisa Hill's attic, Jacob stared through the window towards the small park and Pulteney Bridge beyond. How in God's name had he got here? Worse, why had he allowed conversation between himself and Louisa — and his barely concealed care for her — to secure her confidence that he could protect her and the other women living here?

The woman must be half-blind if she could not see what was staring her straight in the face. Or rather who.

He was a man incapable of protecting anyone.

He fought for a living. Beat men black and blue and profited from their pain. Yet, Louisa had mentioned his loyalty, an incapability of fleeing from his problems. Well, guilt was his problem and he had been constantly running from that. Couldn't she see that he possessed an insatiable need to prove his strength to himself? That she had provided yet another facilitating avenue that he would use to try to assuage the continual feeling of failure that resided inside of him? As for him accepting he was anything more than the son of a murderer, he couldn't believe that would ever happen.

That it hadn't been Louisa who came looking for him this morning, but the other way around relentlessly irked him. He had come to Carson Street of his own free will and was now living and working here. So he only had himself to blame for whatever happened next. As soon as he'd left the club — his stitches removed — his feet had found their way here of their own accord and there hadn't been a damn thing he could do about it.

Jacob gripped the walls either side of the window until his fingers ached.

What in God's name would Louisa think of him if she knew he was the product of a man who had beaten his wife to death? That the same violent tendencies that were rife in his father were alive and well in Jacob? But God, he wanted to protect her. To not fail this time. He needed to believe that change in his life and in himself might one day be possible.

That was why the pull towards this house hadn't waned. This job had the potential to prove his life could change. Prove himself worthy of Louisa's interest and trust. So that she might look at him and believe she had found a man who would give his life to protect her and the women under her care.

She was the first woman who looked at him without fear in her eyes. Her instinct and trust in him made Jacob feel ten feet tall.

He was attracted to her spirit and the fire that burned in her violet eyes.

Eyes that made him want her. Or maybe it would be her smile that would eventually be his undoing. She was more woman than any he had ever met and her kindness to others only made it more difficult to keep the ice around in his heart firmly in place.

The fact it was beginning to splinter was terrifying. Dangerous and ultimately painful, if the unfamiliar stirring in his chest was anything to go by.

There was a knock on his door, and Jacob dropped his hands from the window, exhaustion pressing down on him.

'Come —'

'Only us, Jacob.' Nancy strode into the room, her auburn curls swaying about her face and her smile wide. 'Now you're settled, Octavia and I thought it only right and proper that we tell you a little about what's what when we open for business on Friday night.'

Amused by her swagger, the self-loathing Jacob struggled with slightly diminished and he smirked as he walked to the bed. 'Go ahead.'

She glanced at Octavia who met his stare with narrowed eyes. Nancy waved towards a chair in the corner of the room. 'Have a seat, Octavia. You have as much to tell Jacob as me, don't you?'

The other woman sat, her eyes still on Jacob.

He crossed his arms. 'Do you ladies have a problem with me being here?

Think Louisa was wrong in selecting me to look after you? If you do, I can't say I entirely disagree with you.'

Nancy gave a dismissive wave. 'Of course you're the right person to look after us. I've told you before, and I'll tell you again, if Louisa pursues something, it will always turn out right. She is stronger than steel.' She sat next to him on the bed and scowled. 'The only person who managed to slew her intuition was that cheating husband of hers, but that's another story.'

Jacob kept his face impassive. The last thing he

wanted was to be drawn into conversation about the man who'd once had the honour to share Louisa's bed. 'So, what is it you want to tell me?'

'Well, as you know, we are going to be servicing clients . . .'

'I gathered that much. Go on.'

'Well, for me, it's been a while. We left the brothel several years ago and I haven't . . . been with a man since.' She glanced again at Octavia and surprise flashed in her eyes before she looked towards the window. Nancy faced Jacob. 'What I'm saying is, I'm a little out of practice. It might take some time for me to get back into the swing of things.'

Jacob frowned, unsure where Nancy was going with this. 'All right.

And . . .'

'And men who have the lust in them haven't patience with a whore who isn't confident in what she's doing.'

He looked between the two women who both stared back at him expectantly. What in God's name did they want him to say? 'Which means?'

Nancy sighed. 'Which means I'm probably going to need a lot more looking out for than Octavia here. At least, I will until I find my . . . feet again. I'm sorry to put extra pressure on you not to let Louisa down, but I owe it to you to tell you what's what. The fact is, I'm glad you're here, Jacob. Really glad. I don't think I'd be so keen to do what we have to do if you weren't around.'

Jacob studied her. The woman was afraid, or at least, nervous. Her bubbly personality and easy smile when she was with Louisa had vanished, leaving behind a vulnerability he hadn't foreseen or imagined. His gut lurched. Christ, Nancy was at least three years younger than Louisa; Octavia at least two years younger again.

Sickness rolled through him as he looked at Octavia. 'And what about you? Do you have any reservations about what you're expected to do?'

'None whatsoever.'

Her face was set, her colour pale, and further concern knotted Jacob's gut. These women appeared to be of an entirely different nature to one another yet had ended up in the same occupation in order to survive

'Octavia, be honest with me. Do you welcome my protection or resent it?'

She held his gaze. 'Only time can answer that question, Mr Jackson.'

Jacob studied her. The first time he'd met her, Octavia had been dirty, her hair somewhat brushed but her clothes as soiled as her face and arms. Her bosom had been covered, but an inch or two of leg visible between the top of her split boots and the hem of her skirt. There would have been no mistaking the service she offered, yet her posh way of speaking hadn't rung true to her appearance.

Now she was dressed in satin, her face clean and dark hair gleaming.

Octavia could easily pass for a lady of status, her articulation more than fitting. Uncertainty about her, Louisa and Nancy continued to harangue him, but he was here now, come what may.

He uncrossed his arms and stood. The whole idea of these three women working together sent his head into a spin. Never before had he come across such a mismatched trio. Would this venture of Louisa's really work? He had no idea, but it wasn't his place to question her plans.

Taking a few paces about the room, he faced Octavia. 'It's important we trust one another.'

'I agree.'

'But, for me, trust has to be earned.'

'Indeed.'

Her eyes never left his, her back straight and her chin tilted. Her wariness was palpable and in complete contrast to Nancy's candour. How was he to look after Octavia without knowing anything of her thoughts, preferences or choices? At least with Louisa he understood her ambitions and her deep care for Nancy and Octavia — even if he had yet to understand her reasoning that opening a brothel was her only option.

'Fine.' He returned to the bed and sat. 'Then we agree trust between us will need to grow. So, to that end, why don't we each pledge to respect one another through our conduct and amiability? I am here to do the best I can for Louisa, and I suspect you are, too. Why? Because she has promised each of us that she will neither undermine nor cheat us in any way. Right?'

'Right.' Nancy grinned. 'I knew you were a good one, Jacob. I just knew it.'

'Octavia?'

She stood and studied him before walking towards the door. 'I'll never let Louisa down, Mr Jack — '

'Jacob.'

'Jacob.' She nodded. 'Because if there is even the

189

smallest chance that doing well here means I never have to return to the streets, I will do all that she asks of me.' She put her hand on the door. 'Lying with men for money used to be to my humiliation but, over time, what I do has become my strength. An act for which I no longer feel shame, but power. Each day is a new day where unexpected opportunities might reveal themselves. Louisa bringing me here, to her home, has proven that.'

She walked from the room and Jacob stared after her.

'You know . . .' Nancy stood and shook her head, a soft smile at her lips.

'That woman just might be one of the strangest I've ever met.'

26

Opening night had finally arrived.

Louisa breathed deep, but it did nothing to suppress the nerves fluttering in her stomach. She walked slowly down the stairs to where Nancy and Octavia waited for her, each of her friends' faces reflecting their deep wish that tonight would be a success.

As she stepped from the bottom stair, Louisa nodded. 'You both look wonderful. Now, it is almost nine o'clock. Once I open the door, I have no idea if we will welcome one man, five or none. Whatever happens, I want you to remember that neither of you needs to entertain a single cull who makes you uncomfortable. Just try to focus on the fact that the success of this house is the key to our future independence and I'm sure we will have a fabulous opening night.'

Octavia stepped forward, her pretty face sombre, her blue eyes intense. 'I will work as tirelessly for you as I would for myself, Louisa. The triumph of this house and it remaining my home is all I have to care about. I want you to be assured of that.'

Louisa felt deeply touched by Octavia's show of solidarity. 'It pleases me to hear it. Nancy? Are you ready?'

'Of course.' Her friend grinned. 'Aren't I always?'

Louisa laughed, her shoulders lowering as she

looked along the hallway.

'Where's Jacob?'

'Here.' He emerged from the lower stairs and walked towards her. 'You ladies will have no trouble tonight. I can promise you that, at least.'

Louisa's heart picked up speed. His hair was freshly washed, his constant shadow of beard and moustache around a mouth she had shamefully kissed in her dreams for the last two nights. He wore the suit and waistcoat she had bought for him; his boots were polished to a shine.

Jacob Jackson had never looked more handsome or imposing.

They had been living in the same house for just two days, but her attraction towards him only grew. Her desire was unwanted and foolish . . . even if there was the slightest chance of her unforgivable yearning ever being returned.

She lifted her chin. 'Good. That is, after all, why you are here.'

With a final nod at Nancy and Octavia, Louisa walked to the front door and opened it. She stood on the top step and looked along the street. It stood empty of people, the dark March sky filled with clouds obscuring the moon and stars. She shivered and cursed the ominous trepidation that whispered through her. Everything she had arranged, everything she, her friends and Jacob now did would be for their greater good. Each of them represented an integral part of a business that Louisa was determined would thrive.

Turning, she re-entered the house.

Jacob came towards her and stopped, forcing her to tilt her head in order to meet his eyes. The desire to kiss him — to take strength from him — tingled on her lips and, as he continued to stare at her, heat crept into Louisa's cheeks. Aware of Nancy and Octavia watching this silent, intense exchange between her and Jacob made Louisa want to break the moment, but she remained perfectly still.

His gaze grazed her face, lingered at her lips before he nodded and took his position outside.

Dragging her eyes from him, she forced a smile. 'Let's retire to the parlour, shall we, ladies?'

Brushing past her friends, Louisa steadfastly refused to look at either Nancy or Octavia for fear of what she would see on their faces. Whether either was surprised or disappointed by what Louisa deemed to be an obvious connection between her and Jacob, neither of her friends would have missed the brewing heat that only grew the longer she and Jacob spent time together.

And Louisa hated its dangers as much as her friends undoubtedly would.

But what could she do? Sack him? Send him away? Impossible choices when she had so ardently pursued him. It never occurred to her that Jacob — or any man — would ever again arouse her interest in any other way than what he could do for her. Now Jacob had become an unwelcome weakness and Louisa only had herself to blame.

She led the way into the parlour and closed the door.

The three of them sat, each drawing their hands into their laps, their faces looking forward. The mantel clock counted each passing second, the silence only intensifying the tension that permeated the room. Who knew what type of men would come? Who knew if opening this house would be the biggest and most unwise decision Louisa had ever made?

Who knew if she was opening her friends, two women who had pledged their allegiance to her and her ideas, to untold mistreatment?

There was a knock on the parlour door.

Louisa snapped her gaze to Nancy and Octavia who nodded simultaneously, their backs straightening as they rose to their feet.

Her heart hammering, Louisa faced the door. 'Come.'

Two well-dressed men entered behind Jacob and openly stared at Louisa, Nancy and Octavia. Taking their time to assess them, their lustful stares glided over their faces and bodies.

Jacob's brow furrowed, his lips pinched.

'Thank you, Jacob.' Louisa smiled and strode forward, her confidence sliding seamlessly into place. 'Welcome, gentlemen.'

One of them was the man who had been accompanied by his wife at the theatre. His male companion tonight seemed to be around the same age of forty years, each immaculately groomed. Yet, there was no mistaking the hunger in their eyes as they looked past Louisa towards Nancy and Octavia.

Louisa turned and held out her hand towards her friends. 'Won't you join my associates in a drink, sirs? Nancy, Octavia, please pour these gentlemen a glass of whatever they'd like.'

The men stepped forward and gave a semi-bow to her friends, their smiles wide and their eyes alight

194

with avid interest. Nancy and Octavia greeted them with enthusiasm, every trace of their occasional mistrust obscured in an easy professionalism.

Softly closing the parlour door, Louisa walked along the hallway to the front door. Sensing or hearing her, Jacob turned from staring along the street and stepped inside.

When he looked at her, a faint possession gleamed in the brilliant blue depths of his eyes. 'Everything all right?'

'Of course.' Louisa stared into the street. 'Nancy and Octavia know what they are doing, and the gentlemen seem to broach no threat.'

'At least they don't on the surface.'

She turned. Jacob stared at the parlour door, his strong jaw set and his gaze glazed with annoyance. Once again, Louisa was reminded of his strength, of the ability he held to send a man crumpling to the floor with a single punch.

She crossed her arms. 'You know what I intend for this house, Jacob. Are you having doubts about being here again?'

'There is a lot more to do than what you expected of me.'

'What do you mean? I expect nothing more than you to keep things in order. To ensure Nancy and Octavia are not subjected to any physical or verbal mistreatment.'

He faced her, looking irritated. 'The moment I permitted access to those men was the moment I truly understood, worse, *felt* why I am here.'

'Which is? Because I won't ask more of you than what we've already agreed.'

'No, I don't think you will.'

'Then what — '

'My reservations, my past, are my own to deal with, but now I've seen the reality of what will happen here, I'm even less convinced I'm the man to protect you.' He exhaled, his broad shoulders rigid. 'Violence runs in my blood, Louisa. My hatred of a situation can be ignited quickly and deeply. If any of these gentlemen lay one finger on you — '

'Listen to me.' Louisa gripped his strong forearm, stared deep into his eyes and the pain she saw there sent a tremor through her heart. Words flailed on her tongue.

My God, he is hurting. Really hurting.

Surely, it couldn't be the brothel that so clearly disturbed him? He was a man who understood the underbelly of this city. He couldn't possibly be surprised or perturbed by the sex trade.

She pulled forth as much bravado as she could muster, lest he see how much his barely suppressed torment had affected her. 'I intend for this house to be one of good standing. Your presence alone will be enough to separate the congenial customers from the aggressive. Those types of men play on vulnerability. Nancy, Octavia and I are far from vulnerable alone, but with you here, no man of a cowardly nature would dare to try to gain entry. In my opinion, it is only cowardly men who choose to abuse women.'

She squeezed his arm. 'Trust me, Jacob. Please.'

He stared hard into her eyes and Louisa tried to calm the heavy thud of her heart. *Please stay . . .*

At last, he nodded before he returning to his post at the door.

27

Jacob left the house at first light.

The house had been open for a week, but what went on there continued to torment his thoughts and make him further doubt his decision to come to Carson Street.

Nothing extraordinary had happened and only four gentlemen had arrived each night, Nancy and Octavia performing their duties to perfection, considering the men's satisfied faces when they passed Jacob at the door and walked out into the night.

Claustrophobia at being in the house had come and gone, but at least he'd managed — so far — to be civil to the men who came there. Even if he very much doubted he'd ever raise a smile to any of them.

But his hardest challenge had come last night and possession still simmered inside him. Possession that spoke of his growing care for Louisa — a woman he now felt more bound to than he ever had anyone else.

Last night, Louisa had taken her first client to her bed.

Sickness had rolled through him as he'd been forced to watch her smile and laugh as she'd led the man upstairs to her bedroom. She'd said she wouldn't take clients unless the need came — well, Nancy and Octavia's popularity had already soared and men arrived at the house with an

197

increased frequency that Louisa could not have imagined or, most likely, hoped for.

The rapid rise in status of the house pleased her as much as it worried him. But what else had he expected? Louisa had never promised him anything other than the house's success and his employment.

He walked aimlessly along Pulteney Bridge, the shops on either side drawing neither his eye nor his interest. With each stomp of his boots, Jacob attempted to stamp out his nonsensical jealousy. Just as he reached a set of steps that led to the riverside, he halted.

Damnation.

He swivelled around to walk back the way he'd come, but it was too late.

'Well, looky here! Jake, hold on a moment,' Henry yelled, loud enough that people turned. 'Jake!'

Jacob briefly closed his eyes before turning around. Doreen hurried along behind Henry, the basket over her arm overflowing with vegetables and ribboned boxes and the tension that immediately stretched across Jacob's shoulders when he'd seen Henry loosened. He would not allow his annoyance with his manager to mar the opportunity to check Doreen was well.

'Henry.' He nodded curtly and then smiled. 'Doreen.'

'Oh, Jake.' She beamed, and put her hand on his upper arm, her eyes happy. 'It's so good to see you.'

'You too.' He looked at Henry. 'You too. To a point.'

198

Henry laughed and shook Jacob's offered hand. 'I was expecting you back at the house before now. Your little arrangement with your lady friend working out better than expected, I assume?'

'Better than *you* expected is more accurate, wouldn't you say?' Jacob arched his eyebrow. 'I knew I was making the right decision when I left.'

Liar.

'Oh, come on. You belong with me and you know it. It's only a matter of time before you come crawling back.' Henry looked along the street, adjusted his red top hat. 'After all . . . ' He faced Jacob. 'You and I know fighting is deep inside you, Jakey boy. There's only so long you can stand outside a whorehouse.'

Jacob glowered, his hand curling into a fist at his side.

'Why don't you go along with your business, Mr Bertrum?' Doreen stepped between them. 'Jake will walk with me while I finish up my shopping. Won't you, Jake?'

Jacob dragged his eyes from Henry's smug face and nodded.

'Right you are then,' Henry touched the brim of his hat. 'I'll see you soon, Jakey. Very soon, I don't doubt.'

Slowly uncurling his fingers, Jacob glared after Henry until Doreen touched his arm. 'Hey, ignore him,' she said, her brow furrowed. 'It would be a lot easier between the two of you if Mr Bertrum just admitted how much you mean to him.'

'How much I mean to him?' Jacob huffed a laugh. 'How much I mean to his pocket more likely.'

'I'm not so sure about that.' She pushed her hand into the crook of his elbow. 'Walk with me.'

Jacob fell into step beside her, looking over the riverside below as they walked back along Pulteney Bridge. 'So, how's Colin? Tell me Henry hasn't got him lined up to fight the Killer because I wouldn't agree to a rematch.'

'No, he hasn't gone that far, but he is signing Colin up to more fights than what's good for him.'

Guilt immediately pressed down on Jacob and he stopped. 'Why the bloody hell hasn't Henry scouted for someone to replace me? I didn't expect him to have Colin filling the space I left behind. There are a hundred fighters looking for management. If Henry's as good as he claims to be, he should have boxers falling over themselves to work with him.'

'Mr Bertrum wants *you*, no one else. And that little show of his just now is him doing what he does best.'

'Which is what exactly?'

'Playing with your emotions, just as he always has. I don't doubt for a minute he knew you'd ask about Colin, or that I'd tell you how much the poor lad has been fighting. I suspect Mr Bertrum thought your annoyance about that would lead to you —'

'Coming back. Slimy bastard.' Jacob shook his head. 'Well, he's wrong.

Colin is his own man and will tire of Henry sooner or later, just as I have.

You tell Colin I said he has to remember Henry is working for us, not the other way around.' He rubbed at his jaw, irritation swirling through his gut.

'Anyway, Henry's wrong. I'm not coming back. Not yet, maybe never.'

'Then you'd better tell me more about your new life.'

They continued walking and Jacob struggled with what to tell Doreen and what to keep to himself. He doubted she was interested in the ins and outs of the brothel . . . then again, she'd probably love to know what went on inside the house. The truth was, it would be his feelings for Louisa that would most interest his old housekeeper.

'Well?' Doreen raised her eyebrows. 'Tell me.'

Blowing out a breath, Jacob shrugged. 'Fine. Louisa Hill is like no woman I've ever met, if I'm honest. Neither are the two women working with her. They're as different as night and day, but have a common bond that joins them together like . . .'

'Like only mutual experience can? How only sex can?' Doreen smiled.

'You've still got a lot to learn about women, haven't you?'

'Meaning?'

'Meaning, I'd hazard a guess, considering they're prostitutes, that they each have their own story, right?'

'Without a doubt.'

'When a woman is hurt, really hurt, she doesn't tend to crawl into a corner, curl into a ball and not come out to play again, Jake.'

'Neither do men, as far as I know.'

'Ah, yes, but men show their anger like you do whereas a woman's anger manifests itself in a different way entirely.'

Uneasy with what the pointed tone of her voice implied, Jacob's defences rose. 'I was paid to fight. My boxing has nothing do with me being angry.'

'Liar.' Her green eyes shone with amusement. 'What you admit to and what you don't is fine by me. I've never pushed you too much and I'm not about to start now. I'll let you in on a little secret. Broken promises and broken trust usually result in a hardening of the heart. I'd say that's true of the whole human race, but for women it tends to go deeper than a little self-protection. We make a decision that is unshakeable once it's set deep inside of us. A decision that can often mean we seek comfort and support from other women who truly understand our pain in a way that a man never could. When that happens, Jake, women are the most powerful species in the world.'

He attempted to read between the lines of what Doreen was trying to tell him. 'So you're saying Louisa wants me at the house as a means to an end, nothing more? If you are, I know that. I'm there to do a job.'

'No, you're not . . . at least not the job you think.'

His patience thinning, Jacob tipped his head back and looked to the sky before dropping his chin. 'Will you just impart your words of wisdom so I can enjoy the rest of my day?'

She laughed. 'Temper, temper.'

He scowled and looked away from her wily gaze.

'Jake, Louisa Hill *employed* you. You, on the other hand, agreed to work there because something inside of you prevented you from choosing not to.

202

I have no idea what that something was, but this is the first woman who has struck you like lightning the first night you met her. And I'm glad.'

'You're glad?' Annoyed, Jacob glared. 'Why are you glad if you think I'm being used?

'Who said anything about you being used?' She smiled and cupped his cheek. 'She's paying you to do a job, isn't she?'

'Yes.'

'So, everything is as it should be. At least, it is for her. As for you . . . ' She raised her eyebrows. 'You're in a bit of a mess. A mess that will do you the world of good.'

'What are you talk — '

'You met her for a reason, Jake. I believe that deep in my bones.' She eased her hand from his face. 'Stick with it. You need each other. I don't why yet but, mark my words, you need Louisa Hill and she needs you.'

Before he could respond, Doreen wiggled her fingers in a semblance of a wave and walked away, her dyed blonde curls bobbing beneath the wide brim of her hat. Jacob's feet remained welded to the ground, shoppers walking all around him as he stared after Doreen until she disappeared into the crowds.

His gut clenched with fear. For all her chattering, he couldn't deny Doreen had been absolutely right about one thing at least. Louisa Hill needed him . . . but he as sure as hell didn't need her *or* her brothel.

He would make sure Louisa, Nancy and Octavia were all right, the business running smoothly and then he would be on his way. Now that he'd witnessed Louisa taking a cull to her bed, he knew his ability to witness that night after night was a stretch too far. Once he was confident they weren't in danger or he had persuaded Louisa to find someone else to stand at her door, then he'd go.

Walk away, without looking back.

Jacob cursed. 'Yeah, 'course you will.'

28

Louisa stood at her back door and stared at the garden, her mind unfathomably peaceful. Maybe it was because she had the house to herself for a couple of hours. Or because she could feel a tentative warmth from the sun and the first daffodils had begun to sprout from their slumber. Or maybe it was because for the entire month she had been in business, every single client had left Carson Street happy and eager to return.

Time and again, she had expected Jacob to disappear but, for now at least, he was still here and that pleased her immeasurably. It was clear he occasionally struggled with what she, Nancy and Octavia did for a living and he wasn't shy about voicing his opinion either. Yet, despite his threats of not being at Carson Street forever, something kept him from leaving.

Whatever that something was, Louisa had no idea, but she was grateful for it all the same.

She had been able to step back from the physical side of things more than her friends so far, giving her time to concentrate on their outgoings and income, paying off the remainder of household debts left by Miss Warwick and making future plans for the renovation of the house.

None of which would have been possible without Nancy, Octavia and Jacob supporting her with the household duties on top of everything else.

She had woken that morning determined that

her friends would have the day off to enjoy what felt like the beginning of spring. Their unbending friendship had pushed Louisa forward, even on the days when she felt she'd made a mistake or feared Nancy and Octavia might one day think she used them to her own ends that had nothing to do with their own fortune.

Nothing could be further from the truth, but the thought of losing their trust was heartrending.

Louisa swallowed, fighting the tears that pricked her eyes. It seemed for their whole lives, true security had eluded her and Nancy, possibly Octavia, too. Louisa stared blindly ahead. She still knew so little about Octavia's life before she came to Carson Street, but Louisa had vowed she would not press her for more than the young woman was willing to give.

Occasionally, Octavia's seriousness would crack a little and her eyes would shine with delight. Other times, she proved her hidden wit with a quick retort or jab at Nancy when she tormented Octavia over one thing or another. Although seemingly abandoned or possibly alone of her own free will, Octavia held her secrets close.

Maybe she, like Louisa and Nancy, had once believed she had sanctuary — whether with their parents or, for Louisa, with Anthony. However, that precarious existence had been proven to be little more than a fragile house of cards for all three of them.

If a woman wanted security, she had to build the fortress herself. Plank by plank, brick by brick until her prosperity was guaranteed.

Yet, the occasional flashes of uncertainty in

206

Nancy's eyes slashed at Louisa's conscience and heightened her culpability that her friend had returned to selling herself. It was clear Octavia had no such qualms and, in turn, she had been in much higher demand than Nancy or Louisa.

Shaking off her thoughts, Louisa walked to an arbour arcing a stone seat.

Flowers and vines, wilted through the winter, lay in brown and grey through the lattice and her mind drifted to her and Anthony's garden in Bristol — once a haven where she'd spent blissful hours digging and pruning, designing and bringing into bloom. Never before had she had a garden of her own and it was for such things that she owed her gratitude to Anthony as much as she did her anger. He had given her a home and freedom, four years of married happiness, even if she had been ignorant to the full extent of his masquerade.

If she was to flourish in her endeavours now, she must remember the good times amid the maelstrom of problems he had left behind.

Glancing upwards at Jacob's attic window, Louisa exhaled, thankful his drapes were drawn and he still abed. It bothered her that he was less at ease with her transacting business than Nancy or Octavia and hoped Jacob's resentment was because of the predicament Anthony had left her in, rather than any growing feelings Jacob might or might not have for her.

To muddy the waters with emotion would be catastrophic and Louisa had fought her own feelings for him religiously every day.

Whatever his judgement of her and her friends,

they were not selling sex for fun or kicks. They were in this situation out of necessity. Using their youth and beauty to make money in order to keep this house. God knew, their sexual allure wouldn't last forever. Jacob could think what he would, but he was here to work, nothing more. He knew nothing of what it was to be a woman alone in such an unforgiving world.

She glanced again at his window. The drapes were now open.

Her heart treacherously stumbled, and she turned away, tipping her face towards the sky. Would he seek her out? Sit outside with her? Cursing her anticipation, Louisa sat a little straighter, tension inching across her shoulders.

The crack and brush of twigs sounded behind her and Louisa stilled.

'Good morning, Louisa.'

Forcing a smile, she closed her eyes, not quite ready to look at him.

'Good morning.'

'Quite a day, isn't it? Where are Nancy and Octavia?'

'I sent them out for the day. They've worked hard. They deserve to enjoy some time to themselves.'

'Didn't you want to join them?'

'No, it's been a while since I've had some time alone.' She looked out over the garden. 'Moments of solitude are precious.'

Either ignoring her hint or missing it entirely, he sat down beside her. 'I guess a need to reflect on these past few weeks is understandable. I can't imagine it's easy doing what you do.'

She snatched her gaze to his. 'No, it's not easy, but it is necessary.'

'I understand, but — '

'There is no *but*, Jacob. I've received three more letters this week demanding payment on Anthony's outstanding debts despite him being declared bankrupt. The satisfaction I felt penning letters to these men, inviting them to call at the house for full reimbursement was unquestionable.' She glared at him, daring him to contradict her. 'What Nancy, Octavia and I are doing is not without purpose. There is an end goal in all our minds.'

'Which is?'

'Liberty. And if you don't understand what that will mean to each of us, then you are not the man I thought you to be.'

His jaw tightened, his eyes darkening with annoyance, which poked satisfactorily at her own rising displeasure.

She turned away. 'I want security for all of us. Despite our success thus far, our nicer clothes and surroundings, do not think me unaware that I am encouraging prostitution, or relying on my body rather than my mind most of the time.' She faced him, pride burning inside of her. 'But that will change. In time. For now though, I have deep, hateful moments when I fear I'm doing wrong by Nancy and Octavia and I really don't need you judging me.'

His expression was indecipherable and then he nodded, sitting back and opening the space between them. 'I apologise.'

Birds chirped and squawked, horses' hooves

209

and wooden wheels running over the cobble-
stones beyond the fence punctured the silence.
Yet, despite the awkwardness that rose between
them, Louisa refused to speak. She had said her
piece and he had apologised.

He suddenly stood and held out his hand. 'Let's
go out.'

'What?'

He smiled and winked. 'Come out with me,
Louisa. Please.'

Her heart beat fast, her mind jumbled from his
apparent change of mood and his stupid, disarm-
ing smile. 'Where?'

'Does it matter?'

'No, but . . . '

'Then, let's go.'

'We can't.'

'Why not?'

Her mind scrambled with an unforgivable lack
of excuses. 'Because . . . because . . . '

He raised his eyebrows, his stupid blue eyes
gleaming. 'You're not scared of spending some
time alone with me, are you?'

Despite knowing inevitable disaster loomed,
Louisa tossed him a glare and slipped her fingers
into his outstretched hand. 'It would be a mistake
to ever underestimate me, Jacob Jackson.'

29

Jacob had no idea if he looked like a vagrant beside a lady, or a gentleman walking with his beau. Either way, he'd felt compelled to smarten up for this outing he'd prompted. When he and Louisa had gone their separate ways into their bedrooms to change, Jacob had shaved his stubble and trimmed his moustache, donned a clean shirt and necktie and finished by taking a brush to his jacket.

It was important that Louisa felt proud walking beside him — that he didn't invite curious glances from passers-by wondering how a man like him could be in the company of such a beautiful woman.

When he'd returned to the kitchen, she had packed a picnic basket, complete with an unopened bottle of ale, napkins and plates. The excitement on her face had swept across the breadth of the kitchen and straight into his damn chest. Now, they were here, sitting side by side on a blanket in Victoria Park, staring out at a thousand and one others who'd decided the day's unexpected sun was too good to waste.

Satisfaction swelled inside of him, a contentment and sense of rightness that he'd neither expected . . . nor particularly welcomed.

He admired the beauty of her profile as she smiled at a group of children playing ball with their mothers. Louisa's eyes were alight, a slight laugh tinkling in her throat. Jacob looked away as protectiveness towards her ballooned behind his chest once more, kicking his heart into high speed.

The more he considered how he'd come to be living in her house, spending time with her, the more he was forced to accept that from the first night they'd met, Louisa had intrigued him. That curiosity had evolved into gratitude when she'd nursed him after his run-in with the Killer, laying down the law to Henry in a way Jacob suspected his manager had never been exposed to before.

Then he'd seen her with Nancy and Octavia, learned of her iron will that often darkened her eyes and reddened her cheeks. She was undoubtedly a woman of substance. Someone who could match his strength and barbs, blow for blow. He was here, with her, weeks later because it had somehow become an impossibility not to be.

No danger could befall her. Not after all she had done for him. And for Nancy and Octavia. Yet, Louisa was a brothel madam and, day after day, she was exposed to untold dangers and now Jacob was trapped in her circle.

No, not trapped. Bound willingly . . .

She turned and slightly jumped, her smile widening. 'Does it amuse you to see me laughing at the children?'

He turned from the violet eyes he saw in his sleep and lay flat on his back, closing his eyes. 'I'm glad to see you so relaxed. The fresh air suits you.'

'And so it should. I spent days and days outside when I lived in Bristol.'

There was a rustle of clothes and she sighed

212

before her arm lay alongside his. Jacob squeezed his eyes tighter. The woman had lain down, seemingly completely uncaring of what others might think. Instead of urging her to sit, he relished her confidence.

He slowly opened his eyes.

She watched him, her eyes dancing with happiness, her grin devilish. 'If you can lie around in the grass, why can't I?'

'You are trouble in fine clothes, Louisa Hill. Make no mistake.'

They fell into companionable silence before she blew out a breath. 'So, Jacob Jackson, I think it only right that I learn some more about you, don't you?'

He stilled. 'What?'

'We've lived and worked together for a number of weeks now and I still know so little about you.'

Dread unfurled in his gut, but Jacob stayed perfectly still, not wanting her to know that her inquisitiveness rattled him. Thoughts of his father, his mother, the men he'd left beaten and bloodied, ran through his head.

He swallowed against the dryness in his throat, his body tense. 'What do you want to know?'

'Firstly, have you always lived in Bath?'

'Yes.'

'When did you learn to fight?'

'Henry took me in when I was young. Probably too young. Taught me all I know.'

'I see.'

Jacob's heartbeat pulsed in his ears.

'Do you have family here? Friends? Only, you never seem to leave the house to see or visit anyone. I hate to think you feel you can't do whatever

213

you like during the day.'

He closed his eyes. Tension ran like a tightened rope through the centre of his body, his mind scrambling for something to say so that he might not have to explain his self-enforced solitude. Every now and then, Doreen or Colin had commented on his lack of real friends, but he'd only ever answered their prying with a shrug or dismissive grunt.

Diverting Louisa's inquisitiveness would be a different kettle of fish altogether.

'Jacob?'

'No family, but I have friends. Of a sort.'

His mother's murder screamed in his head and Jacob curled his hands into fists as images of his father beating her flashed behind his closed lids.

His isolation had been sealed that day. The choice to go through life detached and void of feeling or care bringing the security that he would never have to endure such devastating pain again.

'Jacob?'

Louisa's voice came from above him. She had sat up, which meant she was staring straight down at him. No doubt her pretty brow was furrowed and her violet eyes devoid of light in her confusion.

'Have I said something wrong?'

Slowly, he opened his eyes. The sun was low behind her, making her curls glow almost white. Her concern was clear in the depth of her eyes. He rose to sitting and put his arms around his knees, pulling them tight to his chest.

'Of course not.'

'You're angry.'

'No, I'm not.'

Her stare burned into his before she pulled the picnic basket closer and opened the bottle of ale. Guilt twisted inside him as she filled two mugs and handed him one.

'Thanks.' He drank deep. 'How about you? I haven't known you to go visiting since I've worked at the house either. Surely you had many friends in Bristol you'd like to see?'

'No, not really. And, like you, I have no family.'

The sadness in her voice forced his gaze to hers, the comfort he wanted to offer her sticking in his throat, stilling his arms.

'What happened, Jacob? You are a good and kind man, yet all alone.'

Fear whispered through him, his heart hurting to see such worry for him in her eyes. God, had she come to care for him as he had her? He wanted to kiss her, hold her and tell her that he was all right. The one thing he still had despite all that had changed him was his integrity. He had never lied to anyone and wouldn't start now. Even though to lie to Louisa would most certainly be kinder and spare him a heavy load of guilt.

He took another drink. 'I — '

'Sometimes I see such anger in your eyes. Such hatred. It happens when you've seen me with culls or when I wish to go out alone. It happens when Nancy or Octavia are just a little longer than usual behind their closed doors with certain gentlemen. What evokes such rage in you in those moments?'

Jacob looked across the park. All around him people smiled and laughed with loved ones, children played, and dogs barked as they gambolled

215

on the grass. Such ease was so far from his reach, he knew it would never happen for him and, until now, that reality had never bothered him.

The care in Louisa's eyes shamed him. He had once embraced the dislike and distrust in people's eyes, thinking their fear of him equated to proof of his power, his strength. Nothing could be further from the truth. Now, he realised, their fear was merely a reaction to his solitude, distance and anger.

And what was worse, was that he now wanted to share the depth of his self-delusion with Louisa and apologise if he had done anything to add to her already heavy burden.

'My father . . .' Words lodged in his throat and Jacob clenched his jaw.

'My father killed my mother in front of me when I was a child.'

'Oh, Jacob.' She put down her drink and stole her fingers onto his knee.

'As well as anger, I have seen such hurt in your eyes. I suspected it was something bad, but never that. I'm so sorry.'

To his shame, tears burned behind his eyes and he quickly blinked. 'I never told the police. Instead, I ran and never looked back. A couple of years later I learned he'd been hanged. I can only assume someone found my mother and pointed the finger at my father.' Sickness coated his throat and he stared across the park. 'My father is the root cause of my hatred and I'm sorry you've had to witness it.'

'But what happened to you? Did you end up on the streets? In the workhouse?'

He forced himself to look at her and there was a slash across his heart when he saw tears glistening on her lashes. 'On the streets. I suppose you could say Henry saved me as your husband saved you. Albeit in very different ways.'

She shuffled closer until he felt her breath on his lips.

'I'm so sorry.' Her gaze lingered on his mouth before she raised her wonderful eyes to his, a tear rolling over her cheek. 'Truly.'

The urge to close the few inches between them and capture her lips with his burned through him, his fingers itching to steal along her nape into her thick, blonde hair. For so long he'd avoided women whom there could be the smallest chance he could become fond of, but Louisa had entered his life like a storm, weakening his common sense and endangering his self-preservation.

'It clearly hasn't been easy for either of us,' he said. 'We have both fought to survive. Done things we've had to do.'

When she slipped her hand from his knee, the sudden space between them opened a chasm in Jacob's chest. Why in God's name had he inferred to her prostitution? Brought it into the conversation like poison to a sweetened cake?

'You hate what I'm doing, don't you?' Her voice was quiet and soft. 'Do I disgust you, Jacob?'

'Disgust me?' Disbelief swam through his blood. 'How could you think that? I have more respect for you than I've ever had for anyone. You don't disgust me, Louisa.' Before he could think of the consequences, he reached for her, his hand cupping the softness of her cheek. 'I want to keep you

217

safe, that's all. I don't want anything happening to you. Not to you or Nancy and Octavia. I couldn't save my mother, but this . . . being in your house is my second chance to get it right.'

'But you can't think like that. You are there just in case, nothing more. These men are gentlemen, Jacob. There is little chance of any real violence occurring.'

He stared at her mouth, desire stirring deep in his groin, longing in his heart. 'Louisa . . . '

She leaned forward and brushed her lips so softly and so briefly against his, he wasn't sure if they even kissed.

'The Great Exhibition is on its way!'

'Albert has done it!'

'You there, the Great Exhibition will soon be open!'

Jacob scowled at the trio of men wandering past, drinks in their hands, their mottled cheeks red with excitement. The Great Exhibition. It had been the talk of the city for weeks and now it had somehow sliced through the most intimate moment of his life.

Louisa turned to him, her eyes wide with wonder. 'Can you imagine what extraordinary things will be on display? Oh, I'd give anything to see it. I really would.'

His brain had turned to mush, her leap to excitement proving her kiss was little more than her way of offering him comfort. For him it had meant so much more.

Suddenly he wanted to give her the world, but as he couldn't do that, he took her hand. 'Then we should go.' He grinned, hoping he'd fooled her into thinking their kiss was just as insignificant to him. 'You and me. What do you say?'

'We couldn't possibly. We have the house to take care of. Nancy and Octavia. To close for business so soon after we've opened would be foolish.'

'The Exhibition opening is still a couple of weeks away and closing the house while we take a trip to London will only incite frustration. The gentlemen will be even more eager to re-enter the house upon your return.

Anyway, don't you keep telling me you want to live your life on your own terms?'

'Yes, I do.' She laughed, her eyes shining. 'You're right. Let's go to London.'

30

A knock at the front door made Louisa glance from her paperwork to the mantel clock. The next cull wasn't expected for another hour.

The echo of Jacob's boots along the hallway as he made for the front door filtered through her open study door so she returned to recording in her ledger.

Pulling the light of the candle a little closer to her work, satisfaction warmed her. For the first time since they had opened, the brothel was in the black. Not by any life-altering amount, of course, but they were certainly heading in the right direction.

She brushed the soft feathers of her quill back and forth over the tip of her chin.

Maybe it was time to consider whether to employ more girls. Louisa sat back in her chair. Nancy and Octavia still occasionally showed signs of mistrust of each other and their clients. It was too soon to add another woman to the house.

Jacob entered the room, concern shadowing his handsome features as he clutched a folded letter in his hand. 'Louisa, I need to go out for a couple of hours.'

'What is it?' She slowly stood, trepidation whispering through her.

Disquiet hadn't appeared quite so regularly in Jacob's eyes over the last few days as it had in the preceding weeks. Something was wrong. 'Jacob?'

He came closer and swiped his hand back and forth along his jaw. 'It's a message from Doreen, my old housekeeper. She's asked me to drop by the house. There appears to be some trouble brewing.' His jaw tightened as he raised the letter. 'This has Henry written all over it. I can't leave Doreen to worry.'

'Of course not.' Louisa approached him and curled her fingers around his forearm. 'Go. We'll be fine for a while tonight. I know how fond you are of your housekeeper . . . ' She raised her eyebrows. 'Just as I know how much less fond you are of your ex-manager.'

'Never a truer word said.' His expression marginally softened. 'Are you sure the three of you will be all right?'

'Yes. We only have four culls booked in tonight. Two of which are with Nancy and Octavia as we speak. Everything will be just fine. The sooner you go, the sooner you'll be back. Off you go.'

He glanced towards the door. 'Maybe I should go in the morning.'

She planted both her hands on her hips. 'Jacob, you will not sleep a wink tonight knowing Doreen has asked for you. Go now, I mean it.'

His gaze lingered on hers; her attraction for him that had only been heightened since their trip to the park ignited once more. She dug her fingers deeper into the stiff curve of her crinoline lest she surrender to the temptation to pull him towards her. Why she had impulsively kissed him that day, albeit barely a brush of their lips, she had no idea.

It had only served to torment her desire towards Jacob to breaking point.

221

He blinked and stepped sharply back. 'I'll be back as soon as I can.'

Louisa stayed stock-still until the front door slammed behind him. Only then did she exhale a long breath, her tense shoulders dropping. Her every instinct told her that it was only a matter of time before her lips were on Jacob's again. A reality that was reinforced by the continual, silent tension that hovered between them, whether they be alone or in company. She had thought herself in control of her emotions since Anthony's death, able to make good decisions over bad.

Crossing the line with Jacob would be inevitably bad . . . *very* bad.

Striding to her desk, Louisa forced her mind to her work.

It wasn't until she heard murmured conversation, punctuated with Octavia's laugh, that she realised half an hour had passed.

She closed her ledger and walked into the hallway.

Octavia closed the front door and smiled, holding aloft some cash notes.

'Another satisfied customer. I have no doubt he will return.' Walking closer, she handed the money to Louisa. 'My next cull isn't due for an hour or so.

I'm going to wash and then make a cup of tea. Do you want one?'

'Thank you, that would be lovely.' Louisa counted the cash, her eyebrows raising. 'This is more than our agreed rate. Wasn't Mr Spencer a new visitor? It's most unusual that they give extra on a very first meeting.'

Rare mischief twinkled in Octavia's eyes. 'As I said, he will be back soon enough. I'm good at what I do, Louisa. Even if at times I wish I could be anywhere else but under a man. I'll see to that tea.'

Louisa stared after her friend, sadness creeping around her heart. Octavia was not alone in her sentiments and Louisa prayed prostitution wouldn't be her eternal destiny any more than it would be Nancy's and Octavia's. The business was necessary for the time being, but one day, she hoped for something more in their futures.

A door softly closed at the top of the stairs and Louisa quickly put the cash in her pocket and smiled, expecting to see Nancy with her client.

Instead, Mr Chaney descended the stairs alone, his face still ruddy from his exertions as he shot a final glance up the stairs before putting on his hat.

Louisa's smile wavered as unease tightened her stomach. It was most unusual for Nancy and Octavia not to escort their culls to the door. Their accompaniment to the very last moment of the clients' visits was something Louisa had decided would add a nice touch over other establishments who often left the goodbyes to the madams or the protection.

'I trust you enjoyed your time with Nancy this evening?' Louisa walked to the hallway stand and handed Mr Chaney his overcoat. 'Can we expect to see you again on Friday?'

He pushed his arms into the sleeves of his coat, as he steadfastly concentrated on buttoning it. 'I'm not sure. I will send a message.'

'Of course.' Louisa's discomfort only intensified and she look again towards the stairs. 'Is

Nancy all right?'

He snapped his gaze to hers and then, as if remembering himself, he smiled, his eyes softening. 'Why shouldn't she be? The girl is a marvel. Here.' He pulled some money from his inside coat pocket and carefully counted out the bills before handing them to her. 'I think that should cover it. Anyway, I'll be in touch, Mrs Hill. Goodnight.'

Louisa's smile slightly trembled under the strain of keeping her affable demeanour in place. Warning screamed inside her head as she ushered Mr Chaney towards the door, her desperation to check on Nancy increasing with each harried beat of her heart.

The moment she'd closed and locked the door, Louisa threw Mr Chaney's money onto a side table, lifted her cumbersome skirts and ascended the stairs.

She rapped on Nancy's door before gently pushing it open, fear for her friend racing through her. 'Nancy? Sweetheart, are you all right?'

At first Louisa thought the room empty, but then she looked into the far corner. A shaft of moonlight lit Nancy's stockingless toes where she sat huddled on the floor. Louisa's throat dried as she rushed forward. 'Nancy?'

'Help me, Lou. I . . . I can't get up.'

'What?' Louisa reached for the matches on her friend's bedside table and lit the lamp. The amber glow fell over her friend's nakedness and Louisa's breath lodged in her throat. 'My God . . .' Tears leapt into her eyes at the sight of the bruising already darkening above Nancy's left eye, her lip

224

dripping blood onto her naked bosom. 'What did he do to you?'

Carefully, she helped Nancy to her feet and guided her to the bed.

'Stay there, I'll get the ointment. Lie down.' Louisa attempted to ease Nancy back, but her friend flinched and gasped the moment Louisa put even the smallest amount of pressure on her arm. 'Did I hurt you? I'm so sor —'

'It's my back. My . . . bottom.'

'Your . . . ' Louisa leaned around her and stared at Nancy's back, illuminated in all its horror by the candlelight. 'Oh, Nancy.'

'Don't you dare say you're sorry, Lou. This isn't your fault.'

The inch-wide welts were a violent red and weeping blood, streaking down Nancy's back from shoulder blades to the top of her buttocks. Bile rose in Louisa's throat as she stared, anger mixing with grief, guilt with regret.

She squeezed her eyes shut. 'How did I not hear this happening?' She snapped her eyes open, her body trembling. 'I was talking with Jacob and then working in the study, but the door remained open the whole time. Oh, Nancy, I'm so sorry.'

'I said, don't apologise.'

The curtness of her friend's voice forced a thump into Louisa's throat as she tried and failed to remain as strong. Nancy's courage had always been the firmest and now, in light of her beating, their differences showed more than ever. The furiousness of her friend's expression illustrated Nancy's tenacity over adversity.

'We know his name.' Louisa strode to the other

side of the bed and picked up a blanket to put over the eiderdown. 'He won't get away with this. Do you think you can lie on your front? I'll send Octavia for the physician. Those wounds need to be tended properly.'

'No. No physicians. We can manage our business well enough without interference.'

'But —'

'No, Lou. I mean it. What happens in this house, stays in this house.'

'Don't be absurd. He can't get away with this.' Louisa paced the room, swiping at the tear that rolled over her cheek. 'We are supposed to be entertaining gentlemen, not the lowlifes we've had to deal with in the past.

Jacob . . . oh, God, Jacob.' She stopped and crossed her arms. 'He won't let this go unpunished.'

Nancy smiled and then winced. 'Exactly.'

'How can you smile about this?' Louisa gently took her friend's hand, brushing some fallen hair from Nancy's eyes so she could properly see how she was feeling inside. 'You must have been terrified. Have could I have thought this house would be any different than where we were before, Nance? Anger burned through her blood, as she gripped Nancy's fingers.

'We have to do something.'

'And we will. Just leave this to Jacob. You have big plans for us, Lou. I know you do and, one day, what we're doing now will be a distant memory.'

Louisa's eyes burned with unshed tears that Nancy still believed in her despite her thrashing and undoubted humiliation. 'But —'

'We just have to do all we can to ensure our

safety. Set some rules. Have Jacob sitting outside on the landing and the front door locked between culls.

Check each cull for anything they might use to hurt us. Whatever it takes.'

Nancy raised Louisa's hand to her heart. 'You've given me a real life, Lou.

A chance for something more. Without you, Lord only knows what would've happened to me by now. Beatings are ten-a-penny for whores, rapes and muggings, too.' A tear rolled over Nancy's cheek but she gave a strained smile. 'You gave me a home, food and warmth. More than that, you gave me friendship and trust. I love you. Do you hear me?'

'And I love you.' Louisa gently hugged her, before abruptly standing, her heart aching with love for her most constant friend. 'I'll get something for those cuts, but first we need to get you onto your front.'

Once Nancy was lying down and as comfortable as possible, Louisa left the room and bumped into Octavia.

'What's going on?' Octavia glared towards Nancy's open bedroom door.

'Is she all right?'

Louisa swallowed, resentment towards men and all they could inflict on women simmering dangerously inside of her. 'No, go and sit with her. I'll be as quick as I can.'

She brushed past Octavia and headed for the kitchen. Hurrying to one of the cabinets, she extracted their medical supplies and stopped, clutching the box so tightly her knuckles ached.

This would be the first and last time any of them was hurt. There had to be another way than selling themselves, exposing themselves to cruelty and violence.

There had to be . . .

Louisa closed her eyes and fought the panic building inside her. But what else did she or either of her friends have but their looks and bodies? Nancy and Louisa were barely educated, Octavia held her life behind a wall of secrets she was yet to share.

Louisa swallowed as her frustration swelled. How could she save any of them when she knew nothing and *was* nothing?

Damn you, Anthony. Damn you for everything. If I had not known another life, I would have gone along ignorant of any good in this world. But you exposed me to a better life and, by God, Nancy, Octavia and I will know security again.

31

It had taken over an hour and a lot of fortitude for Jacob to hold his temper while he'd listened to Henry's excuses for setting up a fight that would put Colin in the ring with the Killer.

Now, his patience was close to breaking.

Doreen continued to pace the kitchen under the pretence of making tea, then cleaning the surfaces down, then rearranging the saucepans. She'd got him here and now seemed to have nothing more to add to the increasingly heated conversation going on around her.

'Look . . . ' Jacob stood and shrugged on his coat before snatching his hat off the kitchen table and pointing it at Henry. 'You know the Killer is more than willing to use a knife. You know he's willing to kill. No one, including Colin, needs to be in the ring with a man like that. Lay this ridiculous idea of you managing the fighter who succeeds in putting the Killer in his place to rest before one of us gets killed.'

'Well, there's no fear of him killing you, is there?' Henry scoffed and lifted his coffee cup. 'Especially when you'd rather bow and scrape to a group of middle-class women than save your friend from having to fill the space you left behind.'

'For the love of God, can't you see that no space needs to be filled? You just can't abide the fact that someone might make more money from the Killer being in town than you. Sod our lives as

229

long as Henry Bertrum is making money.'

'I made you, Jakey.'

'As you like to remind me over and over again.' Jacob shoved on his hat and stepped towards the door. 'Carry on as you are, and the Killer will be the least of your concerns.'

'What's that supposed to mean?'

Jacob pinned him with a glare. 'It means there is every chance it will be me throttling you with my bare hands rather than any danger posed by a deranged boxer.'

'Is that right?' Henry huffed a laugh. 'The day you put your hands on me, Jakey boy, will be your last. Mark my words.'

'Is that a threat?'

Henry shrugged and took a drink of his coffee, his eyes on Jacob's over the rim.

Jacob's heart pulsed in his ears. He'd had just about enough of Henry and his misplaced ambition. Louisa had shown him that there was more to life than thinking one day ahead. Why not consider the long term? Have dreams and goals with the potential to last a lifetime? Whenever he spent time alone with her, Jacob started to imagine a future that didn't necessarily equate to blood and punches, but happiness and security.

He moved closer to Henry as protection of the new life that sometimes felt within his grasp stole over him. 'Because if it is a threat, I'd tread very carefully. I've got a different way of life now and it suits me. There's nothing to stop me from helping Colin find a different life elsewhere, too. Then where would you be?'

'You're dreaming, Jakey. Colin isn't you and

never will be.'

'I wouldn't be so sure.'

'Colin knows when he's onto a good thing. That boy wouldn't leave.'

Jacob walked to the door and glared at Henry's turned cheek. 'When Colin comes back here, tell him he doesn't have to fight the Killer, because if Colin dies in a fight you arranged I will come straight back here looking for you.'

Henry waved his hand. 'Oh, go back to your whores, Jake. It's clearly where you belong.'

Resisting the urge to smack Henry in the mouth just for the hell of it, Jacob approached Doreen where she was now studying a mark on the oven that seemed a damn sight more interesting than him and Henry.

He put his hand on her shoulder and she turned, her eyes wide with worry. Jacob's heart kicked. 'You know where I am. You come and get me anytime. Do you hear?'

She nodded.

'What does she need you for?' Henry laughed. 'She's all right with me, aren't you, Doreen?'

''Course I am.' She stared into Jacob's eyes, her gaze bordering on pleading. 'You go, Jake. Look after those ladies for me, but don't be a stranger.'

He squeezed her shoulder, shot a parting glare at Henry and left the kitchen.

Outside, Jacob breathed in the cold March air, glad to be leaving his old home and hurrying back to his new. It had stuck like a claw in his gut to leave Louisa, Nancy and Octavia knowing there were culls in the house, but the risk of Doreen being in any way hurt by Henry had taken priority.

Although his return visit had done little to resolve the situation, fingers crossed, Henry would heed Jacob's warning and not expose Colin to such senseless risk.

He reached Carson Street and let himself in.

The house was oddly quiet, and Jacob immediately sensed something was wrong. His shoulders tensed as Jacob slowly removed his hat, listening for something or someone who could be the cause of hair raising on his nape. Then he heard quiet talking coming from upstairs.

Tossing his coat on the banister, Jacob headed upstairs. 'Louisa?'

There was some urgent whispering, possibly from all three women in the house, before Louisa emerged from Nancy's room, looking entirely harassed despite her overly wide smile.

'Jacob! You're back.'

'I am.' He looked over her head into Nancy's room. 'What's going on?'

'Nothing.' She firmly closed the bedroom door. 'Let's go downstairs. I could do with a brandy.'

Now he knew something was wrong. In the weeks the house had been open, he'd never seen Louisa drink anything stronger than the occasional glass of wine. His mind reeled back to the night he'd met her and Nancy coming out of the White Hart half-cut. Something had been worrying her that night, too.

Stepping back, he gestured for her to lead the way before glancing once more at Nancy's closed door.

As Jacob followed Louisa into the parlour, the tension surrounding her was palpable. He curled his hands into fists, every instinct in his body telling him that whatever she was about to tell him would be the hardest test he'd had to face since meeting her.

He stared through the window into the night blackness, his heart beating a tattoo in his chest. 'What's happened?'

Silence.

He turned sharply. She stood in the very centre of the room, staring at him, her mouth open but absent of words and her eyes wide with fear.

He fought to keep his voice calm as he approached her. 'Louisa?'

The skin at her neck shifted as she swallowed, before she blinked, and her eyes glazed with unshed tears. 'It's Nancy.'

Dread unfurled in Jacob's gut as he reached for her hand. 'Tell me.'

'She . . . She was attacked by a client.' She closed her eyes. 'He beat her about the back and bottom with his belt, struck her in the face when she protested. She is . . . so hurt.'

Jacob's fury rose fast, his vision turning red under a dangerous mist of anger. 'I need to see her.'

'No, you can't. Leave her.'

He stormed from the room and took the stairs two at a time, paying no heed to Louisa's footsteps and shouts behind him. Pushing open Nancy's door, Jacob strode into the room towards the bed where Nancy lay.

Octavia leapt from the bedside and held up

her hand. 'Get out, Jacob. She does not need to be around another man incapable of controlling himself.'

Ignoring her, he hunkered down and gently took Nancy's hand, hardening his heart against the silver tracks of tears upon her cheeks. He had to remain focused. 'I need to see what he did to you, Nancy.'

She closed her eyes. 'Jacob, it's all right. Just leave it for now.'

'No. Show me.'

She opened her eyes and exhaled shakily. 'Look, at first, I wanted you to hunt him down, but Louisa's right. Meeting violence with violence will do no good. We need to — '

'I need to see what he's done to you so when he's standing in front of me, I'll remember what must be done so he thinks twice before ever laying his hand on any woman, ever again.'

A hand stole on his shoulder, but his eyes never left Nancy's.

'Jacob . . . ' Louisa pushed her fingers into his shoulder. 'Nancy wants to forget what happened and I'm certain the man in question will never return here.'

Jacob's pulse beat hard in his ears and he tried not to grip Nancy's hand too roughly. 'What's his name?'

'He gave the name Chaney, but that is no use when so many clients provide false names,' Louisa said quietly. 'I will know him if I see him again but, for now, the most important person is Nancy.'

He straightened and gently cupped Nancy's jaw, anger rolling like a rumbling volcano inside him. 'I'll take care of this. Get some rest.'

Louisa's hand slipped from his shoulder as he strode past her towards the door. 'Jacob, please.'

'Follow me. Now.'

Ignoring Nancy and Octavia's hushed murmurs behind him, Jacob could barely stand still as he waited for Louisa to close the door.

'How dare you command me that way.' Her violet eyes blazed with anger, her cheeks mottled. 'I have put up with men ordering me around my entire life. Things are different now, Jacob. You work for *me*, not the other way around.'

'I don't have time to waste arguing and, for your information, there is a difference between a man berating a woman and a man trying to honour her.'

'Of course there is, but I will not tolerate you bossing —'

'We need to get some paper from your study. I need you to draw me a picture of the man who hurt Nancy. You said he's been here before?'

'Well, yes, last Friday and the Friday before.'

'Good, so there's every chance I'll recognise him too. The house needs to be locked up for the night.'

'It will be and I've already sent word to the men expected that we are now closed.' She put her hands on her hips. 'What do you plan to do?'

'Don't worry about that for now. I want you to promise me you won't open the house again until I find this man.'

'Jacob, answer me. What do you plan to do?'

He held her gaze, his jaw clenched. 'What I must.'

235

'So you beat him to a pulp. Then what? Do you think that will impress or help me, Nancy or Octavia? Do you think by doing that this house's reputation won't be affected? You need to use your brain before your brawn. Your intelligence before your fists. *That* is who you really are, Jacob. *That's* the man I see when I look at you.'

His heart painfully jolted, his hands itching to touch her, to pull her into his arms. He snatched his gaze over her head, unable to bear the loving way she was looking at him. 'I'm a boxer, Louisa. A man trained in violence.'

He forced his gaze to hers. 'I've told you brutality runs in my blood.'

'Don't be ridiculous. Beating someone is a choice, not a compulsion.'

Anger darkened her cheeks. 'Promise me if you have to look for Mr Chaney, you'll warn him off with words, not violence. I might have employed you because I knew what you are capable of, but I'd hoped you would never have cause to prove it. Mr Chaney is no longer here, and I don't want you arrested, Jacob.'

His conscience battled with his need to hurt Chaney, but if he didn't promise her, she wouldn't let him leave. 'All right.'

'Promise me you won't hurt him.'

He swallowed hard against the lie. 'I promise.'

'Fine.' She gave a firm nod. 'But I hope you realise he could be anywhere by now.'

'Which is why I want you to keep the house locked up until I've found him and returned. I will never again leave you, Nancy or Octavia in jeopardy. You must not allow any more men entry ever again if I am not here.'

'It could take days to find him. *If* you find him. We are building up good business. If the house stays closed for too long, these men will seek female company elsewhere. You know exactly what we do here and why.'

Frustrated, Jacob swiped his hand over his face and glared at the ceiling.

'If I don't find this man and he gets away with what he's done, I've failed you.' He faced her, willing her to understand that everything he stood for was at stake. 'You have to meet me halfway if we are to remain working together. What's it to be, Louisa? Will you close the house for as long as it takes? Or do I go and not come back?'

Indecision warred in her violet eyes until she nodded, albeit reluctantly.

'I'll close the house.'

'Thank you.'

Jacob led the way downstairs and into the study. She walked to her desk and plucked a pencil from a small porcelain jug.

'These sorts of men are moneyed, Jacob. If you hurt Chaney, the constabulary will be after you quicker than we could ever manage to hide you.'

'Draw his picture. I'll be fine.' The fact she was prepared to hide him didn't go unheeded and now he knew for certain she cared for him as he did her. Whether that was good or bad, only time would tell. He closed his eyes and tried to calm his impatience to leave.

The swish of her skirts told him she had taken a seat at her desk and Jacob slowly opened his eyes. He paced the room as she worked, each minute

237

passing like an hour.

At last, she stood. 'Here.'

Jacob stared at her beautiful face and fought the urge to comfort her.

Instead, he dropped his study to the paper. 'Him. Yes, I remember this *gentleman* only too well. This won't take very long at all.'

He turned towards the door and Louisa gripped his arm.

Looking deep into her eyes, unspoken words passed between them as his heart weakened with the growing affection he held for this wonderful woman. He had to protect her. Had to protect Nancy and Octavia. Had to protect every woman and mother . . .

He opened his mouth to speak but she stepped forward and lifted onto her toes. She gripped his biceps and crushed her lips to his, her tongue edging into his mouth. Crumpling the drawing to the small of her back, Jacob pulled her closer and poured his fear and frustration into kissing her with all that perilously battled in his heart.

'Be careful,' she whispered as she eased away from him. 'We need you.'

Jacob nodded and walked backwards before abruptly turning and leaving the house.

32

After a fitful night waiting to hear Jacob's key in the door, Louisa closed her itchy eyes as she took a moment alone in the kitchen. She had lain in bed that morning, her body stiff with tension. As soon as she had heard the hallway clock strike eight, she tiptoed up the stairs to the attic room where Jacob slept, praying with all her heart she would find him in bed.

She hadn't, and fear had clutched her heart at the dreaded confirmation that he had been out all night.

Nausea rose bitter in her throat as Louisa opened her eyes and reached for the laden breakfast tray beside her. She had no idea if the man she was coming to care so much for was dead, alive or in jail.

Her feet and heart heavy, she carried the tray into the lilac and cream dining room, its cheerful warmth not brightening her morning as it usually did. This morning everything felt tainted and wrong. The house, Anthony's love nest, suddenly felt like the betrayal it was. All she'd had to start again was this property, the only physical thing left from her mockery of a marriage. She had desperately hoped that by combining the house, her looks and experience, she'd be able to create a new life for her and Nancy, and now Octavia.

Yet, Nancy had been beaten. Octavia could barely look at either of them without an angry, resentful shadow clouding her eyes, which meant there was every possibility she felt Louisa had gone back on her word of her guaranteed protection. As for Jacob . . . he was goodness only knew where.

Louisa laid out the crockery and teapot on the table before picking up the tray to return to the kitchen for the bacon, eggs and toasted bread she'd prepared. Even though her appetite had vanished, she had needed to keep busy and cooking for her friends had felt necessary.

As she emerged into the hallway with the food, Octavia was helping Nancy down the last step of the staircase.

Louisa immediately smiled in a bid to hide her heartbreak. Her closest and usually vivacious friend looked so weary. 'Morning, ladies. How are you feeling, Nancy?'

'Me? I'm absolutely grand,' she panted, gripping the newel post. 'But Octavia seems to have forgotten she's a whore and taken on the job of nursemaid instead.'

Octavia shot Nancy a glare. 'Is it so bad that I want to help you? I like to care for people, but if my ministrations are becoming a burden to you, then —'

'Oh, hush,' Nancy snapped, her brow furrowing as she tentatively stepped forward, Octavia's hand at her elbow. 'Who doesn't like to be made a fuss of now and then, eh?'

Despite the bruising on Nancy's face and the welts hidden beneath her nightgown and robe, it was clear to Louisa that her best friend's spirit was far from broken. Pride swelled inside her as

Nancy slowly past her into the dining room. Louisa smiled at Octavia who met her gaze with a solemn nod.

Louisa inhaled a long breath, her idea for them to take breakfast together gathering reason. The three of them needed to talk.

'Make yourselves comfortable.' Louisa waved her hand towards the table. 'I thought it would be nice for us to eat together. We so rarely wake at the same time when clients have been here the night before.'

Nancy grimaced as she lowered onto a seat, the cushion Louisa had laid there beneath her tender bottom. 'I'm guessing you've barely slept a wink considering Jacob hasn't come home yet?'

'No.' Louisa sighed, as she picked up the teapot. 'But I'm sure he'll be back soon. So, what can I get for you? It's important you keep up your strength.'

Once their plates were filled and the tea poured, Louisa picked up her knife and fork. 'I want to discuss the future of this house with you both.'

'The future?' Octavia hovered her fork at her mouth. 'Do you mean to close it? But you can't.'

The fervour in her tone took Louisa by surprise and she glanced at Nancy who raised her eyebrows.

'I haven't thought as much about closing as asking how you both feel about continuing to work. For Nancy and me, this . . . industry, is something we thought far behind us. For you, I promised safety and a better place to work.' Fearful her love and care for these women would come tumbling out and lessen the business-like manner

241

she needed to convey, Louisa tilted her chin and pushed her emotions far away. 'Now that Nancy has been attacked — '

'Oh, I see what this breakfast is about.' Nancy tutted and grimaced again as she reached for some buttered toast. 'You are still blaming yourself for Mr Chaney's actions. Telling yourself that it was *you* who put me in that position and *you* who directed the man to lash me.'

Culpability warmed Louisa's cheeks. 'Well, wasn't it me who came up with the idea of turning this house into a brothel? Wasn't it me who went out onto the streets and harangued Octavia until she relented to come here?

What else am I supposed to feel but guilt?'

'And what do you want to say next, Lou?' Nancy bit into her toast and continued talking regardless that her mouth was now half full. 'That you understand if we want to stop working or maybe even leave?'

Louisa looked between her friends, who both wore almost identical expressions of nonchalant disregard as though they'd expected no less from her.

Humiliation whispered through her. 'This is not funny.'

Octavia flashed one of her rare smiles, clearly amused. 'Well, it is a little.

I've only known you a matter of weeks, but I know who you are, Louisa.

Your reaction to Nancy's beating is exactly what I expected. We know you care for us, but we also know you hold yourself responsible for far too much.'

242

Louisa laid down her cutlery and sat back in her chair, her arms folded.

'Is that so wrong?'

'Of course not, but our wellbeing is our own responsibility. You are delightful. Caring and considerate. Someone who has shown me more kindness these past weeks than anyone has since I left . . .' Octavia's cheeks flushed and she looked to her plate, then began sawing at her bacon. 'You have become someone very important to me.' She met Louisa's gaze, her blue eyes bright with resolve. 'And I, for one, do not wish to leave here or stop working. I trust Jacob to take care of the gentleman in question and I trust you to devise a plan that will mean we are even more protected than we were before.'

Touched by Octavia's frankly astonishing words when she was usually so reserved, Louisa looked to Nancy. 'And you?'

Nancy stared wide-eyed at Octavia who continued to concentrate on her breakfast.

Biting back her smile as love for her friend bloomed inside her heart, Louisa touched Nancy's hand. 'Nancy? Do you agree with Octavia? You wish the house to remain open?'

She finally turned and shook her head. 'Yes, of course, yes.' She scowled and pointed her fork towards the window. 'The men out there are nothing that we can't deal with. With or without Jacob, no man will ever decide our futures again. When you and I came to Bath, we had no idea what we would find. We haven't heard a peep from Miss Warwick and the house is legally yours. So . . .' She flashed a smile. 'We carry on.'

243

Happiness washed through Louisa and she dropped her tense shoulders.

'Where would I be without you? Both of you.'

Octavia and Nancy smiled.

Tears of gratitude and relief pricked Louisa's eyes. 'I'm yet to come up with a plan going forward, but I wanted to give each of you the chance to leave. I would've given you money to start somewhere else and helped to find you somewhere to stay, but if you want to stay here, that makes me happier than you could ever know.'

She stood and gently embraced Nancy before going around the table to embrace Octavia. Unsure how she would react to physical contact, Louisa braced for rejection but put her arms around Octavia anyway. She momentarily stiffened, before softening in Louisa's arms and dropping her head to hers.

Slowly, Louisa straightened and coughed to clear the lump in her throat.

'Once Jacob returns —'

'*If* he returns,' Nancy sniffed.

Louisa shot her a mock glare. '*When* Jacob returns, the four of us will sit down and come up with a better way to run the house. The money is coming in and, if necessary, I am happy to employ more protection.

Otherwise, we will see what else can be done.' She sat and looked at her friends again. 'No more worrying about tomorrow or the next day. This house will be a success.'

Nancy lifted her fork in the air. 'Amen!'

'You have my loyalty, Louisa.' Octavia smiled. 'Always.'

Lifting her teacup to her lips, satisfaction slipped through Louisa on a tentative thread, but still her gaze was drawn to the window and the hope that Jacob would soon come home.

33

Jacob stared at the door of Tanner's gentleman's club, mentally willing the man who had used the name Chaney while visiting Carson Street to come outside.

Twenty-four hours after the bastard had taken his belt to Nancy, Jacob had finally discovered Chaney's whereabouts.

After a little digging and calling in on a few middle-class chaps who regularly watched Jacob fight, he now knew Chaney's real name to be Mr Phillip C. Morrison. His name conjured up a man of stature, honour and respectability. Not the cowardly, lust-filled reprobate he actually was.

The hour neared eleven o'clock as Jacob settled against some railings, his heartbeat falling into the steady rhythm it always did before he entered the ring. Being a successful, prize-winning fighter took more than the ability to give sharp, hard and accurate punches. It took mental ability, too. Knowing how to calm the mind, as much as the adrenaline, set the stage for a controlled, objective performance that would leave an opponent beaten, but not dead. The Killer drifted into his mind and Jacob thought back to his conversation with Henry about Colin. Time and again, Jacob had a niggle that he still had a score to settle with the Killer.

And if anyone was going to fight the maniac, it

would be him, not Colin.

But as Jacob absently smoothed his hand back and forth across his stomach in the semi-darkness, his healing wound reminded him that the time was fast approaching for him to quit the ring. Over the last few days, he'd begun to feel his professional fighting might have come to a natural end, even if violence would forever run in his blood and nature.

His role at Carson Street felt worthwhile and necessary, things that he'd never really felt in the ring. The desperate need to belong somewhere — to survive the dangerous, crime-riddled slums of Bath's seedier side — had made boxing his entire life. Under Henry's tutelage and — what Jacob had incorrectly assumed as a young lad was Henry's unwavering protection, boxing had meant he would always be safe . . . would always matter.

It hadn't been until he'd reached adulthood that Jacob understood he was little more than a commodity to Henry, but at least the man had put Jacob in good stead to find his way in the world.

And tonight, he would put the traits he'd inherited from his father and the direction Henry had given him to good use for all womankind.

A barrage of laughter from across the street snagged Jacob's attention and he straightened. He stared at the huddle of gentlemen on the top step of the club. Unable to see their faces despite the two streetlamps either side of the steps, Jacob slowly strode across the street, his view momentarily hampered by a passing carriage and then by two horses being ridden side by side.

Once he reached the other side, he moved just

beyond the steps and lowered his face, tugging the brim of his hat over his brows as he feigned interest in something invisible stuck to his overcoat.

The gentlemen descended the steps and passed Jacob, laughing and jesting, entirely unaware and uncaring of the man in the tattered black overcoat and hat. None of the men were Morrison.

Clenching his jaw in frustration, Jacob muttered a curse and looked towards the club.

Three more groups of gentlemen exited before his patience was finally rewarded.

Morrison came out alone, the end of his cigar glowing red as he lit it in the pinkish glow spilling through the club's doors. Enveloped in a plume of exhaled smoke, Morrison strolled down the steps and Jacob took a long breath.

When Morrison came closer, Jacob stepped from the shadows. 'Good evening, sir. I wonder if I might have a word?'

Morrison stopped, his cigar halfway to his mouth. Of medium height and build, his face bore pockmarked scars across jutting cheekbones. Otherwise, it was fair to say Morrison wasn't entirely ugly . . . at least not on the outside.

He lowered his cigar, his eyes narrowing as he appraised Jacob from head to toe. 'Yes?'

Jacob offered his hand, which Morrison promptly ignored. He dropped it to his side. 'I believe you are a man often in the market for the company of a young woman, sir. If that's true, I believe I have a lady who might interest you.' He gestured along the street. 'Maybe we could talk further as we walk?'

Morrison guffawed and moved to walk away. 'You are gravely mistaken.

Good evening.'

'She's a redhead, sir. Petite and lively.' Jacob stepped alongside him.

'She isn't always submissive to a man's needs, but I understand that doesn't bother you and you have ways and means to overcome such problems. In fact . . . ' Jacob smiled and arched his eyebrows. 'I believe a woman with a little spirit is just the type you like.'

Morrison's locked his gaze on Jacob's, his eyes showing increased interest. People passed them, their drink-fuelled laughter filling the air, accompanied by music from the hall along the road and the rumble of carriages across the cobbles.

'How old?'

Jacob smiled. 'Young enough, sir.'

'I see. I'm afraid I didn't catch your name?'

'Knight, sir.'

'Mr Knight, let's walk, shall we?'

Morrison led the way and Jacob followed, his mind calculating just how far to take his beating of this piece of shit and what to say to him while Morrison lay bleeding at his feet. Jacob's ministrations had to be severe enough that the son of a bitch never laid a wrong hand on a woman again, but not enough that a physician would need to be summoned.

After all, the questions and suspicions of a doctor could possibly lead to questions and suspicions from the constabulary. Jacob had no desire to incite a reason for either to find their way to Carson Street.

'Along here, if you will.'

Morrison pointed along the street and turned

into a narrow walkway that led to a circle of shops with the darkened archway of the railway bridge in the corner. Once they were alone, Morrison tossed his cigar to the ground and crushed it with the heel of one gleaming, high-polished boot.

'How much and where?' he demanded as he reached into his pocket. 'I'll give you a small amount of cash now as you've made me aware of this woman, but the rest goes to her. I don't agree with the women who entertain me not being paid for their services.'

'A true gentleman, sir.' Jacob's heart beat a little faster, his anger rising.

'You will find her at — '

And Jacob lunged.

His first punch struck Morrison hard in the stomach and as he doubled over, Jacob gave a swift upwards thump to the man's jaw. His hat and cane clattered to the ground as he crumpled with a rather feminine wail, which would have been amusing if rage wasn't streaming through Jacob's veins.

He grabbed Morrison's collar, pulled him up and repeated the sequence to his gut and face.

He crumpled again and Jacob grabbed a handful of hair at Morrison's crown before whipping his face close. 'Shall I go again?'

'What in God's name is wrong with you?' Morrison whimpered as he drew the back of his gloved hand over his jaw. 'You belong in an asylum.'

'I'll ask you again. Do you want more?'

'For the love of God — '

The man was still talking so he clearly hadn't had enough.

Keeping his hand entangled in Morrison's hair, Jacob pummelled two sharp punches to his stomach before releasing him. Morrison dropped like a stone to the ground and curled into the foetal position.

'Enough. I've had enough.' He held up a hand in supplication. 'Take my wallet. My money. It yours.'

'I don't want your money, you fucking scumbag.' Jacob lowered to his haunches and gripped Morrison's battered jaw in his hand, relishing the sight of the blood around the man's teeth. 'You hurt a woman I have come to care for. A woman who works at Carson Street. Do you recollect beating her yesterday evening before you made merry at Tanner's tonight?'

Morrison's eyes widened and he nodded, his chin still clasped in Jacob's hand.

'Good. Then listen up because I will only say this once. Are you listening?'

Morrison nodded again.

'First things first . . . ' Jacob tightened his fingers. 'You will never come near Carson Street again. Understand?'

Another nod.

'Second, if I ever hear that you have put a hand on a woman in any way other than courteously, I will hunt you down. Do you understand?'

Another nod.

'And thirdly, if the need arises that I have to come looking for you again, I will be carrying a blade. That blade will find its way to your throat and I will leave you to bleed out slowly and painfully. Do you understand?'

Another nod.

'Say it,' Jacob gritted his teeth, his anger making him tremble. 'Say, you understand.'

'I — '

A thundering of boots echoed behind him and Jacob stilled.

'There he is, constables! I knew he shouldn't be following that gentleman. He's killing him. Look!'

Cursing, Jacob shoved Morrison to the ground, straightened and held up his hands. The two uniformed constables bore down on him, each taking an arm before slamming Jacob against the brick wall.

'You are under arrest, sir.'

Two other men helped Morrison to his feet, each smartly dressed in black overcoats, top hats and scarves. Their chatter filled the small space as they exclaimed and gasped over the bloody mess of Morrison's face.

Despite being flanked by two officers of the law, Jacob smiled.

Violence bred violence. A truth that he would never easily forget . . . and neither would Morrison.

34

Louisa stood in the brothel's hallway and finished buttoning her coat, her fingers trembling, all too aware of Nancy and Octavia waiting by the front door for her instruction.

A second night had passed without Jacob's return. She could wait for him no longer.

Fighting back the fears that bounded about her heart and mind that Jacob could well be lying in a ditch somewhere, Louisa prayed he was safe and well. It was terrifying and infuriating that the man seemed to have no regard for his own life. Everything he did and said was founded in his unwavering belief that violence was the only way.

She could hardly think straight, much yet find the wherewithal to ensure that she or her friends managed to locate him.

Louisa straightened her shoulders. 'Right then. Nancy, you can ask around the local coffee houses and, Octavia, you go to the infirmary.

Remember, you are to enquire after Mr Chaney in the first instance. Fingers crossed, that is his real name, and someone will know of his whereabouts, which will give us a good indication of whether or not Jacob found him.'

The other women nodded, Octavia looking a little uncertain whereas the prospect of revenge glinted in Nancy's grey eyes likes pieces of flint.

'If we have no luck locating Mr Chaney . . .' Louisa sighed ' . . . only then do we start asking people if they have seen Jacob. The less attention we bring to him, the better.'

Nancy frowned as she scrutinised the bruises on her face in the hallway mirror. 'If we suspect he's been hurt, I think it would be a good idea to ask a few women down by the river known for patching people up if they've seen him, don't you?'

'Good thinking. I imagine he would go to them before he would a physician or the infirmary.' Louisa pushed a stray curl under her hat.

'Goodness only knows what has happened to him. If Jacob found Mr Chaney, I'm not sure he would have kept his promise to me not to hurt him.

After all, I suspect Jacob has grown equally as fond of us as we have of him.'

'Yes, I believe he has.' Nancy's voice ever so slightly cracked before she coughed. 'So, where will you be looking while Octavia and I are at the coffee houses and infirmary?'

'The police station. There's every chance he's been arrested.'

'Do you think alerting the constabulary is wise?'

Louisa stopped pulling on her gloves. 'Why choice do we have? We can hardly leave Jacob imprisoned. I have a little money for bail, if necessary, but fingers crossed —'

'I'm just thinking it won't do any of us much good if this house becomes known to the police.' Nancy put her hand on her hip. 'Do we really want them sniffing around?'

'Jacob's welfare is more important than worrying about what the police might or might not do.' Louisa finished putting on her gloves. 'Anyway, we might run a brothel, but we keep things low-key and are respectful to our neighbours. The police won't bother us, I'm sure.'

'I'm not, but you're right, we owe it to Jacob to help him.' Octavia tightened her scarf and tucked the ends into her overcoat. 'I hope you have more than a little money though. As far as we know, he could already be known to them or maybe even have a record. If that's the case, Lord only knows how high his bail will be set.'

Louisa stomach knotted with dread. What did any of them really know of Jacob's past? He had shared some of his traumatic childhood and how he came to know Henry Bertrum with her, but scarcely anything else.

'If Jacob is being held by the police I have more than enough money to get him released,' she said. 'I can't imagine they'll want a king's ransom.

Either way, I will not leave the station until Jacob is walking out of there with me.'

They left the house and after a squeeze of her friends' hands, Louisa hurried towards the centre of town. The bright sunshine and cloudless blue sky belied the dark turmoil swirling inside of her.

Every possible scenario of Jacob's whereabouts continued to play over and over in her mind. From lying beaten and bloody somewhere, to his body floating along the River Avon, to him being strung up on a tree in Victoria Park. She had to find him.

Once she reached the stone steps of the police station, Louisa's nerve faltered, Nancy's concerns about seeking information from the police resonating in her mind. The brothel had only been running a matter of weeks, but business was steadily picking up. To have it shut down now could be disastrous. Neither she nor her friends had reason to trust the constabulary and Nancy was right that they should be wary.

Over the years, she had come to learn that the constabulary were often less keen to help, but more eager to judge and punish the poor and struggling. She needed to be on her guard and tread carefully with her questions, manner and responses.

Drawing in a strengthening breath, Louisa ascended the steps.

The interior of the station proved even more depressing than the outside.

Wooden chairs lined the grey walls, the floor muddy and stained beneath her feet. The windows were dark with dust so thick the early morning sunlight had little chance of adding any pleasantness to the dim and drab lobby.

Trying not to breathe in the smoky, sweaty and overwhelming male stench, Louisa forced her feet towards an officer studying some papers at the front desk. Nerves fluttered in her stomach and her mouth dried as she fought her growing intimidation.

'Might I help you, ma'am?'

Louisa jumped before her smile automatically slid into place. 'Good afternoon, officer. I am very much hoping that you can.'

Suspicion was rife in his dark brown eyes. 'Is there something you would like to report?'

'Um, no, I am here on behalf of a friend.' She grimaced and feigned an uneasy glance around her before lowering her voice. 'She is too embarrassed to enquire herself, but it seems that her brother may have got himself into a spot of bother.'

He straightened and crossed his arms, his eyes showing his deepening suspicion. 'I see.'

'No matter how much I've tried to convince her he will undoubtedly return unharmed, she is convinced that he might have been arrested and brought here.'

'A brother of a friend, you say?' His tone was rife with amusement and wholly patronising cynicism. 'And what might this gentleman's name be, ma'am?'

Louisa held his gaze, refusing to be deterred. 'Jackson. Jacob Jackson.'

'Mr Jackson?' His mouth curved into a smile. 'Well, well, well. I wouldn't have thought someone like you, or your *friend*, would associate with a man who claims to have no fixed address, Miss . . . ?'

Ignoring the officer's attempt for her name, Louisa dropped her shoulders as though relieved and smiled. 'So, I assume Mr Jackson is here? Oh, thank goodness.'

'He is, but he won't be going anywhere unless the man Mr Jackson attacked decides to withdraw his charges. If that doesn't happen in the next six hours or so, Mr Jackson will be taken to prison to await trial.'

Sickness coated Louisa's throat as she gripped the counter, all pretence of relief vanishing. 'But surely — '

'Now, I suggest your friend leaves her brother to face the consequences of his actions. There is little chance Mr Morrison will retract his charges when he has every reason to pursue them. Good

257

day, Miss.'

'Mr Morrison?'

'The unfortunate victim of Mr Jackson's assault.' The officer frowned, suspicion clouding his gaze once more. 'I had assumed by your friend sending you here you knew, or at least suspected, who her brother had assaulted.'

'Mr Morrison, of course. I will report back to my friend with what you have told me. Good day, officer.'

Louisa hurried from the station with as much dignity as she could muster.

Mr Morrison? So that was Mr Chaney's real name. For all Jacob's impulsiveness towards violence, he would never risk attacking a man if there was even the slightest chance of mistaken identity.

She rushed back across town, heedless to the people, horses, muck and mess all around her. She had to find Nancy and Octavia and tell them they were now seeking a gentleman named Mr Morrison.

35

Jacob had no idea of the time, but the numbness in his backside confirmed he'd been sitting on the hard, steel seat inside the station's small holding cell for hours. He stood and reached his hands up until they almost touched the stone ceiling, his joints popping and cracking. Lowering his arms, he bent his head to one shoulder and then the other.

The stomp of heavy boots sounded along the corridor and then stopped outside the door.

The small opening slid back with a loud clang.

'Mr Jackson, it's your lucky day.' The sergeant grinned, but his eyes were filled with scorn as he peered into the cell. 'The charges against you have been withdrawn. You are free to leave. Under caution, of course.'

Withdrawn? Jacob crossed his arms and kept his face expressionless as he nodded towards the cell door. 'Let's be having you then, Sergeant.'

'Careful, Jackson,' the sergeant said, his gaze fixed on Jacob as he slid the key into the lock. 'It won't take much for me to make an adjustment or two to the paperwork and you'll be transferred to a cell that will make this one look like a bathroom at Buckingham Palace.'

Thinking it best not to push his luck, Jacob held his tongue as the door was unlocked. With a wave of his hand, the sergeant gestured for Jacob to lead the way along the cold, dank corridor scarcely lit

259

by the flickering gaslights lining the walls.

After receiving his caution and signing the release papers, Jacob was sent unceremoniously on his way. As he stepped outside, he squinted against the bright, spring sun, half-smiling to see the tentative warmth meant some brave souls, or maybe souls who couldn't afford coats, walked in their shirtsleeves. Standing on the side of the busy street, Jacob battled with which direction to take. Left would lead him back to Carson Street. Right would take him to the White Hart.

Aggravation or alcohol? Which did he need more?

There was no question in his mind that Louisa was behind the charges being retracted. The question was, what had she had to do in order for Morrison to agree? Protectiveness simmered dangerously in Jacob's gut as he turned right and strode in the direction of the pub.

Morrison would have been in no fit state to have sex with anyone last night, so payment for Jacob's release could not have been made in that way, at least. Yet, that knowledge did nothing to assuage the unrest swirling inside him like a tropical storm. If she had paid money to the piece of scum, that meant her precious accumulation of funds she'd so conscientiously put by for herself, Nancy and Octavia's futures had been jeopardised by Jacob's choice of justice.

Shame threatened and he welcomed its gnawing culpability. Hadn't he known that fate would prove him unworthy of ever being more to Louisa than a set of hired fists? Hadn't he always been someone incapable of illustrating passion or care by any other means but violence?

Continuing towards the White Hart, his boots hammered heavier and heavier on the pavement as more and more guilt pressed down on him. If his release wasn't due to Louisa, it could only mean Henry had somehow become involved. If that turned out to be true, it would be all too obvious what he'd expect from Jacob in repayment and gratitude.

A rematch with the Killer.

Well, Henry could go to hell. Jacob hadn't asked for his help and so owed Henry nothing. Jacob scowled. He suspected his stupid conscience would catch up with that sentiment sooner rather than later.

Christ, he needed to get well and truly plastered.

Shoving open the White Hart's doors, Jacob strode straight for the bar and although friendly faces made to greet him, people took one look at him and backed away again. Good. The last thing he wanted was company.

'Pint of my usual, please, Maura.'

His favourite barmaid raised her eyebrows. 'It might be just as well if you have something stronger.'

'What?'

She tilted her head towards a corner of the packed and smoky pub. 'She's been in and out of here all bloody day looking for you.'

Jacob turned and his heart damn near leapt from his chest.

Louisa stood just inside the door, dressed so finely, her hat flowered and feathered, her blonde curls falling past her shoulders and black baubles dangling at her ears. Even though her violet eyes pretty much shot him in the chest with the intensity of their glare, her pink lips drawn tightly together, her beauty amid such stale ugliness inside the pub took Jacob's breath away.

Nearly every patron watched her, yet not one moved to talk to her. The reason why was obvious. She was way out of any of their leagues . . . and his.

With his eyes on hers, Jacob slowly walked towards her until he stopped in front of her, so close, he noticed she had to tilt her head to meet his eyes.

For some unfathomable reason, the fact she had to do that, that he was taller, stronger — at least, physically — unforgivably pleased him. He wanted her to need him as he was somehow coming to need her.

'Let's go outside,' she said, her eyes never leaving his. 'I'm glad I found you.'

Her annoyance was palpable, and Jacob stepped back, gesturing with a wave of his hand that she walk ahead of him. She was far from happy and whatever the many reasons — considering his actions and their consequences over the last twenty-four hours — he felt sick to his stomach.

He'd disappointed her, broken his promise to her and failed her. After all, she'd specifically asked him to avoid violence, to *talk* to Morrison and prove himself the better man.

Now she knew Jacob for who he really was, she would want him gone.

They walked to an alleyway at the side of the

pub and stood far back in the shadows among the ale kegs and discarded, haphazardly stacked piles of bottles. The stench of alcohol surrounded them, and all Jacob wanted to do was carry Louisa out of there. But given her angry glare, he sensed if he as much as laid a finger on her, she'd swing for him . . . whether she agreed with violence or not.

'So . . . ' She crossed her arms, her eyes ablaze with irritation. 'It seems I am no less inept at unravelling mystery names than you. Mr Chaney, as you clearly know, also goes by the name of Phillip C. Morrison.'

Jacob opened his mouth to speak.

'Let me finish. Mr Morrison likes to portray himself as a man of the highest esteem and therefore lives on one of the costliest streets in the city.

So, I, Nancy and Octavia found our way to Royal Crescent in order to pay Mr Morrison a visit, but he wasn't at home. Do you know why?'

Jacob had the insane urge to laugh. She was challenging him to deny what he'd done to Morrison — to hold his hands up in mock confusion. Was it wrong that he was beginning to enjoy their spats? That she felt comfortable enough around him, so unafraid of him in every way, that she spoke her mind without care for his reaction?

'Jacob Jackson, answer me.'

Willing the smile that pulled at his lips into submission, he swept his hand over his face. 'I suspect he's banged up in the infirmary.'

'Exactly.' She uncrossed her arms and prodded her index finger hard into his chest. 'And you put him there after I specifically asked you not to hurt him.'

263

'What can I say?' He gently gripped her hand, catching a waft of her scent. His cock treacherously — and inappropriately — twitched. 'The man provoked me.'

'Do you know who I had to speak to in order to get the charges against you dismissed? How I had to humiliate another woman, another wife, as Anthony did me? Do you?'

Guilt punched him hard in the stomach at the realisation of what she'd done so that she might save his stupid, impulsive and violent arse. His smile vanished as he closed his eyes. 'Oh, Christ . . . You spoke to his wife. You told her what that bastard did to Nancy.'

'Yes, Jacob. I stood on her doorstep and told her what her husband is capable of inflicting on a woman. My friends standing either side of me, Nancy injured and Octavia so angry it scares me that one day she will explode as you seem so often to do.' She shook her head, her cheeks mottled. 'The woman was mortified and told me she would take care of everything and you would be released today. Will she ever get over the fact that her husband sleeps with and beats whores, that three whores were on her doorstep? I guess we'll never know, will we?'

He clenched his back teeth. 'Don't call yourself that.'

'Why not? That's what am I, isn't it?'

'Not to me.'

'No? And neither are you the man who beat Morrison within an inch of his life to me. You are good and kind, caring and strong.' Her voice cracked. 'Why are you intent on allowing your past to define your future? To continue allowing past hurts to provoke future disappointment and pain?

It stops today. Right now.'

The tears in her eyes slashed hard at Jacob's chest and he swallowed, fighting the weakness gathering inside of him. 'You can't say that to me.'

'Why not?'

He straightened his spine against the pain he knew he was about to inflict on her, but he didn't like being the only one cornered — the only one questioned. 'Isn't the same true of you, Louisa? You can't say you haven't resurrected all you once were, all you once did, so that you might have the chance to rebuild what your husband promised and then stole from you by taking his own life. You are repeating a life you should have had the chance to leave behind. You are no different than me. No different at all.'

'This isn't about me.' She tried to pull her hand from his, but he tightened his grip. 'Let go of me.'

'No.' He stared at her, the sadness in her eyes killing him. 'If you ask why I keep doing this, then you must ask yourself the same thing. Don't you agree?'

The seconds passed, his heart beating fast.

She lifted her chin. 'I might be running a brothel, I might be taking men to my bed again, but I *am* changed, Jacob. Maybe that change isn't big, but it *is* a change. I am living free. Under no obligation to anyone else. What about you? Are you not still fighting people? Using your fists when you are intelligent enough to talk anyone down?'

The fact she thought him capable of placating

someone, of solving a dispute with words, made him want to puff out his chest and kick his damn heels in the air but how could he when her assumptions had no proof? 'Do you feel yourself coming to need me, Louisa?'

'What?'

'Because I feel myself coming to need you.'

The tension in her arms softened and a single tear slipped over her lashes to roll down her cheek. 'I don't want to need you.'

'That's not what I asked.'

'Jac —'

'Are you coming to need me?' He stared at her mouth, her eyes, her hair.

'I need to know.'

She closed her eyes. 'Yes, I need you.' She opened her eyes and they glistened in the semi-darkness. 'I really do.'

Relief washed through him and Jacob smiled. 'And I need you.'

He dipped his head and kissed her. She immediately leaned into him, seemingly oblivious to the station grime and stench clinging to him.

Hungrily, she returned his kiss. Their tongues tangled, the heat between them growing stronger and more urgent as though each fought for supremacy over the other. Jacob pulled her tight to his chest, his fingers in the hair at her nape.

'Don't make me go, Louisa,' he whispered against her mouth. 'Not yet.'

She eased back and lifted her hand to brush some fallen hair from his brow, her touch gentle and tender. 'Why would you think I want you to go?

You can't go. Not now.' She softly smiled. 'Oh, you're an impulsive, egotistical man, Jacob Jackson, but you promised me a trip to London. You're going nowhere.'

36

Louisa eased back in her chair and picked up her wine, happy and inexplicably peaceful as she watched her friends and Jacob banter back and forth around the dining room table. Her and Jacob's shared kiss and confessions of needing one another, of acknowledging that they both had so much personal healing left to do might have brought them closer, but it had also made things strangely tangible between them.

It was something she was certain her friends had noticed, but neither Nancy nor Octavia had broached with her. *Yet.* She looked at each of them now, Nancy wiping tears of mirth from her eyes and Octavia softly smiling, her distrust of Jacob diminishing day by day.

Maybe it was the sense that the four of them now relied on one another that brought Louisa such confidence things would turn out all right for all of them in the end. Or maybe it was the self-protecting barriers each had dared to lower just a little at a time over the last few weeks. Maybe it would even be proven that their individual destinies had dictated they would one day meet under such unorthodox, yet necessary, circumstances. Only time would tell.

'So, you plan to leave for London in the morning?' Octavia asked, turning to Louisa as she lifted her wine glass. 'And while you're away, we're to keep the house closed?'

268

Always so concerned and serious, Octavia already held a huge part of Louisa's heart whether the younger woman realised it or not. She had stepped in as the sensible one. Pragmatic and forthright, she was an integral part of the house and Louisa hoped she always would be.

'Yes, the house will remain closed.' Louisa glanced at Jacob who nodded, his expression showing the decision was not up for negotiation.

'Without Jacob or I here, I would not enjoy our trip knowing you are allowing clients to enter the house.'

Nancy snorted. 'Or anywhere else.'

The women laughed, as Jacob scowled and took a long drink of his wine.

'And . . . ' Louisa fought her smile. 'We will only be away one night, and it will do you both good to have a night to do with as you will.'

'We could catch a show, Octavia.' Nancy grinned and eagerly sat forward. 'Dress up a bit and sup at the Pump Rooms afterwards. What do you think?'

'The Pump Rooms?' Octavia paled, her usual confidence seeming to drain away. 'Me?'

Louisa touched her friend's arm. 'Why not you? You are as deserving as anyone else, aren't you?' She raised her eyebrows and pinned her with a stare. 'After all, you earn a good living, know how to use a knife and fork and can engage in intelligent conversation. Why should you not be as welcome there as anyone else?'

'But I'm not a lady, I'm a —'

'A woman,' Jacob interrupted. 'Who deserves a show and to sup at the Pump Rooms.'

Louisa smiled as Octavia's eyes glazed with

269

tears before she quickly blinked and gave a curt nod. 'Yes, I am.' She turned to Nancy. 'Let's do it.'

Jacob stood from the table. 'Well, if you ladies will excuse me, I have a book I need to return to one of our neighbours.'

'A book?' Nancy's eyes danced with teasing as she picked up her wine.

'Must be a picture book. I've only ever seen you poring over sketches of machinery and such like. I look forward to the day I see you reading a novel, Jacob Jackson.'

He placed his hand gently on Louisa's shoulder as he passed her towards the door. She feigned a glare at Nancy. 'I wish you wouldn't torment him.'

She grinned. 'Why not? It's so thoroughly enjoyable.'

Octavia grinned. 'Oh, but it is, Louisa.'

Rolling her eyes, Louisa took a sip of her water. 'Well, then, I suspect he'll be glad of a night away from you both.' Excitement tumbled in her stomach as thoughts of all she and Jacob would see in London filled her.

'This trip to London might just be the most exciting thing I've ever done.

Anthony . . . ' She looked at Octavia. 'That was my husband — he would never entertain taking me with him whenever he travelled there.'

'Hmm.' Nancy sniffed. 'No doubt the reason being there was another mistress living there.'

Heat leapt into Louisa's cheeks but before she could respond, a sharp bang sounded at the front door and her whole body tensed. They were not expecting visitors or clients.

Nancy and Octavia abruptly stood and stared

towards the dining room window.

'Are we expecting anyone?' Nancy asked, her shoulders high.

'No.' Louisa stood, hating how obvious it was that all three of them were entirely aware that Jacob wasn't in the house. 'Stay here. I'll answer it.'

But just as she had expected, her friends were right behind her as she strode from the room, down the stairs and into the hallway, trying to calm her stretched nerves. Ever since Jacob's arrest, she had feared Mr Morrison might reconsider his decision to withdraw the charges against Jacob. The more time that passed, the more uneasy she felt. What if it was the police?

A reprobate like Mr Morrison could not be trusted. Yet, the enraged determination in his wife's eyes gave Louisa little doubt that anything she demanded of her husband in the future, he would have little grounds on which to dispute.

Louisa walked to the front door, threw a quick look over her shoulder at Nancy and Octavia and then pulled it open. 'You!'

Caroline Warwick stood on the doorstep alongside John Hardman.

Anthony's mistress wore an expression of cat-like satisfaction as she smiled, her green eyes gleaming. As for Mr Hardman he stood ramrod straight, his gaze flitting to Miss Warwick as though awaiting her instruction.

'What the hell do you — '

Louisa raised her hand, cutting off Nancy, and pinned Miss Warwick with a glare. 'Did I not make myself clear that if I saw you again I would not be

271

responsible for my actions?'

'Oh, you did, Mrs Hill but I think you should refrain from any unnecessary assault and listen to what my associate and I have to say.'

'Your associate?' Louisa huffed a laugh and turned to Mr Hardman. 'And you are he, I presume?'

He puffed out his chest, his rheumy eyes boring into hers. 'Indeed I am, ma'am.'

'Then I can only assume your rather scathing opinion of Miss Warwick has changed since our last meeting.' Louisa turned to Miss Warwick and crossed her arms expectantly. 'Well?'

'We are here to claim back what is rightfully mine.'

Louisa huffed a laugh. 'I don't think so.'

'For the love of God . . .' Nancy murmured.

Louisa looked at Mr Hardman. 'So now you are willing to help her?

Why?' She shook her head. 'Oh, what does it matter? You're getting absolutely nothing from me. Just leave.'

Louisa trembled with suppressed anger that her past with Anthony had once more appeared on her doorstep when she had started to relax into semi-contentment.

'No.'

Miss Warwick pushed past Louisa into the hallway, Mr Hardman following and tipping her a triumphant grin.

'Hey, you can't come in here!'

'Get the hell out of here before I — '

Louisa held up her hand, halting Octavia's and Nancy's protests. 'It's all right, ladies.'

Turning her back to the open front door, Louisa slowly walked towards Miss Warwick. 'Why don't you tell me what it is you think rightfully yours? This house? The furniture? Or maybe it's a list of Anthony's debts, now paid by me. Or maybe you'd like to know where you can find the jewellery and trinkets that were once here, but now donning the ears and necks of his creditors' wives? What is it you want exactly? I'm all ears.'

The other woman's gaze darted to Mr Hardman before she faced Louisa again. 'This house was meant to be mine forever. Anthony said so.'

'Anthony said a lot of things to both of us, I don't doubt.'

'But as he deemed to leave it in his will to you, I will be satisfied if you give me half of its worth. In cash.'

There was a prolonged silence before Nancy let out a screech of delight and then Louisa joined her friend's hilarity, Octavia grinning from ear to ear.

'She was your husband's mistress.' Nancy laughed. 'For God's sake, Lou, just get her out of here.'

Miss Warwick stamped her foot and planted her hands on her hips, which only succeeded in sending Louisa and her friends into another barrage of laughter.

'Stop laughing!' Miss Warwick stamped her foot again. 'I mean it. You owe me that money!'

Louisa wiped her eyes with the back of her index fingers and walked closer to Miss Warwick until barely a foot separated them.

Dissolving her smile, Louisa spoke very softly. 'I

273

owe you absolutely nothing. Do you understand? And if you come back here again, my friends and I will see that you are gone, vanished, never to be a problem to us or anyone else ever again.' She pulled back and smiled. 'Now, if there is nothing else ...'

Miss Warwick's throat moved as she swallowed before she stepped back, two spots of colour darkening her cheeks. 'You can't threaten me. Mr Hardman and I only wish to make a living as you and your new man are.'

'My new man ...' Heat warmed Louisa's cheeks as defensiveness for Jacob burned inside of her. 'He has nothing to do with you and you are sadly delusional if you think Mr Hardman would ever come anywhere near being the man that Jacob is.'

'Is that so? Well, in that case ...' Miss Warwick turned to Mr Hardman, a triumphant gleam in her eyes. 'Why don't you present our second option to Mrs Hill, John?'

Louisa could not believe the woman's audacity. 'Your second option?'

Nancy sniffed. 'Oh, this I must hear.'

Miss Warwick gripped John Hardman's arm and pushed him forward.

'Go on, tell her.'

He pulled back his shoulders and theatrically cleared his throat, his squinty eyes moving from Louisa to Nancy and Octavia and back again.

Louisa crossed her arms once more, trying hard to suppress the smile tugging at her lips. 'Well, pray continue, Mr Hardman. I'm all ears.'

'Ahem.' He tilted his chin. 'If you will not give

274

Miss Warwick what is duly hers, then we have an investment proposition. Miss Warwick has a little money put by and would like to make an investment in your brothel, with myself as her silent partner. In return for that investment, she will receive a third of all and any profits that you and your ladies earn. On top of that — '

'There's more?' Louisa raised her eyebrows, her smile breaking. 'Well, I ask that you refrain from elaborating further until I have had time to consider the first half of your investment proposition. Once I have done that, I will be in touch.'

Nancy shot to her side. 'Lou, you can't be serious.'

Louisa nodded at Mr Hardman and then Miss Warwick before holding her arm out and turning towards the door. 'Now, if you don't mind — '

Further words caught in her throat as her eyes met Jacob's where he stood at the front door, his face a mask of fury, his blue eyes burning with rage.

She swallowed. 'Jacob.'

His gaze stayed on Hardman. 'I believe the lady asked you to leave, John. I recommend you heed her request right now and take this woman with you before I lose the last thread of my patience.'

Neither of their unwanted visitors needed asking twice and John Hardman and Miss Warwick swept past Jacob and into the street.

Jacob stepped inside and slammed the door.

Louisa turned to her friends and laughed, swiping her hands together.

'Good riddance to bad rubbish. I don't think we'll be seeing them again.'

Nancy laughed and slipped her arm around Louisa's waist. 'Probably not, but I really wish we do. That was the best fun I've had in a really long time.'

Louisa met Jacob's eyes as Octavia came to Louisa's other side and put her arm around her shoulders.

United. Together. Strong.

'Well, Mr Jackson . . .' Louisa smiled. 'I do believe I am well and truly ready for the Great Exhibition.'

His gaze lingered on hers for a long moment before he gave a curt nod and headed for the stairs. Louisa frowned after him but let him go. No doubt the sight of John Hardman on their doorstep had once again triggered Jacob's tendency for violence.

All would be well come morning.

37

By the time Louisa had settled into the train compartment, Jacob sitting beside her on their way to London, she had accepted she was slowly, apprehensively, falling in love with him. Sometimes she was entirely convinced he felt the same way about her and the only thing preventing them from consummating that love was the mutual fear of what a deeper, more intimate relationship would ultimately mean for them, the house, Nancy and Octavia.

Every time Jacob was near, it took every ounce of Louisa's strength not to reach for him, to touch and kiss him. Yet, each time that pivotal, life-altering boundary came close enough for either one of them to cross, she or he moved away — afraid and unsure, resurrecting the distance between them to a more manageable and safer place.

It hurt a little that the space between them had become peppered with moments of almost palpable tension emanating from Jacob since Miss Warwick and Mr Hardman's unexpected visit to the house. Time and again, Louisa had raised the subject with him, but he always shut down any conversation with a curt response or shake of his head.

She gazed at his profile as he studied the pamphlet of sketches depicting what they could expect to see at the Great Exhibition, the pages crumpled and smudged from his constant perusal. The strong cut of his jaw, his defined cheekbones and brilliant blue eyes were just the beginning of what made Jacob . . . Jacob. He was everything Anthony had not been.

Jacob would never think of indulging her, buying her flowers or gifts.

Neither would he laugh at her mistakes or insist she do something she wasn't quite ready to do. Anthony had done all of these things, more often than not relishing in her discomfort, or heralding her smile as something only he could evoke.

She moved her gaze to the window as humiliation spread over her in a toxic wave. Anthony had held the power to make or break her and now, as she looked back in retrospect, he had basked in that dominance over and over again. With her, Miss Warwick, and possibly ten or twenty other women who had come within reaching distance of being the next Mrs Hill.

Louisa breathed deep, trying to calm the harried beat of her heart as a dark resentment threatened to take root inside of her. Even though she had managed to explain to Jacob how she had known nothing of Miss Warwick and the house's existence, of how Anthony had kept his mistress for two years without Louisa's knowledge, Jacob still retained his distance. She could only presume his anger was anchored towards Anthony rather than her. At least, she hoped so.

A fresh wave of humiliation swept through her. Not once had Jacob been judgemental, maybe a little terse but little else. Swallowing hard, Louisa sat a little straighter and shook off her melancholy. In time, Jacob would tell her whatever it was bothering him and, meanwhile, she would fight the instinct to add another layer of hatred towards a person or situation that had wronged, hurt or limited her chances of climbing out of an abyss mined throughout her adolescence. Her naïveté diminished with each experience and now she was becoming someone wiser and stronger.

She was her own woman now — Jacob his own man — and she wanted him to join her on a quest to heal themselves, whether that be together or apart.

He, too, carried the heavy wounds of his past: pain and frustration over his mother's death and the father who'd killed her continually festering beneath the surface. Sometimes Jacob looked at her and she thought him capable of being all she'd ever wanted, and then she would catch him in thought, in a place far, far away. The most terrifying darkness fell over his features, his hands unconsciously pulled into fists, and Louisa would shiver, retreat from him, unsure if she was brave enough to support someone so completely trapped in such deeply embedded and historical pain.

But she wanted him. So much. And she *would* have him. Even if it was only ever on this trip.

'They say it is impossible to see the entire Exhibition in a single day.'

She forced her thoughts into submission and smiled, her heart skipping to see the excitement in Jacob's eyes. 'Maybe they do, but I have a funny feeling you will ensure we try our best to disprove them.'

'When I was a boy . . .' He hesitated, his cheeks ever so slightly colouring.

279

'I had dreams. Dreams so big that they took me away from the bleak hopelessness of my upbringing, away from my father.'

Louisa's heart beat a little faster as the tiniest vulnerability pierced through the strong, outward presence that she often wondered if Jacob fought to constantly maintain. To see him exposed, however fleetingly, filled her with joy because these were the moments when she believed she saw the real Jacob — not her protector or doorman, but the man she loved.

Her confidant, her lover, maybe even her husband and father of her children . . .

'Tell me.' She smiled gently and took his hand, silently chastising herself for allowing such imaginings to get the better of her. 'Tell me what you once dreamed of.'

His gaze slowly inched over her face, lingering at her mouth before he looked at the pamphlet. 'I dreamed of playing an important part in industry.

In design and architecture. Of using my hands at the levers of mammoth machinery and engines, being the founder of great innovations with the potential to change the country . . . the world.' He turned, his beautiful smile so wide, her heart stumbled. 'I'd dream of my picture on the front of the newspaper . . . ' Stretching out his hand, he swept it in front of them like a banner. 'Mr J. Jackson, engineer extraordinaire, married to his beautiful wife and father to their three wonderful children.'

Shock reverberated through Louisa and she laughed, the sound nervous.

'Marriage and children? I never thought once

of you wanting — '

'A life without uncertainty and violence? Where I would come home every night to the same place, the same people?' He shook his head and turned away from her again. 'As I said, I was a boy when I dreamed these things. Back then, I believed anything was possible for everyone. By the age of fourteen, I had learned such achievements are only possible for a few.'

'That's not true. They are possible for everyone. We have to believe that or give up entirely.'

'Do *you* believe it?'

She looked away from his unrelenting gaze, doubt twisting and turning inside of her. 'I want to.' She faced him. 'I really do, but it's hard, isn't it?'

He nodded, uncertainty shadowing his eyes. She sensed he had more he wanted to say, but yet another of her sought-after moments had already passed as Jacob remained silent.

'Do you know what I've come to accept over the years?' she asked softly.

'That we have to use what God has given us in any way possible to bring us happiness.'

'And what has God given you?'

She shrugged, embarrassed of how little she had that really mattered in a world where she longed to believe her future might be unrecognisably different from her present.

'My face and body, of course.' She tried to smile, but it was so strained her bottom lip trembled. 'People have called me pretty since I was a child and, as I grew, men would look, stare . . . try to touch me. I soon learned looks and a nice figure can be commodities in this world as much as intelligence and wit.'

His jaw tightened. 'You are so much more than your looks, Louisa.'

'I'm not so sure. My looks have given me, however briefly, some wonderful moments of happiness. Of course, my face and body have also been the cause of some of the worst moments, too. That is my truth, Jacob and, like your father's cruelty taught you violence, my mother's abandonment taught me we only have ourselves to rely upon. She left me and never came back. I had no money, no home or security, yet — '

'You're still here.'

She nodded, relieved that he understood. 'Yes.'

He took her hand and looked hard into her eyes. 'Which means you have used more than what you claimed saved you. You are also resourceful, savvy, kind and strong.'

Unable to believe his compliments true, Louisa shook her head.

'Throughout my life, despite every reason to do so, I have never lost my ability to like and trust people. And right now, I trust you, Nancy and Octavia. That's what matters.' She squeezed his hand. 'It makes me sad that you have given up wanting a family of your own one day, or an occupation that you love. You shouldn't, not yet.'

He studied her and a little of the hardness left his eyes before he looked to the pamphlet again. Louisa pretended to search for something in her purse, but the trembling in her hands belied her confidence that one day they would both be truly happy, whether apart or together. In trying to bolster Jacob, she had tried to fortify herself and had undoubtedly failed on both counts. He probably thought her foolish or a liar.

How could she really be happy and live as a whore or even a madam?

Why would he believe her assertion that his dream of a wife and family could still come true when he was currently living with a woman who had shared her bed with so many others? That situation alone was enough to make him think this world a vile and lowly place.

Her own marriage had been a complete sham and Anthony had only married her because he'd wanted to own her. For all Nancy's insistence he had loved Louisa, she now knew his desire was to have a woman beneath him, not beside him . . . in every way.

Jacob would want commitment, faithfulness and loyalty and she was quite sure he would never consider her as a life partner after everything she had done . . . was still doing.

When tears leapt into her eyes, Louisa quickly looked to the window.

'How about just for today and tonight, we be those people?'

She froze, her stare still directed towards the passing buildings and bridges. 'What?'

He touched his finger to her chin, turning her head.

He smiled that toe-curling smile of his. 'Why don't we be the people we want to be just until we get on the train to come home tomorrow?'

'Jacob . . . ' Her heart swelled with love for him and Louisa fell a little deeper, the tension in her shoulders subsiding. 'We can't.'

'Why not?'

'Because . . . because it won't be real.'

He took her hand and lifted it to his lips, his fingers tight on hers. 'We'll make it real. Just for a single day and night.'

Louisa stared at him as he dropped her hand and looked to the pamphlet once again, his grin nearly stretching the breadth of his face.

Come what may, she was in love.

38

Jacob stared at the interior of the Crystal Palace's enormous dome, its magnificence welding his feet to the floor as hope, passion and possibility flowed through him.

When he and Louisa had arrived at London's Hyde Park hours before, a kaleidoscope of colour had greeted them as they were enveloped by the crowds. People had stormed towards the great structure, coats flapping in the breeze, dresses and hats glinting in the sunlight, parasols, canes and wheelchairs interspersed amid a blanket of human bodies.

'Come on, Jacob,' Louisa had laughed, pulling him forward. 'You look like a little boy at the circus.'

Barely able to contain his excitement, Jacob had been in awe of the Palace, its roof soaring towards the sky. He'd stepped forward, marvelling at the way the sun bounced from thousands of panes of glass, seeming to spark the Palace on fire. A glittering pyre of possibility set among bracken, leaves and foliage. Flags fluttering along its sides above arched windows and pillared entrances, fancy decoration and ornaments on every corner and plinth.

Crystal Palace was indeed a sight to behold.

And the country's consort — Prince Albert — was the man who had made it all a reality.

Louisa tightened her grip on his elbow and Jacob

blinked from his reverie as she leaned her temple against his shoulder. 'Are you happy, Jacob?'

'What do you think?' He laughed and clasped her hand where it lay on his forearm. 'We have walked around for hours, tasted, seen and heard things I'm not sure we ever will again and, still, I cannot believe any of these machines, inventions and ideas possibly can or will happen in our lifetime. Or even the next.'

'I don't think you're alone thinking that way. The looks I've seen on people's faces are almost comical.' She tugged on his arm and he dragged his gaze from the interior of the enormous glass dome. 'What was your favourite discovery?' she asked.

He stared deep into her violet eyes and suddenly he wasn't standing in an exhibition that felt as big as the entire country. There weren't thousands of people passing back and forth around them, chattering, laughing and exclaiming. Animals, machines and mystical wonders seemed to still in their glass boxes and metal cages; their screeching, cawing and lowing moving farther and farther away until all he saw and heard was Louisa.

'Jacob? I said, what is your fav — '

'You.' Jacob swallowed, the care he felt for her burning deep inside of him, palpable and real. He brushed a curl from her brow. '*You* are my favourite discovery.'

Surprise, and then delight, shone in her gaze before she blushed, a rare and beautiful thing that led Jacob to dip his head and press a brief kiss to her lips. She immediately stepped back, her eyes darting all around them.

'Trust me,' he said. 'No one is looking at us. Louisa . . . ' A sudden, urgent need to share with her all that he had been thinking and feeling since Hardman turned up at Carson Street coursed through him. Now was not the time. What he had to say, what he had to ask her, would surely spoil this wonderful time. 'Louisa . . . '

She frowned, her eyes concerned. 'What is it?'

'I need to matter to you.'

'What?'

'I need . . . to be important to you.'

She gripped his hand, two spots of colour darkening her cheeks. 'How could you think you are not important to me? You are so much a part of my life now, I can't imagine it without you.'

'Do you mean that?'

'Of course.'

Words battled inside his mind, tingling on his lips but he couldn't say them. Not yet. Not here.

He forced a smile. 'Shall we go?'

She grinned and nodded.

Wanting this once-in-a-lifetime experience to last as long as possible, Jacob walked slowly. He concentrated on every wonder they passed, soaking in the atmosphere created so skilfully by the designers who had displayed each of the world's discoveries and innovations the best way they could. From the British-produced, power-driven and manually operated agricultural machines, to the magnificence of the Indian Court, complete with every glinting treasure imaginable, to the great stuffed and richly adorned, life-sized elephant.

Onwards they walked, Louisa exclaiming at the

beauty of the stained-glass gallery and the wonder of the brightly coloured and intricately patterned wallpapers.

The wonders of the Great Exhibition were endless and the claims that it was an impossibility to see all in a day had been proven true.

Once they had left Hyde Park and merged with the crowds on the busy street, Jacob flagged down a carriage to take them to their hotel. Although they were both too exhausted to walk, Louisa clearly wasn't too tired to refrain from pointing out every famous landmark they passed, her beautiful eyes wide with wonderment and her smile captivating as she exclaimed and gasped.

'Can you believe everything we've seen?' She leaned closer to the window, craning her neck to see the top of a building. 'I can't believe we are actually here, can you?'

Jacob tried to focus on her words, yet saw nothing but her eyes, her hair, her smile . . . and all increased his desire to have her, to make love to her.

He turned away lest he reach for her and make a fool of himself.

This day away from Bath had allowed them the freedom to be true to themselves and each other. Her arm had barely left his, his fingers constantly finding their way to the small of her back. Tension to be alone with her only continued to grow, his trousers tightening across his groin as want of her formed the tenderest of images in his mind.

To touch her skin, kiss her breasts . . .

The carriage slowed to a stop and Jacob opened the door, offering his hand to Louisa. Once he'd paid the driver, Louisa took his arm and they climbed the stone steps into the hotel lobby.

She smiled up at him and his heart stumbled before she reached into her bag. 'Just a moment.'

Unease writhed in his gut as she reached into her purse and pulled her wedding ring from a small velvet drawstring bag. She discreetly slipped it onto her finger, her gaze lingering on the glittering circle of gold before she met his eyes, her smile strained. 'There. Let's go inside, shall we?'

He nodded, words painfully cutting into his tongue and jealousy stabbing mercilessly into his heart.

Walking through the wood-panelled lobby, the tap of their shoes echoed on the tiled floor. Decorated in bright white and glistening gold, the hotel should have felt more than a little overbearing, but somehow its smaller size created just the intimacy Jacob craved.

He looked towards some small circular tables bearing shaded lamps and ashtrays where guests enjoyed an afternoon drink. Women were dressed sedately, men suited and booted, their chatter and laughter bouncing from the walls and sash windows. He should suggest they indulge in a drink themselves even if all he wanted was to be entirely alone with her after the vast crowds of the Exhibition.

'You wait here,' he said. 'I'll collect our room key and then I'll see if I can find us a table for coffee.'

'Jacob?'

He stopped.

Her extraordinary eyes burned brightly with

something akin to expectation, but also a quiet confidence that only served to enhance his attraction.

She stepped forward and touched his arm. 'I don't want coffee.'

'Then what — '

'I want to go upstairs.'

His heart picked up speed and his groin twitched fully awake as though he were an adolescent barely growing whiskers, not a worldly-wise, street-savvy man of twenty-seven. Pure, heartfelt desire enticingly shadowed her gaze. Not the flirtation he'd seen her exhibit a hundred times in front of clients or with clients.

This was want of *him* ... of *them*. Together, alone, naked.

He lifted his fingers to her cheek, lower to her jaw before drawing them slowly along the curved line of her neck. She shivered, her eyes never leaving his and Jacob winked. 'I'll be right back.'

Anticipation, and maybe a little trepidation, twisted inside of him as he impatiently waited in line at the reception, almost snatching the keys from the man's hand when he finally handed them over. 'Thank you.'

He rushed back to Louisa, ignoring the amused arch of her eyebrows and twitching lips.

'Say nothing,' he said, barely able to contain his own smile. 'I am but a man.'

'Oh, Jacob.' She slid her hand into his elbow. 'I hope you are so much more than that.'

They walked upstairs as tormenting thoughts of her being with other men inched into his consciousness. Jacob straightened his spine, steadfastly pushing the taunting imaginings far away where they could not spoil this time with a woman he thought the world of, cared for more than he ever had anyone else.

He wanted to show her what she meant to him, how he would like to be with her even though they both knew it was an impossibility after this one precious night. Their agendas were not in line; their wants and wishes were too far removed. All Louisa wanted to focus on was the success of the Carson Street brothel and all he wanted was to find a place, an occupation where he truly fit.

More than that, there was Nancy and Octavia to think of. He couldn't imagine either of Louisa's trusted friends would be happy with him being on such intimate terms with the woman they looked up to in every way.

And they would be right to think him not good enough for Louisa — not constant enough in temper to be a man she could rely upon past day-to-day protection. He was flawed and impulsive. He knew it and so did Louisa's friends.

Otherwise, why would she be considering Hardman's suggestion of investment?

She might have said she trusted Jacob, but part of him knew Louisa would bolt if he ever asked for more than she was willing to give. Her husband had betrayed her, turned her life upside down and Jacob would keep his distance so that he could never inadvertently do the same. It was inevitable that one day he would have to leave Carson Street.

He unlocked the door to their room and Louisa entered ahead of him.

Dropping her bag to the floor, she walked to the dresser and slipped off her wedding ring. Turning, her eyes on his, she discarded her coat before walking to the bed. Facing him, she started to unbutton the tiny pearl buttons on the front of her dress. Slowly, Jacob closed the door and locked it, his erection straining. He needed to gain some control; take his time loving this wonderful creature who would be his for just a few more hours.

Walking towards her, he tugged at his necktie and unwound it. They stood in front of one another, eyes locked as they slowly undressed. Neither looked at each newly revealed inch of skin or moved another step closer.

Tension hummed between them on an invisible thread, connecting and joining. Desire permeated the room, filling it with an erotic, tangible aura.

He was naked, yet still her violet eyes never left his and he didn't know whether to laugh or cry at her composure, that she still hadn't risked a single glance over his body, over his . . .

She lifted her chemise over her head and stood naked.

His restraint lasted all of two seconds before his eyes drank in every inch of her. Words stuck like stones in his throat. She was perfect.

Habitual unworthiness edged in and Jacob's confidence faltered.

'No, Jacob.' She stepped closer and cupped his jaw. 'Don't think.'

He stared at her and fought his insecurities until a groan rose inside him and he covered her mouth with his, lifting her sharply off her feet making her gasp into his mouth as her fingers dug hard into his shoulders. Carrying her to the bed, Jacob's heart hammered as the weeks of trying to not look at her for too long, not to touch her too intimately or kiss her as often as he longed to, fell away, leaving him open, raw and consumed with longing.

They tumbled onto the bed and he pulled her on top of him, her breasts pressed hard against his chest as she rained kisses over his jaw, neck, collarbones. Fire burned through him as the urge to stop her screamed in his mind, but his resistance was parchment-thin as her beautiful, perfect figure writhed against him, sending sensation after sensation hurtling through his body.

He reached down and eased her onto her back. Staring into her eyes, Jacob relished the fire and lust he saw there. She pulled him to her, and they kissed, her leg coming up to rest her heel against his buttock. Her pubic hair teased and tempted his cock, but he wouldn't take her.

Not yet.

Pulling his lips from hers, he moved slowly downwards, darting kisses over her breasts and ribs, stomach and hips until he reached her core.

'Jacob . . . ' Her fingers scored into his hair. 'Please.'

His flicked out his tongue, used his fingers to excite and stimulate, over and over again, he tasted her and loved her until he knew she was ready for him, physically, emotionally . . . totally.

And then, only then, did he finally allow himself to satisfy his hunger.

39

Carson Street had been open for two months and pride filled Louisa as she descended the stairs. Business was building and over the last few weeks, the flow of customers had turned from sporadic to constant . . . and exclusive.

Neighbours either knew nothing of what went on inside the house, or else it didn't bother them due to the pains Louisa and Jacob had taken to ensure — after the repellent Mr Morrison — that only the most amiable of gentlemen entered.

As was usual, the moment Jacob came into her mind, Louisa's heart stuttered. They had lain in each other's arms, made love and talked late into the night as much as they could since their sojourn to London.

Although their attempts to keep their love-making to just a single night had dismally failed, neither had asked for more from the other, their personal feelings about their new intimacy never spoken of. After all, there was little need when such a connection anchored them. The only tension that continued to hover between them were the moments Louisa caught Jacob studying her, his thoughts hidden behind his stare as though he was deep in thought and did not see her at all.

But she suspected the opposite to be true. How could she not if he appeared so angry as he considered her?

Yet, no matter how often she pressed him, his

concerns remained unspoken. Only this morning, he had said, 'I will share my thoughts when the time is right.'

This, of course, had done little to reassure her and, instead, enhanced her foreboding.

What surprised her was that neither Nancy nor Octavia had mentioned the change in her relationship with Jacob. Not that she couldn't feel their curiosity or the need for answers brewing.

Talking and laughter echoed through the open parlour door as Nancy and Octavia entertained two gentlemen who were now their regulars. Well-bred and polite outside of the bedroom, the gentlemen's wants behind closed doors would have been unforgivable in polite society. Yet, their sexual kicks neither shocked nor appalled her friends. In fact, they were a walk in the park for Nancy and Octavia considering what they'd had to endure during their time hawking on the streets.

Times that neither Louisa, Nancy nor Octavia knew for certain would not, one day, return. The threat of regressing back to the lives they once lived hovered above them like a heavy axe waiting to fall, no matter how much they liked to imagine it wasn't there.

Walking into the parlour, Louisa forced a smile and nodded hello to the gentlemen as they sat on the sofa, Nancy and Octavia on their laps, feeding them fruit plucked from the basket on the table in front of them.

'Good evening, gentlemen. I was going to ask if there is anything you need.' Louisa raised her eyebrows, teasing. 'But I can see you're being ably taken care of.'

She walked to the drinks cabinet, lifted the crystal stopper from a decanter of claret.

'Mr Jameson has just proposed marriage, Louisa.' Nancy ran her finger down his whiskered cheek. 'But I've told him I couldn't possibly considering I am already weighing my options from the four other proposals I've received this week.'

'She's a hard woman to catch, Mrs Hill.'

Louisa sipped her drink, pleased with the playfulness in her friend's and Mr Jameson's eyes. 'Indeed, she is. I wonder if I might have to take in more girls to keep up with demand. Sooner or later, some lucky gentlemen are going to make my friends offers too good to refuse.'

Octavia rose from Mr King's lap, her usual seriousness vanished under her flirtatious smile, her eyes alight, making her more beautiful than ever.

'And Mr King has given me the most exquisite pearl necklace, Louisa. Look.' She reached into her bosom and slowly extracted a double string of glistening pearls, the silver clasp glinting under the gaslight. 'I think we should go upstairs, Mr King. I think the evening is warm enough for me just to wear these to bed, don't you?'

'I couldn't agree more.' Mr King slowly rose from the settee, his dark eyes glazed with lust as he studied Octavia. 'Excuse us, Mrs Hill.'

Louisa raised her glass in farewell as Octavia led him by the hand from the room. She turned to Nancy. Mr Jameson's face was obscured by her friend's, her fingers trailing back and forth over the front of his trousers as they kissed.

Smiling, Louisa left them alone and walked from the room.

Strolling into her study, her glass hovering at her mouth, Louisa came to an abrupt stop.

Jacob stood with his back to her staring through the window into the darkness, his arms crossed and his shoulders rigid.

Slowly putting her glass on her desk, she approached him and slipped her hand over his back and onto his shoulder. His corded muscles were stiff with tension. 'Jacob?'

He continued to stare through the window. 'Are the girls all right?'

'They're fine.'

'Good.'

Unease knotted her stomach and Louisa slipped her hand from his shoulder. She walked to her desk and sat. 'When are you going to tell me what is bothering you? I can't bear these moments of silence between us.'

Slowly, he turned and leaned his backside against the windowsill, his arms still crossed over his broad chest. His blue eyes bored unblinkingly into hers.

Resisting the urge to turn away, Louisa put her glass to her lips and drank, watching him over the rim.

'What are your plans, Louisa?'

'My plans?' She lowered the glass. 'With regards to what?'

'This house. Your future. Your work . . .'

She raised her eyebrows, her heart beating a little faster as her defences automatically heightened. 'And you?'

Almost every day she woke and wondered if this would be the day that Jacob told her they couldn't go on as they were — that things had to change.

It wasn't just the times she noticed him watching her, but also the way his jaw grew tight when she laughed or flirted with a client. Then he'd sweep from the hallway or parlour as if unable to witness any more.

'Although I'm just a small part of everything that goes on here,' he said, dropping his arms and gripping the sill either side of him, 'I think I have the right to know what you have in mind for the future.'

Protectiveness for the life she was building swept through her. This house, Nancy and Octavia would always remain her priority, no matter what. She might be falling in love with Jacob, but surely he understood what would always be of paramount importance to her? She had not hidden Anthony's death or betrayals from Jacob, and he knew almost all of her struggles and desires.

She sipped her wine. 'I've only thought ahead in terms of making the house as successful as it can be. The business continues to grow and I'm toying with idea of finding new girls. Not to live here, but to work each evening. What do you think?'

He pushed away from the windowsill and walked to the bureau; lifting some papers, he looked down at them. 'What do *I* think?'

His tone dripped with sarcasm and she glared at his turned back. 'You are as much a part of this house as the rest of us. You know that.'

'Do I?' He dropped the papers and turned, his blue eyes angry. 'Then I suppose I have every right to know if you intend to ever take another client to bed.'

There it was.

She had suspected his irritability was grounded in her occasionally sleeping with culls but had hoped it wasn't so. Since their trip to London, she had purposefully avoided it and, so far, it had been easy enough as the house settled into a steady flow of regulars for Nancy and Octavia. It had always been Louisa's intention to take care of the business side of things as much as possible and her friends had wholeheartedly agreed with the arrangement.

However, she had never said to them — or Jacob — that she would not take a cull if necessity demanded it.

Lifting her glass, she sipped, slowly lowered it to the table. 'I never promised you that I would stop entirely, Jacob.'

'Is that any kind of answer?'

'What other kind of answer is there? The way I run this house gives me complete control over my life for the first time, even if I have had to return to my past in a way I never wanted or expected. I'm in charge now and can make life better, not just for myself, but for Nancy, Octavia and possibly others who are in the situation that I once was.' She shook her head, anger burning hot in her chest. 'How can you not understand that I once trusted Anthony, my husband, but he left me without warning and only this house to my name. I will not make the mistake of giving away what is mine ever again.'

His gaze locked on hers and a strange battle

took up arms inside of her.

Freedom and possibility versus vulnerability and fear until she worried she had made a dire mistake allowing their relationship to deepen. Yet, deep inside, she treasured the joy and happiness that came with being with a man she thought saw her as an equal. A man who she'd thought understood her past and why she was working to ensure a different future.

'So, it is as I thought.'

Fighting to keep her irritation under control, Louisa kept her voice purposely controlled. 'Why are you asking me these things now, Jacob? Is it because we have made love? That you now consider me yours?'

'Of course not.'

'Then what —'

'Why haven't you spoken to be about the fact you are considering Hardman as an investor?'

She stilled. 'What?'

'You heard me.'

She stood and planted her hands on the desk, unsure whether to laugh or cry at the ludicrousness of his suggestion. 'I never spoke to you of it because I dismissed the proposition from my mind the moment the words came out of that man's mouth, that's why. I didn't raise it with you again because I assumed you'd find Caroline Warwick and John Hardman as ridiculous as I do.' She briefly squeezed her eyes shut, her heart racing as she tried to contain her temper. 'My God, Jacob, even Nancy hasn't mentioned the investment and she isn't one to sit on any major change lightly.'

'This isn't about Nancy, this is about us, Louisa.

300

You should have spoken to me. I've been waiting for you to tell me exactly what Hardman said. To ask my advice or opinion.' His cheeks mottled as Jacob came forward and gripped the back of the chair opposite her. 'But you've said absolutely nothing.'

'And now I've told you why. If that is not enough —'

'Do you know how hard it's been for me not to hunt Hardman down? To warn him not to come near you again? But I didn't, for you.'

'Meaning what?'

A muscle twitched in his jaw. 'Because I thought eventually you'd reach out to me. That you'd need me past standing at your damn door.'

Anger bubbled inside Louisa at the threat to her new life, her independence and self-preservation. How dare he demand such knowledge of the business from her? 'This house is *mine*, Jacob. What I do with it, what decisions I make have nothing to do with you.'

He glared until a wry smile curved his lips and he pushed hard at the chair and straightened. 'I see. Well, I'm sorry, Louisa. It won't work that way for me.'

She crossed her arms, her body trembling. 'It won't work with me having more control than you? More ownership of the decision-making in my own house. How dare you?'

'How dare I?' He paced a few steps away before whirling around, his eyes blazing with fury. 'I dare because I've told you things I've told no other living soul. I dare because I've made love to you over and over again.

I dare because I care about you, Nancy and Octavia more than I ever have anyone else since my mother. That, Louisa, is why I dare.'

Her self-confidence wavered as the way Anthony assumed her a fool, used and humiliated her, rushed through her. 'You are here because I want you here. You are important to the success of this house and you are important to me. But that doesn't mean — '

'That I am important enough to ever be your true partner.'

Shock, disappointment and blind stupidity washed over her. Had he planned all along to one day have a hand — an investment — in her business?

'What?'

He put his hands on his hips and paced back and forth before stopping abruptly a second time. 'When I left Henry to come here, I vowed that I would never feel under obligation to anyone ever again. I would come and work for you, but for how long would be decided by me and only me. Yet, it seems I'm right back where I started. I thought we had something special, that you trusted me. I won't stay where I am, little more than another damn cog in someone's else wheel to make money.'

Louisa shook her head, unsure what to say or think when so many conflicting emotions warred inside of her. 'If anyone should feel that way about me, it should be Nancy and Octavia. Lord above, Jacob, you are our muscle. I don't ask you to do anything more than protect us if we need it. I am not using you. You knew what the job was when you came here.'

302

'The job has changed, Louisa.'

'Why?'

'Because I lo . . . because I need more from you.'

Every instinct to protect herself rose. Just the thought of handing over even a single piece of the house, even to Jacob, made her recoil. 'The house is mine and always will be.'

Disappointment, anger . . . hurt passed through his gaze and her heart ached, but she didn't move or retract her words.

Stepping back, he raised his hands in surrender. 'Then it's time for me to go. I'll start looking for someone to replace me. You should too.'

He walked towards the door and Louisa fought the panic rising on a tidal wave inside of her. 'Jacob, don't . . .'

But he'd gone.

Pressing her lips tightly together, Louisa lunged forward and snatched her glass from the desk. She drained it, tears burning behind her eyes.

40

Staying at Carson Street the night before had been the hardest thing for Jacob to endure since he'd arrived. Since their return from London, he had crept into Louisa's bedroom night after night, the house quiet and them finally alone to make love and talk until sunrise.

Now, after a fitful night's sleep, he strode across town towards his old lodgings, his heart a mess and his thoughts dangerous. As he passed the Abbey, he bought some roses and a bag of fresh oranges before making his way through the crowds. Stopping by a young lad and mother as they lay huddled together beneath a blanket, he dug into the paper bag and offered the boy an orange.

He took it slowly, his gaze wary before Jacob plucked one of the roses from the bunch and handed it to his mother. He winked at her and the boy's smile gave Jacob a little cheer to his otherwise heavy heart.

One good deed deserved another, isn't that what they said? He hoped Doreen would be as generous with her advice once he arrived at the house.

God knew, he needed someone to ground him amid the storm that only raged harder and deeper in his heart. His argument with Louisa had sent his emotions into turmoil and his usually quick decision-making was all over the damn place.

To add to his aggravation, he'd heard on the grapevine that the Killer was back in business and fighting in the underground club by the river within the hour. The rumour all over town was that today's challenger wasn't much of one at all but the boxing-loving public were braying for the Killer's blood regardless, hankering for someone to come and finish his reprehensible fighting once and for all.

The excitement surrounding this afternoon's fight seemed to be reaching fever pitch and Jacob just hoped his instinct that Henry and Colin would be there spectating was right. He needed to arrive at the house and find Doreen alone. Otherwise, Henry would be on Jacob's back the moment he walked through the door. A potential rematch on his lips. Jacob had heard the prize money being offered to anyone who defeated the Killer was astronomical, which proved just how badly people wanted the man's face in the sawdust beaten and bloody.

Reaching the lodgings, Jacob knocked on the door, furtively looking over his shoulder. If he could avoid it, he'd prefer that Henry didn't learn of his being here at all. His ex-manager would only count it as another triumph and evidence of Jacob's weakness.

Which he couldn't deny was entirely true.

The door swung open and Doreen's face immediately lit with fondness.

'Well, look who it is! Come in, come in. You are a sight for sore eyes, I can tell you.'

'Are you alone?' Jacob stepped into the hallway. 'I could do without Henry's crap today.'

She raised her eyebrows, her green eyes glinting with knowing. 'Like that is it? Well, it's your lucky day. He and Colin are at the club.'

'As I'd hoped they'd be. Here.' He thrust the roses and bag of oranges towards her. 'For you.'

'Aren't you the charmer?' She stuck her nose into the blooms and inhaled. 'Thank you, sweetheart. Come on, the tea is brewing.'

Hanging his coat and hat on the bottom of the stairs, Jacob followed her into the kitchen and sat at the table. Rare nerves leapt and jumped in his stomach as he listened to Doreen's familiar humming as she made the tea.

In truth, he had no idea how Doreen was supposed to help untangle the mess he'd got himself into over Louisa.

'Here we go.' She placed the teapot next to the cups and saucers that lay in permanent residence on the table. 'I'll pour, you talk.'

He exhaled a shaky breath, hating his feebleness . . . hating that he was here at all. 'I think I'm going to have to leave Carson Street.'

She slowly pushed a filled cup towards him, her canny gaze studying him. 'There are two things I question about that statement. One, you *think* and two, you *have* to.'

Staring into the depths of his tea, Jacob tried not to fidget under her scrutiny. 'She's . . . made it pretty damn impossible for me to stay.'

'Hmm . . . ' Doreen lifted her cup to her mouth. '*She's* made it impossible?

Or, as I suspect, you and that stubborn head of yours have made it impossible?' She sipped and lowered her cup. 'Is this because you've gone and

306

fallen in love with the woman?'

He swallowed, his mouth dry. 'No.'

'Liar. And I'll stake ten guineas that you fear for her as you did for your ma.'

Pain burned hot and fast around his heart. He tightened his jaw. 'Of course I don't.'

'Liar. Do you want her to want you as you want her?'

Irritation hummed dangerously inside him and he glared. 'No.'

Doreen raised her eyebrows, her eyes shadowed with disbelief. 'Three lies. Three pretty hefty denials. Seems to me, Jacob Jackson, our Mrs Hill has got you hook, line and sinker.'

He curled one hand into a fist under the table and opened his mouth to speak —

'The question is,' Doreen continued, her fingers drumming up and down on the table, 'are you going to be a damn fool and let that woman get the better of you? Or are you going to stand up and own what's messing with your heart and decide what you're going to do about it?'

'You don't know what you're talking —'

'Because the way I see it, you've never shown anything but kindness to a lot of people, but this is different. Whatever pulled you to that house had nothing to do with kindness then, and it certainly has nothing to do with it now. It's clear from the look on your face that you love her, Jacob. You want to protect her.' She lifted her tea and smiled. 'But I reckon Mrs Hill is her own woman. Strong. Knows her own mind and that is driving that thick head of yours mad.'

He scowled. 'So I'm thick *and* weak. Thanks a

lot.'

'You're welcome.'

He glared as she continued to smile before squeezing his eyes shut. 'Fine.

I love the woman.' He opened his eyes. 'But that doesn't change anything.'

'It changes everything. What does she want?' Doreen's smile slowly dissolved, her eyes sombre and caring on his. 'What does she fear that's stopping her from loving you back?' She reached across the table and gently gripped his fingers. 'I find it hard to believe any woman on this earth would not give themselves to you freely unless something big, something genuinely frightening, held them back. Do you know what or who has put the fear in her?' She squeezed his hand. 'More importantly, what can you do to help her really see you for who you are?'

Sickness rolled through his stomach and Jacob slowly pulled his hand from Doreen's before swiping his fingers over his face. 'She's been hurt.

Let down.'

'And?'

'And now she won't allow anyone too close. Her life, her terms.'

'Well, to my mind, there's nothing wrong with that. Isn't that the way you've led your own life up until now?' She sipped her tea. 'Although I'm thinking your way of looking after your own interests has fallen to the wayside since moving into Carson Street.'

'And I'm a bloody fool for allowing that to happen. What the hell was I thinking by agreeing to this job?' He shook his head, self-loathing twisting and turning in his gut. 'I know how the world works. Time and time again, I've stopped myself feeling anything for anyone. Kept my head down.

Boxed and earned a wage. I'm not a man for settling down. I need the rage that runs through my blood. *That* is my lifeline, not a woman, and certainly not a damn brothel housing three of them.'

'Calm down.'

His pulse thundered in his temple. 'How in God's name could I have let things go this far? I've made love to her, laughed with her. Went to bloody London with her, for crying out loud.'

'You did?' Doreen grinned. 'Well, Jake, that's wonderful. You went to the Great Exhibition, didn't you? All these years you've talked about invention and Lord only knows what else. What was it like?'

'I don't want to talk about that. I don't want to remember that day. That's when everything went down the bloody pan.'

'Codswallop. That's when you fell for her, wasn't it?'

He turned away from her, concentrated on digging his finger over and over into the surface of the table. 'I'm my father's son. I thrive on violence and bad feeling. I'm strong and I've proven it over and over again.'

'Then bloody well be strong.' She abruptly stood and stalked to the larder in the corner of the room, took out a couple of plates. 'This is your chance to prove that strength. You need to go back to Carson Street and see where this new path leads you.' She put a covered cake on the table and walked to the drawer, extracting a knife. She turned and pointed it at him, anger blazing in her eyes. 'What are your plans otherwise? To box until you're killed? Do you really think now you've found love that you can live the rest of your life resisting it?'

She jabbed the knife into the cake and cut him a generous slice, putting it on the plate. 'Eat.' She sat down. 'You're afraid. "Course you are, but you're not stupid. Give her time. Mark my words: some way, somehow, you'll come together if it's meant to be.'

'How is that likely when she won't even meet me halfway? I have to be more than a lackey to her, Doreen. I want to be her partner. In everything.'

She stopped slicing a second piece of cake and stared, the confusion in her eyes slowly changing to comprehension. 'Ah, I see. This is about your own self-importance.'

'It's got nothing to do with my bloody — '

'You're a man, aren't you? Of course it's to do with you and your feelings. The question is, how can you be her partner? Is it money? Is that what she wants?'

He closed his eyes and pushed his fingers into his closed lids.

'Everything was going along nicely until some bastard not worthy of licking her damn boots offers to invest in the house.'

'Why did that change anything?'

He opened his eyes. 'Because it made me furious.'

'Because it never occurred to you to ask her

310

such a thing?' Doreen pushed a slice of cake onto the second plate. 'Then raise the damn money, Jake. If that's what it takes to make you feel you have something real to offer her, to enable you to protect her, to be with her. Raise the money and prove to her that you're here to stay and you respect what she wants to do with her life.'

Jacob stared at her. Was she right? Would offering Louisa his investment in the house prove to her that he didn't want to stop her ambition? Ease some of the rage in his heart? Would it be enough for her to know he believed in her?

He met Doreen's gaze as the possibility of some potentially easy cash coming his way poked and prodded at him. His heart raced with adrenaline.

'I've heard the Killer is back in town again.'

41

Louisa stared at the man sitting across her desk and battled the horrible feeling she was committing adultery. It felt so wrong to be considering other doormen behind Jacob's back. Yet, it was he who had left the house before dawn that morning without communication of where he was going or even if he would return.

The only saving grace had been when she'd shamefully crept into his room, relieved to find his belongings strewn about the place as usual.

She was doing nothing wrong by interviewing this man. Jacob's obstinance had put her in this situation. The fault lay with him and him alone.

Inhaling a long breath, Louisa forced a smile. 'The hours are from eight in the evening to two in the morning. You will be expected to be here on time and not leave before the last gentleman has departed. The safety of my girls is more important to me than any client or any amount of money they might spend. It will be your continual task to ensure the women who work here are happy and unharmed at all times.'

Gruff, in no way handsome — and certainly no Jacob — the man grinned as he leaned forward, his eyes alight with lust. 'I'll protect them, Mrs Hill, don't you worry about that. How many girls work here exactly?'

The lecherous glint in his eyes caused revulsion to twist inside her and Louisa made up her mind.

He was leaving. Right now.

He glanced towards the closed study door. 'Do you offer them for free to your doorman?'

'What?'

He wiggled his eyebrows. 'Your girls. Do they come as part of the job?'

Louisa stood. 'I think we're finished here, Mr Fielding. I'll see you to the door.'

'Hey, wait a minute. All I'm asking — '

There was a knock on the door before it was pushed open and Nancy peered into the room, her smile wide. 'Sorry to interrupt, only there's someone here to see you.'

Before Louisa could agree or deny the visitor access, Nancy had reached behind her and grabbed someone's arm. She practically threw Jacob into the room before slamming the door closed behind her.

Shock reverberated through Louisa as Jacob's eyes briefly met hers before falling on Mr Fielding.

'Who's this?' Jacob demanded.

She put her hands on her hips, hoping her pleasure and surprise at Jacob's return didn't show on her face considering his rude arrogance. 'Mr Fielding, this is Mr Jackson. Jacob, Mr Fielding.'

Mr Fielding narrowed his eyes and cautiously held out his hand. 'Mr Jackson.'

Jacob ignored his hand and blatantly appraised the other man from head to toe. His eyes blazing with anger, his cheeks mottled. 'What do you want?'

Foreboding whispered through Louisa. What did he think he was doing?

313

Did he intend to punch Mr Fielding where he stood? Jacob glared at Mr Fielding with the same look on his face that always scared her. Whenever Jacob wore this particular expression she remembered his fighting; remembered the violence he often felt and had used when necessary. This side of him was discomfiting and she had to make it stop.

'Jacob.'

He continued to glare at Mr Fielding even when the other man took a step back, the colour seeping from his face.

Nerves rippled through Louisa even as her annoyance rose. She rounded the desk and stormed to the door. 'Thank you for dropping by, Mr Fielding.'

She pulled open the door and looked at Nancy where she stood a little way along the hallway, feigning interest in a vase of flowers. 'Nancy? Would you please see Mr Fielding to the door? Thank you.'

Louisa stood straight-backed, her body humming with awareness of Jacob's proximity, tension permeating the air around him. Mr Fielding tossed a scowl at Jacob and then Louisa, before stomping from the room.

Shoving the door shut, Louisa locked it and rounded on Jacob. 'What is wrong with you? You can't come in here, throwing your weight around like a damn ape. Was it really necessary to speak to someone I'm in conference with that way?'

'In conference?' He took off his hat and threw it onto her desk, heedless to the papers and bundles lying there. 'He was here for my job, wasn't he?'

'*Your* job?' Indignant, she fisted her hands on her hips. 'Didn't you leave, Jacob? As far as I knew, never to return. What were your intentions just now? Did you think to pummel the man? Beat him senseless and then throw him over your shoulder and into the street?'

He held her gaze.

'Answer me.'

'I might have if he hadn't left so swiftly.'

'And you think that makes you a man? To punch and hurt people?' She stood in front of him, hating that his height meant she was forced to tip her head back. 'I don't like violence, Jacob. How many times?'

'Then why the need for a doorman? If there is any trouble here, what do you expect me to do, Louisa? Pat the offender on his bloody shoulder?'

'You know very well what I mean. Unnecessary violence. I hate it.'

'Unnecessary violence? Violence is a necessary evil whether you like it or not.'

'Oh, when are you going to stop believing such nonsense?'

He gripped her wrist as she brushed past him, his blue eyes burning with fury. 'You're glad I'm back, violence or no violence. I daresay you've checked my room. Everything I own is still there so whatever you might say, you were safe in the knowledge I hadn't disappeared.'

Louisa's heart thundered, her pulse beating under his fingers. God, she longed to pull his face to hers and kiss him. Press her body hard against his, have his hands rip at the hooks on her bodice . . .

She swallowed and snatched her arm from his grasp. 'I'm not a mind reader nor a fortune teller.

How was I supposed to know you did not mean every word you said? You told me to replace you and that's what I am trying to do.'

'And can you replace me?'

The innuendo hung heavy in the air as Louisa struggled to retain her dignity when all she wanted to do was tell him he was entirely irreplaceable to her. Personally and professionally. Pride battled with desire as his beautiful blue eyes stared into hers, his handsome face unmoving, his strong shoulders still with tension.

She swallowed, her body trembling. 'No, Jacob. As much as it pains me, I don't think I can.'

He came closer, his gaze on her mouth, her hair, her eyes. Gently, he cupped her cheek before lowering his mouth to hers. To her shame, she slumped against him, her tongue finding his as she grasped the wide, strong circles of his upper arms. They kissed deeper, their tongues tangling until she could feel bruising branded on her lips.

She pulled back, her strength renewed. 'I won't give up what I'm building here. Nothing's changed.'

'Everything's changed and you know it.'

'Not my wish to be free of a man's control. Not my wish to not have to lean on anyone ever again. Including you.'

A flash of frustration sparked in his gaze before he closed his eyes, his jaw a hard line. 'Well, then, I suppose we'll have to find a way to make it work.' He opened his eyes. 'Because I want you, Louisa. I think I'm coming to love you and I can't — I won't — leave you alone in this house or have someone other than me ensure your safety, Nancy's and

Octavia's. So, what's it to be? Do we find a way to make this work? Or would you prefer finding a way to live with me being here and hating me?'

She planted her hands on her hips, her whole body wanting him, yet despising him. 'Are you telling me what I can and cannot do?'

'No.'

Annoyance made her heart beat faster and she glared. 'Yes, you are.

You're not listening to me. I won't be held hostage to any man ever again.'

'Then somehow I'm going to have to become your partner. I'll wait for as long as it takes for you to trust me, maybe even love me, but I'm not leaving.'

She stared into his eyes, her fear escalating at the pure, unadulterated sincerity in his gaze. Weakness threatened and she fought against it, writhed against it, but the power of him was too strong, too powerful to resist. She was falling for him and her stupidity was only deepened by how vehemently he'd displayed his honour despite her rejection.

'Kiss me.' She tilted her chin. 'Just damn well kiss me.'

He slowly smiled and stepped closer, grasping her waist and lifting her atop the desk. Roughly, he parted her legs and stood between them despite the barrier of her skirts and gripped her face in his hands. 'I love you. Do you understand? I bloody love you.'

Tears pricked her eyes and she defiantly blinked them back. 'Then show me how much. Right here, right now.'

He heeled off his boots, reached for his belt buckle, his fiery gaze on hers. 'And afterwards?'

'You can show me again.'

42

Jacob walked into the underground club and squinted through the dense fog of cigar and pipe smoke. The place stank of ale and male sweat, the sawdust beneath his feet scattered with spat tobacco, horse shit and God only knew what else.

These types of places were once his norm, but not anymore. Now he was only here as a means to an end. Tonight's fight against the Killer would be Jacob's last and even though it bothered his conscience that Louisa might not forgive him for fighting, he had to focus on the money: the money he could invest in Carson Street, in Louisa and her ambitions.

Deciding to fight had been cemented when Henry and the Killer's manager had set the match on a Monday night. The one night each week the brothel was closed. Jacob's being here was fate.

Of course, the chosen night also had a lot with the club's hope that, even though the Killer had become a crowd puller, the spectators should be fewer than they would be on a weekend. Fingers crossed, the reduced crowd meant there was less chance of the constabulary coming knocking.

'All set, Jakey?'

Jacob turned from watching the men and women around him roaring and cackling, baying for blood as the warm-up fighters sparred and punched, fuelling the audience's excitement in anticipation of the main event.

'Yeah, all good,' Jacob murmured and raised his eyebrows. 'We're still agreed that you only get quarter cut of the winnings, right?'

Henry's jaw tightened as he looked towards the ring. 'It's not as though I've much choice in the matter, is it?'

'No, you haven't. So we're agreed?'

'Yes, Jake, we're agreed.'

Henry turned. 'But if you win, I'm betting you'll want me to sort out who you fight next.'

'There won't be a next time. If I come out of this match alive, it will be my last fight. After tonight, we're finished as far as boxing is concerned. Got it?'

The silence stretched as Jacob stared straight ahead, ignoring the strength of Henry's glare as it drilled into his temple.

'You're a bloody fool,' Henry said as he snatched his hat from the bar. 'I hope he smacks ten bales of shit out of you.'

Jacob smiled and raised his bandaged hand in acknowledgement before Henry walked away.

A wave of quiet hushed through the club and Jacob pulled back his shoulders before inhaling a long breath through flared nostrils. The first fight had finished and now the audience looked towards the back door of the darkened club. Tension hovered over the spectators, every face etched with barely suppressed excitement as they stood on their toes, necks craned to watch the Killer emerge.

A huge rumble of applause and cheering broke out as he came out and stopped in front of Jacob.

Tension rippled through every muscle in Jacob's

body as he calmly held the intensity of the Killer's pale eyes. Adrenaline pumped through Jacob, his heart picking up speed as he clenched and unclenched his fists.

This was one fight there was no chance he'd lose.

The Killer nodded and smiled and Jacob did the same before the Killer led the way to the ring, his huge bulk swaggering from side to side, his smile stretched the breadth of his face.

Jacob narrowed his eyes. There was little point in denying the man's size or muscle. After all, Jacob knew first-hand just how powerful the Killer's punch was as much as he was familiar with his potentially lethal tactics.

Tactics that had, hopefully, been dealt with tonight as he and the Killer were checked over by the docker who was acting as referee, their bandaged hands and trousers patted over for any weapons, rudimentary or otherwise.

Once done, the referee stood back, raised his hand, looked at Jacob and then the Killer . . .

'Begin!'

The roar of the crowd grew in volume as spectators bounced on the balls of their feet, their fists punching the air in Jacob's peripheral vision. He mentally blanked them all out until his only focus was the Killer.

Hands raised, they slowly circled each other.

Jacob watched him, gaining strength and confidence from the new sombreness in the Killer's gaze, the unusual rigidness of his body. Suddenly Jacob saw with complete clarity and understanding that the Killer was nothing without a weapon.

A legal and moral fight was beyond the man's ability, beyond his skill.

Winning this fight would not take long at all.

Pulling back his fist, Jacob whacked the Killer a hard punch to the jaw and his head whipped back before he came back with a right-hand swipe of his own that juddered through Jacob's face, his teeth clattering.

Again and again, Jacob pummelled the Killer's face and body, jabbing hard and precisely, pushing every ounce of his fire, anger and experience into the onslaught. Time and again, the Killer caught Jacob a worthy punch but it wasn't enough. Nowhere near . . .

Clenching his teeth, Jacob pulled back his arm and punched the Killer hard in the ribs with his right fist before swinging his left and ramming in full force into the Killer's face. Bone cracked, blood flew, and the audience erupted as the Killer hit the sawdust, sending dust flying.

The referee bent over the Killer, his hands on his thighs. 'You out? Can you stand?'

The Killer's eyes met Jacob's, his humiliation and mortification flashing quickly before he closed his eyes and dropped his head to the dust.

'And he's out!'

The referee straightened and grabbed Jacob's wrist, thrusting his arm into the air. 'And the winner is Jacob 'The Man' Jackson!'

The applause swept over Jacob, his gaze still locked on the Killer as he willed him to come around. Nothing mattered until he spoke to the man for the first and very last time.

His manager came into the ring and gave a few

slaps to the Killer's cheeks until his eyes opened. He looked at his manager and then Jacob before allowing his manager to duck under his arm and lift him to his feet.

They moved to shuffle past Jacob when he stuck out his hand, planting it to the Killer's chest.

'I hope it's as clear to you as it is to me that you are no fighter. You're nothing at all without a blade. It ends here, got it? No more illegal boxing, no more fucking bloodshed.'

'To hell with you,' the Killer sneered, blood lining his teeth. 'This isn't over, Jackson. Just watch your back now and forever, you son of a bitch.'

Jacob smiled and stood back, letting the Killer and his manager fight their way through the crowd waiting to get to Jacob. Their congratulatory slaps landed on his shoulder, the occasional rub to his head as he watched the Killer until he disappeared into the club's back room.

'You're a rich man, Jakey.' Henry laughed as he came up beside him, his arms crossed as he stared towards the back-room door. 'A rich man who has a few years of fighting left in him yet, I reckon.'

Jacob pinned him with a glare. 'It's over. I'm collecting my money and I don't want you to speak to me about boxing ever again. If I stop by the house it will be to see Doreen and Colin. If you're there, I'll be glad to see you but one word about fighting, Henry, and our association is finished.'

Walking away from him, Jacob made his way through the crowd to the makeshift bar. One pint and he'd collect his winnings . . . then it would be time to return to Carson Street.

43

'Louisa, you need to stop pacing about the room. Jacob will be back soon.'

Louisa spun around and started another circuit around the parlour. 'It's almost eight o'clock, Octavia. Where in the world is he?'

'Why does it matter? You know he likes to visit his old housekeeper.

He's probably been waylaid somewhere.' She put the novel she was reading in her lap, her brow furrowed. 'I'm sure he's fine.'

'Fine? Jacob is never fine.' Louisa walked to the window and peered out into the street. 'Is Nancy at the White Hart?'

'Yes, and I'm sure she would have sent a messenger if Jacob was there.'

'Which means he isn't.' Louisa spun away from the window and planted her hands on her hips. 'Tell me again what she said Jacob told her before he left.'

Octavia's frown deepened as she took a fortifying sip of wine. 'He said he was heading into town, but Nancy had seen him earlier poring over an article about the Killer's fight tonight. She suspects he was heading to the club. Here.'

Louisa practically snatched the newspaper from Octavia's hand, her eyes shooting straight to the tiny column that had been circled and mentioned the Killer's fight at the club this very night. Strangely, there was no mention of his opponent, only a lot of insinuation and speculation.

'This tells me nothing,' Louisa cried, tossing the paper onto the chair beside her. 'What if it's him?'

'Who?'

Impatience thrummed through Louisa, nerves tightening her stomach.

'What if the Killer is fighting Jacob tonight?'

'Surely not?' Octavia's eyes widened with alarm. 'He wouldn't . . . would he?'

'Oh, God.'

'What?'

Louisa pressed a hand to her stomach, her mouth dry. 'Of course. This is all my fault.' She closed her eyes before snapping them open and storming towards the parlour door. 'Oh, Jacob.'

'Where are you going?'

Louisa put her hand on the doorknob and faced Octavia, now standing, her face pale. 'Louisa?'

'He's going to fight again, Octavia. He's going to raise the money he thinks he needs to invest in the house.'

'Jacob wants to invest in the house? Why?'

'Because he thinks by doing so, he and I will become true partners in every sense of the word.'

Octavia flashed one of her rare smiles. 'Well, all power to Jacob.'

'All power? That's the last thing I want for him and so should you,'

Louisa snapped, irritation warming her cheeks. 'The man is not thinking of our partnership at all. He is most likely thinking how he could run this house better than me. What changes he would make.'

'Louisa, Jacob would never think like that. He adores you.'

'Hmm. Funny that Nancy once said the same thing about Anthony.' She trembled, her worry for Jacob incredibly annoying and undoubtedly misplaced. 'How will he ever invest in the house, in us, if he is lying on the floor of a ring dead to the world? Right, well, that's decided then.'

'What is?'

'We're going to find him,' she said, yanking open the door. Then she stopped. 'We can't leave Nancy to come back to an empty house. She'll panic and then all hell will break loose.' Louisa gave a curt nod, ignoring the warnings screaming in her head. 'I must go alone. You stay here and when Nancy returns I want you to convince her that all is well and I'll soon be back.'

'But everything is not well.'

'Octavia, please. Just do as I ask.'

Louisa strode into the hallway and hurried upstairs to her bedroom. Once inside, she retrieved her boots and hat, her gaze continually drawn towards the window and her hearing strained as she hoped against hope that she might hear Jacob's voice downstairs.

With her shoes on and her hat pinned in place, she grabbed her purse before hurrying downstairs.

Octavia waited with her arms crossed, her blue eyes dark with concern. 'I really don't think this is a good idea. What if something happens to you? How will I know? Not to mention Jacob's reaction should he return and find I let you walk about the streets at night alone.'

'Let me?' Louisa snatched her coat from the

326

stand. 'Jacob Jackson knows better than most that no one *lets* me do anything. I do things of my own accord.' She buttoned her coat, her fingers trembling as she reached for her purse and forcefully pushed it under her arm. 'Lock the door and do not open it until Nancy comes home.'

Octavia nodded and dropped her arms, her chin lifting. 'Fine. If you insist.'

'I do.' Louisa stepped forward and quickly embraced her friend. 'I'll be as quick as I can.'

Racing from the house, Louisa hurried along the cobbled street and hailed a carriage to the underground club across the river.

Once there, she stepped back from the door to allow a group of men to exit before slipping inside. The place stank to high heaven and she screwed up her nose, barely resisting the urge to gag. Through the dense smoke, Louisa walked along the corridors until she came to a half-empty room, partially occupied by the men standing at a makeshift bar, others surrounding a boxing ring in the centre. She scanned the room back and forth, but Jacob was nowhere to be seen.

Then she spotted a man dressed as though he was about to do a turn on stage. Garish, loud and overly confident, the man had to be Henry Bertrum, Jacob's ex-manager. If she hadn't been so concerned, she might have laughed at the accuracy of Jacob's many descriptions of Mr Bertrum.

Louisa approached him. 'Excuse me, sir? Might you be Henry Bertrum?'

He halted his conversation with the man next to him and turned. His smile faltered as he met

Louisa's eyes. 'I am, young lady.' He doffed his hat theatrically. 'And how might I help such a beautiful woman this evening?'

She flashed him a smile, automatically falling into her flirtatious persona in order to solicit the information she needed. It irked to do so but needs must. 'Oh, thank goodness. I'm looking for Jacob Jackson. I wonder — '

'Are you her?' He let out a low whistle, his gaze sliding up and down her person. 'You must be.' He extended his hand. 'Mrs Hill, I presume?'

Impatience hummed through Louisa as she reluctantly took his hand. 'So, have you seen him?' She glanced around her. 'I was hoping to find him here. I have read about a big fight taking place tonight?'

'The Killer, yes. All done and dusted.'

'Done and dusted?'

'Yep. He won.'

'Jacob?' Louisa swallowed and looked around the room. 'Then where is . . . ?'

Her mouth dried as her gaze met Caroline Warwick's where she stood a little way across the room. What was she doing here? Louisa's heart leapt into her throat as Caroline leaned in to say something into the ear of the giant of a man standing beside her, bloodied and beaten, his hair shorn close to his head.

She glanced at Mr Bertrum. 'Is that him? The Killer?'

'It sure is.'

Anger bubbled inside Louisa as she faced Caroline again. The other woman's triumphant gaze burned into Louisa's and she slid her eyes to the Killer. He straightened as he looked at her, a slow smile curing his lips before he lifted his glass as though toasting her.

Fear coated Louisa's throat and she quickly turned away from his menacing study. 'Where is Jacob, Mr Bertrum?'

'Gone.'

'Gone?' Louisa's heart pounded. 'Do you know where he went? It's important that I find him.'

Mr Bertrum picked up his glass of sherry or something equally feminine-looking, the glass glinting under the flickering candles set out along the bar.

'He left over an hour ago. Clutching his winnings without as much as a thank you said in my direction.'

'Thank you? Why did Jacob need to thank you?'

'Because . . . ' His eyes lit with annoyance. 'It was me who got him this fight, that's why.' Louisa held Henry Bertrum's gaze, her worry for Jacob overriding her wish to shake the man.

'Was Jacob all right? Was he badly hurt?'

Mr Bertrum grinned, his brown eyes amused. 'When is Jake not all right?'

'I don't find this funny, Mr Bertrum.'

'Oh, don't get your stockings in a state,' he said, rolling his eyes. 'You should know by now that Jake's more than capable of looking after himself.'

'I do, and it's exactly that aptitude that worries me.'

Storming away from him, Louisa snuck a glance at Caroline and the Killer as they stood huddled in a corner with two other nasty-looking men.

Forcing her focus to the matter in hand, Louisa

left the club and looked left and right along the narrow street. What was she supposed to do now?

Would Jacob go straight home to Carson Street? Go somewhere to clean up first?

Seeing no other choice, Louisa decided the best thing to do was go back to the house and hope he had turned up there in her absence.

She strode past the front of the club, her mind distracted. She blindly weaved among the late-night revellers standing on the club's corner supping gin and ale from dirty glasses. The streets were dark and dingy at this side of town and she stepped up her pace. She needed to get back across the river as quickly as possible.

Two men emerged from an alleyway that ran alongside the club and blocked her path.

Louisa's mouth drained dry. It was the men she had seen talking to Caroline Warwick and the Killer. 'Get out of my way.'

'Or what, darlin'?'

'You going to make us?'

Jacob, help me. Where are you? Tears burned the backs of her eyes and her pulse thundered as Louisa slipped her purse from beneath her arm and held it out. 'Here. Take it. Now let me pass.'

'What are you doing in an underground club, eh?' One of the men's gazes stuck fast on hers, his eyes gleaming with intent. 'You know only whores walk these streets at night. Are you a whore, Mrs Hill?'

Louisa looked from one man to the other, her heart pounding in her ears.

She opened her mouth to scream and the men lunged at her, dragging her deep into the alleyway and flinging her hard against the wall. Her head smacked against brick and the air rushed from her lungs.

'Hold her! Bloody hold her!'

'Just cut her, will you? We haven't got time to mess about.'

Kicking out, Louisa's lungs screamed as she grappled to find her breath, her body shaking as she scratched and clawed. 'Help me! Someone help me!'

One of the men wedged his elbow hard against her throat and held up her chin. 'Damn well cut her! That was the Killer's instructions.'

She kicked out with all her strength and the man's arm left her throat as he doubled up.

'Bitch! Cut her face. Do it now!'

Something slipped across her cheek, so succinctly Louisa wasn't sure what it was at first and then the men fled.

She dropped like a stone to the ground.

Tears burst from her eyes and ran down her cheeks, sending a searing pain through her face. She reached her shaking fingers to her cheek and the flesh moved like it was loose from her bones.

Raising her hand to her eyes, her fingers were dark with blood.

'Hey, are you all right? My God, Mrs Hill?'

Louisa looked to the side of her. 'Mr Bert — '

And the world went black.

44

Jacob ran his tongue over his swollen lip, pleased that he didn't taste blood this time. He smiled, pride swelling his ego like air filling a balloon. He might have taken half a beating from the Killer, but he'd taught the animal a lesson proving just how lame a fighter he was without the added extra of a blade.

Jacob smiled. Best of all, he'd kept his head. The strength that had flooded through him during the fight would have been enough to see him through another couple of rounds had the Killer not hit the sawdust in such a satisfying and quick collapse.

The truth was, Jacob had not used half his strength and had controlled his anger.

It felt like progress — like he could face Louisa and have nothing to apologise for. He'd be fully aware of his actions and strength. The red mist that had become his anger's companion had evaporated quickly, enabling him to fight with purpose rather than blind rage.

He put his hand into the inside pocket of his coat and fingered the wad of cash notes he'd won. And now he had the means to invest in the house. In Louisa.

Reaching Carson Street, he let himself into the house and as he turned to shut the door, shouted along the hallway. 'Louisa? Where are you?'

The parlour door opened, and Nancy and

Octavia emerged, their faces pale. 'At last, where have you been?' Nancy snapped, looking past him to the front door. 'Where's Lou?'

'What?'

She put her hands on her hips, her eyes angry. 'Despite Octavia warning her against the stupidity of doing so, Louisa took herself off to look for you.

I would've stopped her, but I was out doing the same bloody thing. Now, where is she?'

Dread knotted Jacob's stomach as fear for Louisa's safety whispered through him. He shoved his hand in his hair in an effort to stop his head from exploding. 'How long ago?'

'Maybe an hour or so?' Octavia stepped forward, her eyes filled with worry. 'I'm sorry, Jacob. There was nothing I could say to stop her.'

'It's no good looking at us like that, Jacob Jackson,' Nancy glared, her arms tightly crossed. 'You know how stubborn she is when she decides — '

'Jacob! Jacob! Oh, thank God.'

Jacob spun around.

Doreen clambered up the last couple of steps to the front door and into the hallway. She gripped his arm. 'You've got to come with me. Quickly.'

'What's going on?' Nancy demanded. 'You can't just come in here — '

'What is it, Doreen?' Jacob's studied her face, unease writhing like a snake in his gut. 'Is it Louisa? Have you seen her?'

'I had no idea who she was when Mr Bertrum brought her to the door. My God, Jacob, she was covered — '

'Henry brought her to the lodgings? What are

you talking about?' He put on his hat on and turned to Nancy and Octavia. 'You two stay here and for Christ's sake do not open this door to anyone. Do you hear me?'

'Yes, Jacob, we hear you but I'm coming with you.' Nancy held his gaze before looking at Doreen. 'Is Louisa all right?'

Octavia stepped forward, her blue eyes telling little of her thoughts, her face set. 'What has happened to Louisa?'

Jacob stared at Doreen as she flitted her gaze nervously between them, her lips pinched tight and her lower lashes brimming with tears.

He took her arm, fighting the instinct to shake her. 'Doreen? Is Louisa all right?'

She mutely shook her head.

Gently, Jacob released her, his simmering angry building dangerously even as dread began to weigh heavy inside him. 'What's wrong with her? Tell me.'

'She's been cut, Jake. Cut bad.'

Nancy gasped beside him as Jacob felt the blood drain from his face.

'Cut?'

'No. Not Louisa,' Octavia breathed beside him.

Doreen nodded. 'Someone's cut her beautiful face, Jake.' Doreen sucked in a breath. 'I did the best I could with my stitching and bandages, but . . . '

She shook her head, tears escaping. 'She wouldn't let me call the doctor or the surgeon.'

A deep, violent shaking started in Jacob's stomach.

It slowly escalated and spread through his body.

Blood pounded in his ears, lessening the sound of Nancy and Octavia's cries. Then the weight of someone's hand on his shoulder made Jacob flinch and he turned to Nancy, her grey eyes bright with anger, her mouth moving but Jacob could hear nothing over the thundering of his pulse.

'Jacob!' Octavia shouted and gripped Jacob's arm. 'Go. You've got to go to her. Now. We'll stay here and lock the door, I promise.'

He blinked and was thrown back into the here and now.

He curled his hands into fists, as the need to punch something, maim something, grew hot behind his ribcage, encasing his heart in an iron shield.

Pain burned through his body, punching and bruising through his skin and flesh to his very soul.

Louisa.

He snatched his gaze to Doreen. 'Let's go.'

45

Louisa was awake but the effort it took to open her eyes depleted her minimal energy and she surrendered to her exhaustion. Unfamiliar smells drifted into her nostrils and soft breathing ebbed and flowed somewhere close to her.

Her cheek ached and when she clenched her teeth, pain shot through the side of her face to her temple. Cautiously, she lifted her fingers and they knocked against something warm and hard on the bed.

She fought to open her eyes a second time. They prised to a slit and she glanced downwards, her heart jolting and tears immediately springing into her eyes.

'Jacob . . . ' she whispered, her breath seeming to catch on her dried lips.

'Jacob?'

Her eyes fully opened as he stirred, his forehead moving from the bed and across her fingers sending the mussed hair at his brow to brush along the back of her hand.

Love swelled Louisa's heart as he slowly eased his neck from side to side as though releasing the stiffness. At last, his gaze met hers . . .

Concern immediately leapt into his eyes even as he gave a tight smile.

'Hey, you.'

'Where am I?'

'You're at my old lodgings. We . . . ' He stood

and brushed some hair from her face, leaning over to press a lingering kiss to her brow. 'We gave you something to help you sleep. You were in so much pain, Louisa. I didn't know how else to ease it.'

She pushed herself further up the pillows and lay back, exhaustion heavy once more. 'How long have I been here?'

'Two days.'

'Two days?' Her heart stumbled. 'But the house. Are Nancy and Oct — '

'They're fine. Colin has been staying there in my absence.'

'Colin?'

'My friend. He's a boxer and my housemate when I was here. He won't let anything happen to them.'

'Oh.' She looked to the side and tried to reach for a cup sitting on a table beside her. Jacob jumped up and held it to her lips. Sipping at the water, Louisa watched him over the rim, a mix of vulnerability and renewed determination whispering through her. 'I want to go back to Carson Street, Jacob. Today. It's time to get back to normal.'

His expression shadowed with something dark and indecipherable as he slowly eased the cup from her mouth and returned it to the table. 'If that's what you want.'

'It is.' She looked at the purple bruising and scabbed cuts on his face, his bottom lip split and one eye blackened. 'I heard you won.'

'What?'

'The fight. You beat the Killer.'

He nodded, his gaze lingering on hers, his eyes sad rather than victorious.

337

Louisa frowned. 'What is it?'

'Nothing.'

She stared at him before looking past him to a dresser where a mirror had been propped against it. 'Can you get me that mirror?'

When he didn't answer, she turned. His face was set, his jaw tight as he stared at her cheek before quickly looking away. 'Not yet.'

Louisa's heart picked up speed as her new reality came crashing into her, hard and faster than Jacob could ever have punched the Killer. He wouldn't — or couldn't — look at her and, in that moment, she realised her entire world — her only asset — had been destroyed. A phantom pain seared across her cheek and sickness rolled through her stomach on a cruel wave.

'Give me the mirror.' Her voice was dangerously low, not sounding like her at all. 'Otherwise I will get out of this bed right now and get it myself.'

Finally, he faced her, his blue eyes almost black with an emptiness that sent another slash across her heart. So, it had finally happened. What she had always predicted — always known to be true: without her looks she was nobody. Unloved and unattractive to everyone.

Including Jacob.

She lifted her chin, flinched as the cut on her cheek smarted like a reminder of its existence. 'Give me the mirror.'

He walked to the dresser and lifted the mirror. He looked into it and Louisa studied him, trying to read his thoughts . . . look into his heart. All she saw was a man who could no longer be hers — a man she was duty-bound to set free.

338

He walked back to her and handed her the mirror. 'Here.'

She dragged her gaze from his, inhaled a strengthening breath and looked at her reflection. A cat-like mew rose and seeped from her mouth before she could stop it, her eyes immediately filling with tears. The wound had been expertly stitched, but the cut was long even if it was blessedly narrower than she had imagined. Blood surrounded the black threaded stitches, dried and hard. A raw redness bloomed from the top of her cheekbone to approximately two inches from the corner of her mouth.

Bile coated her throat and Louisa lowered the mirror to the bed, closing her eyes as she tried to regulate her breathing. She fought her panic and despair, her heart thundering.

'Who attacked you, Louisa? Did you know them?'

Jacob's voice was gruff. With anger? Disgust? His voice cracking. With tears? Revulsion?

Slowly, she opened her eyes. 'I didn't know them, but I saw them in the club when I came there looking for you . . .' She met his steady, blank gaze.

How could she tell him one of her assailants had mentioned the Killer? 'I'd like to go home now, please.'

'I'll take you as soon as you describe these men.'

His voice was emotionless. Cold. She resisted the urge to shiver.

'Let it go, Jacob. You don't owe me anything.' She forced a hardness around her heart. For as sure as she was of anything, she knew he would

339

soon be gone. 'You have done enough caring for me these past two days.'

'Describe them, Louisa.'

Fear for what he might do if he found out the Killer had ordered her attack clutched like a fist in her stomach. 'I understand that you — '

'You understand?' His jaw was a hard line, his blue eyes dark with the violence she hated. 'What do you understand?'

'That you want to find these men. And if you do, you'll beat them and then leave me. There is no need to find them and there is no need to spend days or weeks searching for a way out of the brothel. Out of my life. I'm letting you go.' Her heart aching, she lifted the blankets from her legs and hesitantly lowered her feet to the floor. 'I'd like to leave now.'

'You think I don't want you now? Because of this? Because of your face?'

Tears burned behind her eyes and humiliation rose hot in her cheeks. 'I have Nancy and Octavia. I'll be all right.'

'Louisa, look at me.'

His voice was laced with pain. She took a deep breath, forced herself to face him.

He came forwards and stared at her with such love, such passion, she thought she might die there and then. Fear mixed with hope, desire with uncertainty.

'I love you,' he whispered, pulling her head gently beneath his chin and holding her close. He kissed her hair. 'I love you and I'm not leaving you. Not ever.'

'Jacob . . . ' She said his name on a sob. 'Don't

340

promise me that. Please.'

'I can and I will.' He gently eased her away from him and looked deep into her eyes, his own glazed with unshed tears, his anger simmering somewhere behind the love. 'I have to find who hurt you.'

Disappointment twisted inside her. No more violence. No more threats and promises. She just wanted to hide; run the Carson Street house from her study with Nancy and Octavia at front of house. It could work with her in the background and her two best friends holding court for the customers.

She would *make* it work.

'Tell me what they looked like, Louisa.'

Regret coiled inside of her. She couldn't lie to him. 'They knew the Killer.'

'What?' His arms stiffened around her, his cheeks darkening. 'Did they follow you from the club?'

'Yes. I saw them with the Killer talking to Anthony's mistress. She must have told them I'm your lover.' She cupped his tightened jaw, prayed he heard her. 'If the Killer sent them after me, he did so as revenge for you winning the fight. Don't give him the satisfaction of succeeding to push you into such stupid, senseless games. Just let it go, Jacob. Please.'

But he wasn't listening, his eyes remained blank on hers, dark with hatred.

'Jacob?' Louisa ran her thumb over his lower lip. 'Listen to me.'

He caught her wrist and lowered it, his grip so tight, her pulse thumped beneath his fingers. 'I won't give him the satisfaction of fighting him. The form of my chosen revenge will act as a pledge to you.'

'What do you mean?'

'I promise to love and protect you for the rest of my life.' He blinked and then finally looked at her as though he really saw her. 'I will think how best to prove that to you.'

'But you don't need to prove anything to me.'

'Then I need to prove it to myself.'

He pulled her close again and Louisa laid her uninjured cheek on his chest. Maybe she could hope that his words of love and protection were true but, deep down, Louisa feared he was unaware of the lies he had told her.

She had never been so afraid of the future, of what Jacob might do or how she would rise again once she'd lost him. Her strength weakened more and more, her belief in love and possibility evaporating entirely.

46

Jacob stared into the bottom of his brandy glass in the White Hart and relished the barely suppressed rage burning hot in his blood. His knuckles ached around the glass as he fought the mounting and desperate need to hit something. Hit someone.

Two days had passed since Louisa's attack and so far he had done nothing to avenge her. The Killer haunted him day and night. His smiling, sneering face looming like a ghost in Jacob's mind.

At Carson Street, Louisa only walked about the house when no clients were around, quiet and thoughtful, her beautiful violet eyes shadowed with sadness. He longed to make her smile and laugh as she had before, but whenever she looked at him it was as though she waited for him to bolt. To leave her.

He clenched his jaw and snatched up his glass, drank deep, welcoming the heat of the liquor as it travelled down his throat, burning his chest and into his empty stomach. He wanted nothing more than to hunt down the Killer and finish him off once and for all. But where would his death leave Jacob and Louisa? It was his fault she was cut, his fault she no longer had the confidence to face the culls coming to the brothel . . . or face anyone at all.

She would never forgive him for provoking the Killer to order her attack and Jacob doubted killing the bastard would change that.

Raising the glass, he caught Maura's canny gaze as she watched him from the other side of the bar. 'Another.'

She took a brandy bottle from a shelf at the back of the bar. 'What's up, Jacob? You're not yourself. You got another fight on your mind?'

He picked up his replenished glass and smirked. 'You could say that.'

'Who is it?'

'Doesn't matter.'

'Well, whoever he is, I don't think it's just a fight you have in store for him.'

He swirled the brandy in his glass, wishing Maura would mind her own business. 'You think you know me well enough to know what I'm thinking?'

'I know you well enough to see you're spoiling for more than a fight.'

She whipped a rag from her shoulder and wiped it along the bar. 'Whoever he is, he's not worth a spell in prison, or for all and sundry to see your beautiful face hanging from a rope.' Maura stared at him expectantly, her eyebrows raised. 'You've got murder on your mind. Am I right?'

'Maybe.'

'Don't be a fool, Jake.' Her cheeks reddened and her gaze filled with anger. 'You mean a lot to me and a lot to others around here. You've finally found yourself a little happiness and now you're going to throw it away? That's just plain stupid.'

'I didn't protect her, Maura.' He took a hefty gulp of his drink, his body trembling with the injustice that the Killer still walked around when he should be buried six feet under. 'Just like I

344

failed my mother, I failed Louisa, too.' He met her steady gaze, his own blurred from drink. 'I have to find him.' He drained his glass and grimaced. 'And I can't see any other choice than to kill him.'

She clutched his hand, her gaze hard on his. 'Listen to me. There are other ways of dealing with people who've wronged us than committing murder. This Louisa woman needs you, right? You love her?'

He nodded, his heart aching and only escalating his need to leave the pub and hunt down the Killer as he should have the second he'd safely returned Louisa to Carson Street and the care of Nancy and Octavia.

'Then damn well stay alive for her, Jacob.'

Maura stalked off along the bar, her smile back in place for the next customer.

Jacob's heart beat fast, his mind whirling with how and when he could finish off the Killer. A few months ago the felonious boxer possessed the nerve to stab Jacob. Then, he'd arranged for the love of Jacob's life to be attacked.

He had to be punished. He had to die.

A man like that did not go from fighting the good fight to using underhanded tactics and violence against women in a single stroke. The cold, icy look in the Killer's eyes spoke of a man who would not stop. He had attacked before, served time and hard labour. Nothing but death would stop him.

Jacob drained his glass.

If he went after the Killer himself, there was every possibility Jacob would end up in prison for a really long stretch or, more likely, he would be hanged. So, to his mind, it was a case of kill or be killed.

Either way, he'd lose Louisa. Of that much, he was absolutely certain.

But how could he be with her — or live with himself — without avenging her attack? It was enough living his life knowing his mother had died due to his cowardice. How was he supposed to walk away a second time when someone he loved had been hurt and left for dead? To live with the knowledge that Louisa would never forgive him for being maimed without provocation? He had to ensure justice was served.

He had to succeed where he had failed with his father.

Pushing up from his stool, Jacob swiped his hat from the bar and walked from the pub.

It was mid-afternoon and the bright sunshine pierced through his brain, deepening his anger. On and on, Jacob walked, breathing deep as plans came and went in his mind.

He came upon the police station and stopped, his heart hammering and his fists clenched.

How could he predict what would happen after he'd murdered the Killer?

After all, Jacob would undoubtedly be caught eventually, hanged and be out of the way, leaving Louisa exposed to what? Further revenge? An attack by one of the Killer's cronies? If they didn't come after Louisa, there was nothing to say they wouldn't come after Nancy or Octavia.

Hardman had returned to Carson Street. Louisa's husband's mistress had brought Louisa to the Killer's attention.

Jacob swallowed. He had to stay alive. Had to retain his liberty and keep Louisa safe from further retribution. The only way he could keep Louisa's love and trust, and ensure the Killer answered for his crimes, was to seek justice legitimately.

He stared at the station doors.

Could he trust the police to ensure the Killer spent the rest of his life behind bars?

Closing his eyes, Jacob pressed his fingers against the lids.

If he didn't attempt to do this the right way, Louisa would never believe him capable of restraint, self-control and loyalty.

He had to prove himself to her. Had to prove his inner strength to himself.

Taking a deep breath, Jacob walked up the steps and into the station.

Squinting, he waited for his eyes to adjust to the dim darkness of the lobby as he surveyed the men and women around him. It might only be mid-afternoon, but that didn't seem to have deterred the actions of the drinkers and brawlers who had found themselves dragged in by the constabulary.

Alcohol fumes, dirty bodies and the cloying stench of stale sweat permeated the space and Jacob straightened his shoulders and walked to the desk.

'You'll have to take a seat, sir,' the duty sergeant said, not looking up from the file in front of him. 'It's going to be a bit of a wait, I'm afraid.'

Ignoring the request, Jacob put his hand on the countertop. 'I want to report an assault on a female friend of mine. She was cut and I know who ordered the attack.'

The officer raised his head, his eyes steely. 'That's all well and good, but you still have to wait your turn.' He looked back to the file. 'A constable will be with you as soon as possible.'

Impatience hummed through Jacob as he stared at a bald spot on the top of the officer's head. 'Have you heard of the Killer?'

The officer's head lifted again, suddenly interested. 'The boxer? What about him?'

'It was him who ordered the attack on my friend. I want him arrested before he can hurt anyone else. Man or woman.'

The officer's eyes slowly swept over Jacob's face before he slid the file to the side and picked up his pen. 'What's your name?'

'Jackson. Jacob Jackson.'

Recognition sparked in the officer's gaze. 'Stay there.'

Considering he had no intention of going anywhere, Jacob turned his back and leaned his arse against the counter as the officer walked away.

He watched the goings-on around him, barely seeing or registering the squabble between two drunks and the flirtation between a man and a whore.

Instead, his mind's eye filled with images of the Killer and then Louisa still as a statue in bed, her cheek cut and bleeding. Jacob crossed his arms and battled the need to burst through the station doors and find the Killer himself.

Why in God's name was he waiting —

'Mr Jackson? Sergeant Kerrigan. I believe you have something you wish to tell me.'

Jacob turned and met the stare of an older man, his grey-whiskered cheeks and silver-white hair offering a modicum of hope that maybe this clearly distinguished and experienced officer of the law might just take what Jacob had to say seriously.

He pushed away from the counter and offered his hand. 'Yes, sir. I do.'

47

As she had every night for the last week, Louisa sat alone in her study, poring over her ledger, making sure the house's finances were in order. She had to ensure that they ran at a continual profit. That she, Nancy and Octavia were making the money they needed in order to survive in the house and not end up back on the streets.

Now that she was unable to service customers, or even act as a hostess, they were effectively down in number and in profit. And the blame lay with Louisa. Plus, it was only a matter of time before Jacob left and then a new doorman would be needed on top of everything else.

She sat back from the papers and touched her cheek. Everything could change in a heartbeat. Love could die with the slice of a blade . . .

There was a rap on the door and Louisa snatched her hand from her face just as the door opened and Nancy appeared, male laughter mixing with Octavia's echoing along the hallway.

'Can I come in?'

'Of course.' Louisa forced a smile, her cheek tightening. 'Are Mr Byrne and Mr Rowland being suitably entertained?'

'As much as Octavia and I can manage without you.' Nancy came forward and plonked herself down in the chair on the opposite side of the desk. 'Although, like almost every single one of our regular customers, they continually ask when you will be joining us for a drink.'

Louisa frowned, nerves immediately taking flight in her stomach. 'I've told you, I will not be seeing anyone.'

'For how long?'

Louisa picked up her pen and dipped it in the inkstand, hating that her fingers trembled. 'For as long as I see fit.'

'You're not being fair, Louisa. Especially to Jacob.'

'Why? Is he asking for me?' She feigned interest in her ledger. 'If he wants to see me, he only needs to walk from the front door and along the hallway.'

'You know what I mean.' Nancy reached across the desk and plucked the pen from Louisa's fingers and put it in the inkstand. 'You are killing him.'

Louisa clenched her hands tightly in her lap, wishing Nancy would leave.

'Don't be ridiculous. Jacob and I are going along perfectly well.'

'Bull.'

'Why do you keep harassing me like this?' Louisa glared, fear winding tight in her stomach. 'How do you expect me to go out there and talk to the gentlemen who come in here, looking as I do? Do you want us to gain or lose business?'

'It's a scar and it's healing, Louisa.' Nancy's cheeks reddened, her gaze, usually filled with laughter instead burned with frustration. 'You are no less beautiful than you were before. And even if you were, it is not because of your looks that people want to see you, why people love being in your company. The gentlemen miss your laughter and smile, your good wishes.

Can you not see that?'

Louisa stood and walked to the drinks cabinet in the corner. 'They miss my flirtation. My servitude and saucy behaviour. That's not who I am anymore. Who I am now is clearly written on my face.'

'What are you talking about?'

Louisa poured herself and Nancy a glass of wine, the crystal stopper clanging against the decanter as she replaced it. 'I am little more than a scarred whore.' She walked to the desk and held out one of the glasses, her gaze steady on her friend's. 'These men come here to feed on us. To fuck us. Nothing more, nothing less.' She took a mouthful of wine, anger burning hot in her chest. 'Jacob is no different.'

'My God.' Nancy slowly shook her head. 'I never thought I'd see the day when my best friend would allow anything, or anyone, make her so bitter and twisted. Make her a bloody shadow of her former self.' She lifted her glass in a toast. 'Well, well done to the Killer. He has indeed succeeded in killing you, Louisa.'

Louisa trembled, tears treacherously pricking her eyes. 'Get out.'

Nancy sipped her drink. 'Make me.'

'Damn you, Nancy.'

Louisa slammed her glass on the desk and lunged, grabbing Nancy's sleeve and heaving her to her feet. Her glass rolled to the floor unheeded as they grappled. Anger surged through Louisa, strengthening her resolve and muscle as she forced

Nancy to the wall and held her.

She stared into her friend's eyes, her heart pounding . . . breaking.

'Everything I do is for us. Do you hear me? Every decision, every penny, every bloody waking hour, I only think of us. Not Jacob. Not Anthony. Us.

If I go out there, I will lose us money and that is something I will not do.'

'It's Jacob you think of all the bloody time these days and I'm glad for it,' Nancy spat through clenched teeth. 'And he damn well thinks of you, you stupid, bloody whore.'

Louisa pulled her friend away from the wall and slammed her against it a second time, her anger escalating. 'He will leave soon enough, don't you worry. I've accepted that but then we will need someone else. I hate it, Nancy. I bloody hate this reliance we are forced to have because of what we do here.'

'You don't rely on him. You love him.'

'Which means what? I still need him, and I don't *want* to need him.'

Louisa's voice cracked and she released Nancy. 'I don't want *him*.'

Silence descended and Louisa stepped back, covering her face with her hands.

'For the record . . . ' Nancy gently took Louisa's fingers away and looked into her eyes. 'Jacob loves you. He loves you so damn much, the change in you, the fact you hide in here day after day and reject him night after night is killing him. Do you blame Jacob for what happened to your face, Lou? Or do you blame Caroline Warwick? The Killer?

Because it is them at fault, not Jacob.'

Louisa shook her head and swiped her fingers over her damp cheeks. 'Of course I blame them. Jacob did nothing but fight, even if his reasons for doing so were entirely founded in his own senseless quest to prove his self-worth.'

'You're not being fair to him, Lou. Do you know he has moved heaven and earth to see the Killer brought to *legal* justice. Damn well swallowed his pride and followed the law instead of his own instincts. For you. No one else.'

'What?'

Sighing, Nancy walked to the door and gripped the handle. 'You can look over your books, spend hours totting up our money and looking for that all-important security that you so desperately think you need, but you're wrong about Jacob. The man is steadfast, strong and completely yours. Talk to him.'

Louisa glanced towards the door, her heart aching. 'I can't.'

'Yes, you can. All you really need is some bloody confidence, Lou. To see how much more there is to you, me and Octavia than our damn looks.

For God's sake, sort yourself out before it's too late. It's not a weakness to want love. To allow Jacob to love you and you both find happiness. Let him love you. Make him a partner in the house. Be happy for once in your life.'

Nancy stormed from the room, slamming the door so hard, Louisa's teeth clattered. Her entire body shaking, she put her hand to the wall for support, her friend's anger vibrating through her. Slowly, she slid her bottom to the floor as her

354

tears flowed, Nancy's wisdom echoing in her conscience.

She could not go backwards. Not return to the dependency she had on Anthony. She had no choice but to shut Jacob out; to protect Nancy and Octavia . . . protect herself. She had to keep strong and focused and not allow herself to care again.

Louisa buried her face in her hands. But how was she to refrain, to resist, when she wanted nothing more than Jacob's arms around her, strong and unyielding, standing beside her forever as she knew, deep down, he absolutely would.

48

Jacob nodded at the happy — and clearly sated — cull as the man passed him at the front door and hurried into the early morning darkness. Glad that the house was finally empty of clients, Jacob returned indoors, locking and bolting the door behind him.

He stared along the hallway towards Louisa's closed study door, indecision swirling in his heart and consciousness. She had not yet gone upstairs to bed, despite the hour being two in the morning. Night after night, he battled to leave her in peace, after having told her that the Killer had been arrested, after the men who had cut her were identified, with Louisa's eventual cooperation, and spilled their guts with knowledge about other attacks the Killer had orchestrated.

It seemed that since his previous incarceration the Killer thrived on getting other people to act on his wishes. A man of menacing and threatening power who used threats like a puppeteer would strings.

Nancy's and Octavia's voices drifted from the open parlour door and Jacob walked into the room. 'Either of you managed to persuade Louisa to come out yet? She's been in her study all night.'

'No, and why would tonight be any different?' Nancy sighed and shook her head. 'It seems all your efforts to be the better man as far as that deranged boxer was concerned have been wasted.

No doubt she's still in there seething or sulking.'

'I can't imagine Louisa doing either of those things.'

'Possibly not.' Octavia walked to the fire and plucked some wilting blooms from the overflowing jug on the hearth. 'But we have to do something about our situation, Jacob. Louisa needs to accept she needs you.

As we all need you.'

He should have felt some pride in Octavia's admission. She had been the hardest of the three women in the house to crack, but with patience and a little tongue-biting, Jacob had slowly but surely gained the young woman's trust. Now it seemed, Louisa had erected an impenetrable barrier against him . . . against her heart.

'I'll see if she'll speak to me,' he said, stepping towards the door. 'I'll take her some food, too.'

'Before you go . . .' Nancy raised her hand, her grey eyes sombre. 'There's something you should know. She's been poring over the accounts again. I suspect there are decisions to be made. Either we find more money elsewhere or we take on more girls. I don't think Louisa has the tenacity to go along either route right now.'

'But she knows I've got the money to invest now. She knows why I took that final fight. Are you telling me even the success of this house doesn't make that fight worth anything to her?'

'Jacob . . .' Octavia sighed. 'You have to give her time.'

'We don't have time,' Nancy snapped. 'He needs to go in there and tell her what's what.'

He looked at them. 'We could make this house

357

work, have it running for as long as we want. I know we could.'

Nancy smiled and winked at Octavia, who nodded. 'Good. Then go and speak to her.'

Jacob walked towards the door again and stopped, wanting Louisa's friends to understand what she meant to him. 'I love her. You do know that, don't you? I'll never hurt her.'

Octavia smiled. 'We know, Jacob.'

He looked at Nancy whose smile was more cautious. 'We wouldn't let you, anyway. Just go and speak to her and make sure you're convincing.'

Jacob walked along the hallway to Louisa's study. Taking a deep breath, he raised his knuckles and knocked.

'Come in.'

Surprised that he didn't receive the expected rejection, Jacob entered the room.

She stood with her back to him at the window, a piece of parchment in her hand. 'Shut the door, Jacob.'

He closed the door. 'How did you know it was me?'

'I don't know how, I just did. I always do.'

As he approached her, he stared at her beautiful blonde hair, twisted in a long plait down her back, tendrils flowing over the gentle curve of her neck to brush her shoulders. She wore a royal blue dress covered in black lace, a pair of jet earrings dangling to her jaw. It was a similar dress to what she'd worn the very first night they'd met.

God, how deeply he'd fallen in love with her since then.

Gently, he lowered his hands to her waist. She

stiffened, the parchment she held slipping from her fingers to the floor. She inhaled a shaky breath but didn't step from his grip. Relief gave him strength and he eased her back against his chest, encased her in the fold of his arms, his hands pressed softly to her stomach.

Resting his chin against her hair, he spoke softly. 'It's time, Louisa.'

'Time for what?' she whispered. 'Time for you to go?'

Jacob closed his eyes, hating that she still thought it possible that he would ever desert her. 'I'm going nowhere. It's time to decide if you just wish me to continue to work with you. Or, if not, if you'll let me love you. You already hold my heart in your hands, but now I have the means to help you keep the house for as long as you wish. It's time to decide if you want me. In everything. Or something.'

She leaned away from him and bent down to pick up the fallen parchment. 'This was the letter my mother left me to find when I came home and learned my family had gone. Read it. Charles is my younger brother.'

With his eyes on hers, Jacob took the letter and lowered his gaze.

Dear Louisa, my darling girl,

There are secrets I have kept from you for as long as I can, but the time has come for my honesty. Your father could soon be arrested and thrown into debtors' prison. We are leaving to go on the run, but I do not want

that sort of life for you, my darling. I have lit-
tle choice but to take Charles. You must stay
here and be strong. Everyone loves you, Lou
and you are a good girl who will make her
own way. I know you will.

Sell your flowers and be good, always.

Love you forever, Ma xx

Jacob raised his eyes to Louisa's, anger and revulsion unfurling in his gut. 'How old were you?'

'Thirteen.' She stepped closer and touched her fingers to his jaw. 'They never came back. Eventually, I accepted they were gone and soon a brothel madam approached me when I was selling lavender on the streets and sleeping on a neighbour's kitchen floor. She took me in and became a surrogate mother who taught me how to use my face and body for money. My life has been whoring, in one way or another, ever since.' She looked into his eyes. 'Until I met you, I've always believed my only gifts were physical. Maybe I'm wrong, but even if I'm not, why do you want to be with a woman who has been with more men than she can count?'

'Because I love you and want you to be mine, Louisa. I want to share everything with you, good and bad and do all that I can to make you happy.'

He brushed his thumb gently over her scar and she closed her eyes. 'You never stop fighting and I wouldn't want you to, but wouldn't it be better if I were beside you in those fights?'

She opened her eyes and they glinted with tears.

360

'This scar will never go away, Jacob.'

'I know.'

'Neither will the scars left on my heart from my family and Anthony. I'm hardened. Angry. Determined and ambitious. Those things will never change.'

'I know, and that just more reason I want to marry you.' He lowered his mouth to the scar on her cheek. 'Trust me, Louisa. Please.'

'Marry me?'

'Yes.'

She closed her eyes. 'I think it best we take it one step at a time, don't you?'

'Fine, but is that a yes?' He smiled. 'You want me in everything?'

She fisted her hand around his lapel, pulling him forward. 'It's a promise I'll try my best to always love you. To trust you. To know it's all right to need you. The rest we can work out as we go along.'

He winked and she smiled for the first time in days.

Jacob crushed his lips to hers.

At long last, his final fight was over . . . and he prayed Louisa's was, too.

Acknowledgements

My first acknowledgement is to my fabulous editor, Rhea Kurien, who accepted my proposal for *A Widow's Vow* and the following two books without hesitation. I have wanted to write a trilogy set in a fictional Victorian brothel for a while and Rhea gave me the confidence to believe my idea for the series was actually quite good!

I'd also like to thank the head librarian at my local library who sourced many books and information that helped me make the house on Carson Street become more and more real in my imagination, as well as adding substance to the women whose lives I wanted to explore and bring to life.

Finally, I'd like to thank all the amazing readers and reviewers who continue to love my previous series (Pennington's) and have written to me eagerly awaiting the release of *A Widow's Vow* — the wait is finally over for all of us!

Rachel x

We do hope that you have enjoyed reading this large print book.

Did you know that all of our titles are available for purchase?

We publish a wide range of high quality large print books including:
**Romances, Mysteries, Classics
General Fiction
Non Fiction and Westerns**

Special interest titles available in large print are:
**The Little Oxford Dictionary
Music Book, Song Book
Hymn Book, Service Book**

Also available from us courtesy of Oxford University Press:
**Young Readers' Dictionary
(large print edition)
Young Readers' Thesaurus
(large print edition)**

For further information or a free brochure, please contact us at:
**Ulverscroft Large Print Books Ltd.,
The Green, Bradgate Road, Anstey,
Leicester, LE7 7FU, England.
Tel:** (00 44) 0116 236 4325
Fax: (00 44) 0116 234 0205

Other titles published by Ulverscroft:

A PLACE TO CALL HOME

Evie Grace

East Kent, 1876: With doting parents and sib-
lings she adores, sixteen-year-old Rose Cheevers
leads a contented life at Willow Place in Canter-
bury. A bright future ahead of her, she dreams of
following in her mother's footsteps and becoming a teacher. Then one traumatic day turns the
Cheevers' household upside-down. What was
once a safe haven has become a place of peril, and
Rose is forced to flee with the younger children.
Desperate, she seeks refuge in a remote village
with a long lost grandmother who did not know
she existed. But safety comes at a price, and the
arrival of a young stranger with connections to
her past raises uncomfortable questions about
what the future holds. Somehow, Rose must
find the strength to keep her family together.
Above all else, though, she needs a place to call
home.